D0985480

THE ALLARDS

BOOK TWO
THE HUNTER

Wilmont R. Kreis

Second Edition

THE ALLARDS

BOOK TWO:

THE HUNTER

By Wilmont R. Kreis

Port Huron, Michigan
2007

Second Edition
2009

Copyright © 2009
By Wilmont R Kreis
ISBN: 978-1-442-10451-8

Library of Congress control number: 2009902424

All rights reserved

Dedicated to my brother, Russell Allard Kreis,
and my Cousin, Dr. Charles Defever
for making my path in life easier
by leaving such wonderful footsteps.

Acknowledgements

I would like to thank Susanna Mason Defever for her role as editor, critic and teacher. I cannot overstate the effect she has had on my work. I would like to thank Carrie McLean for her help with maps and Lorelei Maison Rockwell for her encouragement. I would particularly like to thank my wonderful wife, Susan, for her help as editor and critic and for giving me the idea and encouragement to give life to the stories of my ancestors.

INTRODUCTION TO THE SECOND EDITION

This is a story. More precisely it is two stories. Most of it is true, or should I say based on records thought to be true. Some of it is fiction and some of it based on speculation of what *may* have happened.

First it is a story of my mother's ancestors. Second is the story of the people of which they were a part, their amazing journey from the old world to the new and the two new nations they would eventually help create.

When I initially wrote Book Two, it was entirely for members of my immediate family. I had no idea others would be interested. But they were, and I have written this second edition to improve the rhetoric and make it more readable for the general public. The story has not changed at all. How could it? It actually happened.

PROLOGUE

This is the second in a series of books about my mother's Allard ancestors. The books are in serial form and I recommend they be read in order. There are two stories, first the story of her actual ancestors and the second the history of the period. The stories are faithful to the dates of record of birth, death, marriage and other data available in abundance from the wonderfully preserved Archives of Québec and numerous other sources.

These are superimposed on the events of the period. I have tried to be faithful to facts and particularly to the nature and personalities of prominent people such as Cadillac and LaSalle. At the end of the book I will try to confess to any fabrications of my own. Whereas Jean-Baptiste* Allard may not have participated in each of these events, it is possible that he did participate in some of them. Some ancestors, however, did participate in each historical event in the book. It is, however, foremost a story. Don't use it in your term paper without checking the details.

Names: Unfortunately the early French-Canadians had few surnames. A great number of the girls had names beginning with Marie (Marie-Anne, Marie-Charlotte, etc.). Most of the families were large and the use of names of fathers, grandfathers, and siblings was common. As a result there are five second-generation Allard families each with many of the same names. Some families even used a name more than once! In their time, nicknames were common. However, I have little record of these from this period. I try to use last names and middle names to try to alleviate confusion.

Asterisks: As before, an asterisk appears after the first name of all ancestors. I began this to help navigate a genealogy program, but it is also useful to keep track of which Jean-Baptiste* is which. There are many ancestors who appear as characters in the story. Unless otherwise stated these were all real people in the settings in which they lived. As one looks back in time, each generation has twice as many ancestors as the next. As this story is three hundred years in the past, several of the people in Québec are ancestors, and for the most part they lived and interacted with the Allards. As the stories move forward there will be fewer ancestors in each successive generation. In future books we will see how these people "join" the family. I like to think of these people as families that are on a historic and genealogic collision course with the Allards.

Indians: Although I may have used some license, I have tried to be accurate in the portrayal of Indians. Indians who lived in civilization did occasionally speak French; they seemed to have found it easier to learn than the southern tribes found English. The French missionaries made a great attempt to teach French to the Indians. Marie l'Incarnation, see Book One, went so far as to write an Algonquin dictionary. Although many French could speak various Indian dialects, she found it much easier for Indians to learn French than for French to learn Algonquin.

Maps: I have included maps of the major voyages. Some are adapted from Francis Parkman.

THE ALLARDS BOOK ONE: THE NEW WORLD
SUMMARY

At 26, the son of a Normand Shoemaker, François*Allard, hears of the new world of Canada and signs on for a three-year indentured service, leaving in the spring of 1666 from the port of Dieppe. Among storms, plagues and pirates, he meets Guillaume* Renaud, a Normand soldier. Their families will travel together in new world adventure for many generations.

When the ship stops at the beginning of the Saint-Laurent River, François*, sent hunting but separated from his group, happens upon an Indian. He helps the man save his son and is given a wooden necklace as a wampum or sign of friendship. In turn François* gives the Indian a family medallion given to him by his father as he left France.

François* is hired by a wealthy widow, Anne* Ardouin, who, with her Indian helper, Henri, teaches him the ways of the wilderness. At the end of his three-year service, he obtains his own farm in Charlesbourg, a village outside of Québec. Henri's son, Philippe, goes with him to start his own family.

Marguerite Bourgeoys, a nun, arranges a marriage with Jeanne* Anguille, daughter of a French landholder who travels to Canada as a *Fille du Roi*. François* and Jeanne* marry; their farm prospers, and the story leaves them at the birth of their third son.

THE ALLARDS
To 1723

François* Allard~1671~Jeanne* Anguille
Québec
1639-1725   1647-1711
Normandie, France   Loire Valley, France
I
Jean-Baptiste*Allard~1705~Anne-Elizabeth* Pageot
Québec
1676-1748   1686-1748
Québec   Québec
I
Pierre* Allard
1716
Québec

THE ALLARDS
BOOK TWO
THE HUNTER
MAIN CHARACTERS

François* Allard: First immigrant Allard ancestor.

Jeanne* Anguille: His wife.

André Allard: b. 1672, their son.

Jean-François Allard: b. 1674, their son.

Jean-Baptiste* Allard: b. 1676, their son, the hunter.

Anne-Elizabeth* Pageot: His wife married 1705.

Indians

Henri: Algonquin brave, best friend of François*.

Philippe: His son. Lived on François* and Jeanne*'s farm.

Marie: His wife.

Joseph: Their son, best friend of Jean-Baptiste*.

Voyageurs

Antoine de Lamothe Sieur de Cadillac: Explorer who founded Michilimackinac, Détroit, and New Orleans.

Joseph Parent: Voyageur and first resident of Détroit also went to Louisiana.

Pierre Roy: Voyageur and Parent's perennial sidekick. They accompanied Jean-Baptiste* and Joseph to Louisiana.

Jean* Casse dit Saint-Aubin: Former officer of Cadillac, early resident of Détroit, also led the trip to Louisiana.

Jean* Gauthier: Voyageur lived in Kaskaskia and went to Louisiana.

Marie-Suzanne-Jeanne* Richard (Capieioufseize*): His Indian wife went to Louisiana.

Robert* Reaume: Voyageur brought Madame Cadillac to Détroit and also went to Louisiana.

Nicolas* Reaume: Robert*'s son, went to Louisiana.

Jacob* Thomas: English colonists who was captured by Québec militia and remained in community. Went to Louisiana.

Tom le Baptiste: Slave captured with Jacob* Thomas, stayed in Québec, went to Louisiana.

Chapter 1

Northern Lake Michigan - Summer 2006:

John Chartier meticulously scanned the instruments in the deckhouse as his boat made dead slow forward progress. He had a feeling that this was to be the long awaited moment. "Look!" he shouted as he froze a screen, "It's the right shape and size and this is the right place!"

His colleague, Ben Champine, looked critically and replied, "It's at almost 700 feet, one of the deepest points, we'll have to launch a robot."

Chartier had been following this boyhood dream for the past five years. He was born and raised in Algonac on the shores of the St. Clair River, an area that had been populated with Chartiers since the French colonial days. His great-grandfather was a farmer and his grandfather used his knowledge of earth moving to form an excavating company. John's father in turn had turned it into a major industry. At the age of forty, John was offered $100 million for the business. He took it in a heartbeat and knew exactly what he wanted to do with the fortune.

He purchased a small shipyard in the resort town of Leeland in northwest Michigan, and he spent the next two years directing the construction of a state-of-the-art dive ship equipped with every bell, whistle and toy available. He named the boat *Le Castor,* an odd name to the people in Leeland even if they realized the English translation was 'The Beaver'. To Chartier, however, it was perfect.

As a young man, John was a good student with no interest in the excavation business. He attended the University of Florida and studied North American History and Marine exploration. After graduation he worked on various marine dive projects for everything from oil to shipwrecks.

His interest arose from a book he had found in the small Algonac library as a young boy. It was about the life of the French explorer LaSalle. John was particularly intrigued by the story of LaSalle's boat 'The Griffon' which was the first sailing vessel on the Great Lakes. It was built in a makeshift boatyard near Niagara and launched in 1679. LaSalle took it through the Straits of Mackinaw to the area of Wisconsin now called the Door Peninsula. There he traded for an unbelievable quantity of beaver fur. After LaSalle left the ship in Lake Michigan, the boat began to return to Niagara, but was never seen again. No trace of it had ever been found.

Through his studies, John Chartier had learned everything about this voyage. He even discovered a book that claimed that the man who captained the craft was named Chartier. The *Griffon* and his boyhood dream had become his adult quest. He had even considered naming his new boat *Le Griffon* II, but that seemed a little too 'pushy'. When he inherited his father's business at the age of thirty, he returned to Algonac but never let go of the dream.

Champine and Chartier went on deck with the crew and attached a small oblong craft to the crane. This was a robotic submarine with amazing capabilities. Alone, it had cost over two million dollars. They lowered it into the water and returned to the deckhouse from where they could control it.

The robot descended the 700 feet and began to explore the floor with its impressive illumination. At this depth there was total darkness and the water was a constant 45 degrees. After a few sweeps they saw the shape they had seen on the sonar. The bottom was hard and the view with the artificial lights was excellent. It was clearly a wood sailing vessel and certainly the correct size and shape. It was in unbelievably good condition and sat intact slightly on its port side. As the robot circled the bow, they could make out a carved board on the side. Chartier's heart almost stopped. Undeniably it said, *"LE GRIFFON"*.

After a brief celebration, they quickly returned to the screen. The robot could enter cabins and even open doors and hatches. They viewed the deck and the upper cabins. Chartier exclaimed, "There is nothing here, nothing in the deck, nothing in the cabins, not even the equipment necessary to sail the boat!"

They entered the hold. It too was empty, no furs or even evidence of furs. There was a large hole, however, in the port hull near the center of the hold. Champine remarked, "At this depth, the furs should be in as fine a condition as the boat. What could have happened?"

Chartier said, "Let's get a closer look at the hole." As they examined it he said, "At least we know why it sank."

Champine looked puzzled, "I'm not so sure. It's miles offshore, with no means of sailing, no sails or lines. There is nothing for miles to put a hole in the boat at this depth; the structure shows no sign of a storm, and look here! The boards are broken outward. Whatever made the hole, made it from the <u>inside</u> of the boat!"

Just as they were about to exit, Chartier noticed something else. "There appears to be a small case against the wall." Indeed there was a small wooden chest. "Let's bring this up." It was a small wooden chest in good condition about two and one-half feet long. It was not locked and the men carefully opened it. They all stared in silence.

Champine broke the silence, "An arrow?"

Chartier added, "And nothing else. It looks like an Indian arrow, wood shaft, carved stone head and feathers on the end, but look! As the feathers are gray-brown, one is very different, a bright red." He turned and wrote a note and handed it to one of the men. "Jerry, take this chest ashore on one of the inflatables. Be very careful. Then take one of the trucks to Detroit. Go to the Detroit Public Library downtown and to the Burton Collection. Ask for this man. I'll call and alert him you are coming. If anyone will know what this means, it will be him."

Later that evening, he received a call from his boyhood friend, Jim Trombley. Both boys had developed an interest in local history in high school. Jim now was an historian working on local history, especially Indian history at the Burton Library. "John, where did you find this?" Chartier gave him a short version of the day. Trombley continued, "It is definitely an arrow from around the seventeenth century, but not definitely Indian. It appears to have been made by someone using more typical European tools."

Trombley went on, "I've been seeing some weird things lately. Just last week I had a chest of bizarre artifacts from the same period unearthed under the foundation of St. Joan of Arc Church in St. Clair Shores."

Chartier returned, "Maybe our ancestors are coming back to haunt us for speaking English." Both men laughed and agreed to stay in touch.

Chapter 2

Southern Lake Michigan - Late October 1679:

Robert leaned on the bow and looked over the endless water. There was no land in sight. When there was land, it was endless stands of the virgin forest of the wild. He loved this savage new land and the wonderful life of adventure that it provided. He paced the deck of his boat. Imagine a respectable sailing vessel sailing on this enormous fresh water inland sea. The project was his idea, but his friend Henri de Tonty had constructed the boat. There were hundreds of miles of water only navigable by canoe between Montreal and the beginning of these grand lakes, and the materials for construction had to be transported or fabricated at the site of the launch just above the Niagara River.

However difficult, the task had been completed and *Le Griffon* at 45 tons with seven guns would soon complete her maiden voyage. They were sailing to the bottom (southern end) of the lake where LaSalle would meet with Tonty and they would proceed by canoes to the River of the Miami where they would travel to the land of an Illinois village and then to the great river of the Mississippi which they were to explore for the King.

The ship would return without LaSalle, traveling north through the straits at Michilimackinac and the small mission of Saint-Ignace down through the lower lakes and on to the Niagara River where they would send their treasure by canoes to Montréal. The treasure was several thousand pounds of beaver pelts obtained trading with the Outaouais Indians in the Green Bay. This was a bounty that would have taken the fourteen men who crewed the Griffon several years to amass and it was certain to make LaSalle even wealthier.

Robert felt that he not only rode with his fortune but also the future of commerce in the new world. A voice ended his dreaming; it was Captain Jean Chartier who was calling, "Monsieur de LaSalle, I believe it is time for you to depart. We will see you in Montréal when you return."

At the end of this adventure LaSalle would return to his comfortable home in Québec and his lively mistress Madeleine de Roybon. She would doubtless be pleased to see him, although neither party suffered much loneliness as they shared a very open relationship. Robert boarded the canoe and it with two other canoes headed south as his magnificent Griffon headed north and east. Little did he realize that he would never see his wonderful invention or its treasure again.

Three days later as the Griffon neared the northern tip of Michigauma, a fierce storm arose from the north and west. Captain Chartier felt that the Griffon was seaworthy but he also knew that she had not been really tested. He knew further that there was a secure natural harbor nearby in a place the Algonquin called *Lee-la-na.* He corrected his course to due east. Chartier had experienced the autumn storms in the Saint-Laurent and he would rather be safe than sorry. That evening he was relieved to have made it to this harbor.

The following morning he realized he had made the correct decision as the storm raged. However another problem had arisen. A man who had come aboard in Green Bay had fallen ill. He had a terrible cough with fever, severe vomiting and diarrhea. Chartier recognized the symptoms of cholera, and ordered the man off the ship. They provided him a small camp and provisions. They all knew that he was not to survive, but this was necessary to prevent the spread to the others.

That evening as the winds died, the men made ready to sail in the morning. Standing on the deck watching the progress, Captain Chartier heard something and turned. The last sight of his life was of a fierce man with the sides of his head shaved shooting an arrow. The small band of Iroquois massacred the crew in less than an hour and threw their bodies into the harbor. They then discovered the wonderful prize in the hold and the leader decided to hide the boat, and at his leisure, trade the treasure back to the French.

They pulled the boat with their canoes to a small river leading inland from the harbor, secured it to the bank and covered it with brush. By morning anyone standing five feet away would not see it. As they finished their task, a man appeared from the woods and shot the leader. The others descended on him and slaughtered him which was not difficult as he was now quite ill. They cut opened his chest and each took a generous bite out of his warm heart.

The first Indian fell ill three days later. By the end of the week, the entire band had succumbed.

Chapter 3:

Larochelle, France - 1683:

Pierre sat nursing a glass of mediocre red wine. He was in a harbor tavern much like all the taverns in which he and Antoine ended the day. Pierre was finally becoming nervous although Antoine was as composed as ever as he sat making a sketch on his napkin. Antoine was never nervous.

The men had met as boys at military school. They both came from lower-class bourgeois families with just enough money to send their third-born sons to a third-rate institution. Neither boy excelled, in fact they were both expelled before graduation. They set off together and Pierre found that life with Antoine was always an adventure. Antoine had one central plan, 'If you act as though you have money, you will not need it.'

Finally Pierre spoke, "Antoine, I fear we are at the end. The authorities from Bordeaux cannot be far behind, and we have only the ocean in front of us."

His friend looked up from his scribbling, "I do not think the situation is so precarious. What do you think of ducks? Do ducks appear regal?"

Pierre could only wonder what was going on in that clever brain. Antoine continued, "I believe we should be to bed as I suspect tomorrow will be a big day. By the way, what was the name of that village we stayed in the night before Bordeaux?"

Pierre replied, "I believe it was Cadillac, yes, Cadillac."

"Good, then off we go."

The following morning Antoine burst into Pierre's room. He was dressed and had obviously already been to town. "Pierre, my boy, there is a ship at the harbor, the *Saint-Michel*. It carries a military troupe to the Americas, Canada I believe, a place called Acadie, wherever in the hell that is. Have our things packed and brought to the ship at once. It sails before midday." And as abruptly as he had entered, he was gone.

Pierre knew any scheme of Antoine's was likely to succeed, so he summoned a boy and he made his way with their belongings to the port. At the dock of the *Saint-Michel* he was greeted by the purser. "I am with Monsieur Lamothe, Antoine Lamothe."

The man replied, "Oh yes, Colonel Antoine Lamothe, *le Sieur de Cadillac*. Right this way monsieur. He is in the main stateroom, next to the captain."

As Pierre was being shown the extremely comfortable quarters, Antoine burst in, dressed as a fine gentleman with a long cape and a large hat with a plume. His cape carried a prominent family crest, which centered on six swimming ducks. Antoine surveyed the luxurious room and regarding the purser as though the man smelled bad, said, "I suppose it will have to do as long as you assure me that it is the best." And in his most condescending tone he added, "That will do my good man, we will summon you if we have need."

With that the purser bowed timidly and said, "Yes, of course, *Monsieur le Colonel,* I will come immediately." And he backed out of the room bowing as he went.

Antoine threw his hat on the desk and sank into a padded chair, pouring a glass of fine wine supplied by the captain. Chuckling, he said "Well I guess it will have to do. I do like the ducks, don't you?" Pierre could only shake his head. The man had done it again.

Chapter 4

<u>Charlesbourg, Québec, Canada - November 1686:</u>

The snow fell softly bringing a total silence to the Canadian woods. The boy sat motionless in his place. The snow slowly covered his fur hat and deerskin coat, but that would only conceal him more effectively. He had only to wait for his prey and he was certain that it would come. He knew his weapon and was certain that he could shoot it straight; but as his father had taught him, that was the easy part of hunting.

His father had taught him as the Indian had taught his father that to be a good hunter one must first be a good trapper. A successful trapper knows the habits of his prey, where it goes and why and when. Other lads would go to search the woods for game and shoot what they encountered, but the boy went to the woods with a prey in mind. He would go to where the prey would be and had only to wait.

His father had also taught him that patience was as important as shooting. "Why can a cat catch a bird who can fly?" the boy's father asked.

The boy replied, "Because the cat is smarter."

The father returned, "Then why can a dog, who is smarter than the cat, not catch the bird?"

As the boy pondered the question, his father continued, "The answer is patience. Whereas the dog will chase the bird, the cat waits for the bird to come to him. The greatest virtue for a hunter is patience. Patience to wait for the prey, and then harder still, to wait for the perfect shot."

So the boy waited as he had most of the afternoon, downwind of the lair and concealed. He would make no motion or sound; he knew that his prey would come. Although he was not yet eleven years old, he was already a skilled hunter. He heard the slightest rustle, and then he saw it in the corner of his eye. Always cautious around its lair, it sniffed the air and searched the surroundings. Then it moved quickly toward the opening. The boy waited for the perfect time and released his shot. He knew instantly it would be perfect, stopping the animal and not hurting the fur.

He approached the animal carefully, realizing a wounded animal is by far the most dangerous, but as he suspected as he saw it lying motionless in a small puddle of red, his shot had been true. This was always the saddest part of hunting as a true hunter learns to respect his prey. Unlike the other boys, he only hunted what he needed and disliked the concept of hunting for sport. He withdrew the arrow and inspected it for damage; he wiped it in the snow and returned it to his quiver. He lifted his prey and headed for home.

On his arrival home, he went straight to the Indian camp. An Indian woman in her thirties was smoking meat. As he approached her he called, "Marie, I have another!"
She regarded the animal and replied, "Why Jean-Baptiste*, it is beautiful, even finer than the first."
He returned, "I know where I will get a third and then we shall have enough. I would like to skin this one

myself, but could you help me as you are the true expert and I want it to be perfect."

They took it to a large flat stone and she instructed him as he skinned the beast. They washed it and hung it to begin the process of curing the skin. Marie said, "It will be good for now. You should get along as your mother will be expecting you for dinner."

As he walked toward the farmhouse, he encountered a number of the neighborhood boys carrying crooked sticks. The boys included his older brothers, André and Jean-François. As the fall harvest was over, the boys could occasionally take the afternoon off after finishing morning chores. These boys had, as usual, been playing their favorite game of lacrosse named for the French term for the stick *la crosse*. Today they had played on the pond on the Allard farm, which had frozen in the last cold snap. When it was on ice, they used the Indian term *Ah-kee*.

André saw him and called out, "Hey Baptiste*, how is the great hunter? Empty handed again?" He used the common nickname, Baptiste, used for all the boys with the common French name Jean-Baptiste.

Jean-Baptiste* replied that it had been a slow day; his project was to be a surprise. His next oldest brother, Jean-François, called back, "Maybe if you had come today we may have won."

Although Jean-Baptiste* was the youngest (André was fourteen and Jean-François twelve), Jean-Baptiste* had an uncanny ability to score. He regarded the game with the same patience as hunting and always waited for the best shot. Like his father as a young man, he was bigger than the other boys his age. He was as tall as Jean-François and almost as strong as André. Although his brothers were fond of him, they both regarded him as rather odd.

As they approached the farmhouse, they were greeted by their younger brother, Georges, age six. Although he was usually allowed to follow the boys to play lacrosse, they had escaped without him today. He took André's stick and began shooting small ice balls. They entered the house and were greeted by their mother who was hard at work at the hearth in the back of the front room. "Get your things put away and yourselves ready for dinner, your father will be here presently." She was being assisted by her oldest daughter, Marie, age eight who was also looking after Marie-Anne, age one, who played on the floor.

Jeanne* Anguille-Allard had come to Québec in 1671 from the region of Touraine along the Loire River in France. She had come to a marriage arranged by her family who was well to do by standards of the seventeenth century, and Jeanne* was well educated. She was taller than most French girls and quite attractive and fit even after fifteen years in the wilderness and seven children, six of whom had survived the hardships of the age and region. The seventh, Marie-Renée, had died one year earlier at the age of one from one of the many diseases that threatened the children of the era.

The door opened and her husband entered. He shook what was left of the light snow from his deerskin coat and fur hat and hung them on a hook. He surveyed the room and said, "*Bonsoir, famille.*"

They responded in unison, "*Bonsoir, Papa.*" François* Allard was tall, stronger, more quiet and thoughtful than most French colonists. He had come as an indentured man in 1666. He came from a small town in Normandie and had worked three years for a widow, Anne* Ardouin-Badeau. François* had gained a good reputation as a hard working, honest man and was well regarded throughout Québec. He had managed to develop one of the more prosperous farms in the region.

As they gathered around the table, they bowed their heads in anticipation of grace. François* gave his usual rendition thanking God for everything from the weather to the price of Calvados (which he had produced clandestinely for many years), and finished with thanks for bringing him to this wonderful new country. In truth, François* thanked God every morning, noon and night for a life of which he could have never dreamed in France.

The main dish consisted of two large pheasant shot the day before by the boys. François* inquired, "Who was responsible for these wonderful birds?"

André, mumbled, "Who do you think?"

François* responded, "You lads should learn from Jean-Baptiste* and hunt with more patience."

Jeanne* added, "You boys all have your talents, André is my student and Jean-François is our farmer."

"What about me?" called Georges.

"You, *Petit,* shall be Governor of Québec."

After a brief laugh, François* continued, "Tomorrow is Sunday and Father Mathieu has asked that Jean-François and Jean-Baptiste* serve mass, so be there early."

The boys were not thrilled at the task but they did like Father Mathieu. He had come from France on the same boat as their mother and they were good friends. Occasionally François* wondered if they were too good. The priest had also served some years in the Huron Missions and was versed in Indian ways and had a wicked lacrosse shot.

François* continued, "Monday and Tuesday we must try to make everything ready for winter. Philippe and his boys will be here at dawn and we will all be ready to go. Georges, we will need you as well."

The youngest boy brightened at being included with the 'men'. He stared back at his father. He always enjoyed his father's stare as he had the most unusual eyes, one brown and one green. François* told them that it ran in the family but it had not appeared in any of the children. He told them that it usually skipped a generation.

Chapter 5

<u>Charlesbourg, - The Next Day:</u>

After mass, the congregation gathered outside in the square. Although it was early winter with a scant inch of snow on the ground, the rugged colonists continued their weekly ritual of an outdoor picnic and would only be sent into the chapel when the great winter storms came later in the season.

As the early Québec farms were long 'ribbons' perpendicular to the Saint-Laurent River, Charlesbourg and some of the newer settlements were built around a square. The town center was about one mile from the big river and the houses formed a circle around the square with the farms extending out like very long pieces of pie. The farms were quite large and none were more than ten percent cleared. Eventually the land would be divided among the children of the various families.

The square was used for gatherings like the picnics and various games. The chapel, which had been built sixteen years earlier, and its cemetery were adjacent to the square. The typical house had a ground floor for storage or a shop, the second for living and a loft for the children. A few commerces were now in the village and they were on the bottom floor of the houses of the proprietors who also farmed.

Charlesbourg boasted a few businesses including an inn and tavern called the *Oie Bleue,* or Blue Goose in

English. There was a small store, a blacksmith, carpenter, cabinetmaker, and next to the Allards, Thomas* Pageot, the tailor. The society of twenty-three families was extremely close. They co-operated on building and many of the heavy farming tasks. The proximity of the houses provided good protection against the constant threat of Indian raids by the Five Nations of the Iroquois originating around Lake Champlain in the British and Dutch Colonies.

Unlike Québec at the arrival of François* Allard in 1666, most clothes, food, livestock, and even some industrial goods were now products of the young colony. Even many of the citizens, like the Allard children, were products of Québec.

The picnic was a grand feast. Adults gossiped and planned, the boys played games and the girls watched the boys. Although most men did not marry before the age of twenty, it was not unusual for the girls to become marriageable at the age of fourteen. Having little interest in girls, the Allard boys engaged in a game of Lacrosse played on the thin layer of snow on the square. Although Jean-Baptiste* was younger than most of the boys in the game, he was valued for his accurate shot due to an unusually strong left arm and his incredible sense of timing and patience.

The Sunday picnic served as dinner and afterwards the Allard children returned home where their mother gave them their lessons. Having been raised near the abbey at Artannes-sur-Indres in France, Jeanne* was better educated than most of the women and was determined to maintain this in her children. She had found her husband a good student and planned to do as much with the children. As there was no formal school for the *habitants,* as the French called the free settlers, home schooling was all that was available.

André, the oldest, was the best student. He was named for his uncle André Anguille, a priest in France who had been an excellent student himself. Jean-François and Jean-Baptiste* were more interested in the outdoor activities of farming and hunting. Marie and young Georges also showed some promise.

As promised, the next morning started early, and François* and his boys were out at dawn to meet Philippe and his two boys, Henri, who was the age of André, and Joseph, who was the age of Jean-Baptiste*. They were an Algonquin family who lived in a camp on the Allard farm. Philippe's father, also Henri, had lived with his family on the farm of Anne* Ardouin and had been a great friend and tutor of François* when he first came from France.

The French settlers enjoyed a close relationship with the native people and they learned a great deal from each other. The relationship with the natives to the south in the British and Dutch territories was not so good and frequently hostile.

The two men and their boys began the early winter ritual of securing the farm for the hard and sometimes cruel Québec winter. Firewood, livestock feed and human provisions were checked to be adequate and appropriately stored in a set place, which was then marked with a tall stick. Other landmarks about the farm were marked with stakes longer than ten feet. They knew that at any time a snowfall could blanket the farm higher than the buildings and these stakes were vital.

In addition, they had to stock and secure the *caveau*, which was a man-made cave, dug in the side of a hill close to the farm. It was quite large and used to store furs and other items to be used in trade. It also contained a certain amount of non-perishable food, candles and other necessities so that it could be occupied. The outside was entirely covered and not discernible even at very close inspection. This was to be used in the event of the rare, but always feared and anticipated, Iroquois raid. Each of the family members had been well trained in the use of the *caveau.*

As the day progressed, Philippe noted that the sky in the north appeared very dark. He remarked, "I predict a big snow tonight." Indian weather predictions were generally quite accurate, and the following morning, the Allard family awoke to three feet of new snow.

The boys were immediately dispatched to make tracks along the common walkways of the farm. Everyone would henceforth stay to these paths, both to prevent becoming lost and also to maintain the visible pathway. After the chores were completed, Jean-Baptiste* took to the woods with his bow. He had a deadline to meet.

Chapter 6

<u>Québec - December 24, 1686:</u>

It was custom in the Allard house to gather on Christmas Eve after dinner to exchange gifts. Gifts were simple and usually useful items. Jeanne* arranged so that everyone gave at least one gift and that each of the children received one but no more than two gifts. Philippe and his family came up to the house for the occasion for a rare inside visit.

At the end of the gifts, there remained one large paper-wrapped item beneath the traditional pine tree. Jean-Baptiste* lifted it up and handed it to his surprised mother, "This is for Mama." Jeanne* unwrapped it and was dumbstruck at the contents. It was a stole made from three perfectly matched red fox pelts. The pelts were of excellent quality as was the stole. She wondered what the local woman would think of her in such a garment. This was something that was produced in Québec to be sent to France and sold to wealthy ladies, not worn by the pioneer wives.

Jean-Baptiste* spoke up, "I hunted the fox and Marie helped me cure the pelts and make the stole. I know how much you liked the one that Aunt Madeleine has."

Madeleine de Roybon was not actually his aunt. She and Jeanne* had come on the same boat from France in 1671, and although they were 'cut from very different bolts of cloth,' the ladies had become very good friends. Madeleine was sent from France by her father, a rich officer of the King, because of her outrageous behavior. Even though she too was a *fille du roi*, she did not marry; rather she continued her scandalous ways and was now the long-term mistress of the rich explorer, René-Robert Cavelier de LaSalle.

Jeanne* realized that she must wear this to mass tomorrow at the Cathedral in the city, but she wondered how she would explain such a fine garment to the other *habitant* wives.

The next day was bright and sunny, and in spite of the early heavy snow, the family was able to travel to Québec for the Noël mass. As the Saint-Laurent was not securely frozen, François hitched their large Perchon horse to the cart and they traveled along the shore road, fording the Charles River and entering the city from the side.

Due to the relatively small size of the colony, most of the Québec residents were acquainted with one another, and the *habitants* such as the Allards were well regarded by the more affluent colonists. After mass, the community gathered in the square of the cathedral in the upper town. Although they were acquainted, the Québec winter made visits quite infrequent.

Jeanne* visited with many of her friends and explained that the stole was a gift from her son. They all seemed to understand but were perplexed at how a young boy could produce something so fine, however knowing that Jeanne* was not one to put on airs, they took her at her word. Finally Madeline de Roybon wearing her fox stole arrived on the arm of LaSalle, and in her fun loving way said, "Why Jeanne*, it would appear that farming is doing well this year."

Jeanne* explained, "It is a gift from Jean-Baptiste* who hunted and made it, but it is rather too fine for me."

Both women realized that Jeanne*'s was of finer quality, but Madeleine said, "Nothing is too fine for a boy's mother. Where is the lad?" Seeing Jean-Baptiste* with his friends, Madeleine greeted him and congratulated him with a hug. Jean-Baptiste* liked being hugged by Madeleine because she always smelled so good.

Madeline returned to Jeanne* without LaSalle, "It seems that Robert is leaving as soon as the ice breaks on some new journey for the King. He's going to some Spanish place beyond the end of the Mississippi, Mexico or something. Anyway it will give me time to meet the new immigrants looking for adventure. Robert has been rather morose after losing that boat that Henri de Tonty had built for him."

Chapter 7

Charlesbourg - July 17, 1689:

After grace at dinner, François* announced. "There is to be a summer fair in Montréal next week, something like the fur market but for agricultural items, and considerably less wild. I thought it would be a good opportunity for the older boys to see Montréal. I will take André and Jean-François, and Philippe will take Henri."

Immediately sensing Jean-Baptiste*'s disappointment, Jeanne* replied. "How wonderful! Baptiste* will be the man of the household." Knowing when he was being offered congratulation for a condolence, the boy's face sank and he remained quiet for the remainder of dinner. He knew that it would be of little use to question his father's judgment.

After dinner François* approached him, "I know you would like to go, but twelve is quite young for this venture. If you were to go, I would have to ask Joseph as well and there is not enough room in the canoe, perhaps next year." As the boy sulked off to bed, Jeanne* said to her husband, "Don't worry, I'll find some special treat for him."

Charlesbourg - July 24, 1689:

As François*, Philippe and the three older boys shouldered their packs and began the hike to the Saint-Laurent where their canoe was stored, Jean-Baptiste* and Joseph helped their mothers with morning chores. Jean-Baptiste* put on his saddest face and inquired, "Since we have missed this trip, perhaps Joseph and I could do an overnight hunt next weekend."

Jeanne* thought and replied, "We shall see, if you work hard and you must be back Saturday night and ready for mass. Don't forget that there is a special festival in Québec and the entire village will go to the cathedral for mass."

Joseph stifled his excitement and replied, "Yes Mama".

The Saint-Laurent - July 27, 1689:

The journey to Montréal was still wild in places but had changed greatly since François* had made his first journey with Philippe's father, Henri, over twenty years ago. The shore beyond Québec was very populated for several miles, but it returned to wilderness for a great while before *Trois Rivieres*. They stopped at the Algonquin camp of Philippe's uncle Anuk for the night.

The boys were ecstatic at the prospect of staying in a 'real' Indian camp. Anuk and his people were not Christian and followed the old Indians ways. François* could never see a real moral difference unless it was that the Indians were, if anything, more honest than the French. François himself always enjoyed these stays as it reminded him of his first years of adventure with the first Henri.

The men sat and smoked into the night, the boys were delighted to be invited to smoke the Indian pipe with the men; though as the night passed they began to feel a little 'green'. Anuk talked of the feared disappearance of the Indian ways. Again, his men who guided near the Dutch and English territories told of the massive encroachment into the wilderness. He also indicated that the Iroquois were again becoming restless.

When asked about his brother, the first Henri, Anuk looked up and said. "I have not seen him for many winters, but in my heart I feel he still lives. Each night I hope to see him appear at my campfire." As the talking died and the men drifted to bed, François* asked that they not treat the boys to the customary hospitality of an Indian maiden, as he felt their mother may not understand.

The following morning they continued on to the wide portion of the Saint-Laurent southwest of *Trois Rivieres*. The following day they passed an isolated farmhouse that had burned to the ground. When the boys asked about it, François* had a worried look but replied. "People need to be more careful of their fireplaces." Two days later they reached their destination.

Montréal - August 3, 1689:

Montréal had grown considerably since François*'s first visit many years ago. It was larger and now clearly the hub of the fur trade as well as the frontier exploration. It had a stone cathedral, a small seminary, government buildings and many fine homes. The streets were improved and the people more civilized. It did, however, still possess a more wilderness allure compared to Québec.

The fair was a grand event. There were livestock shows and exhibits of new farming method and machinery. There was even a device to pull behind a horse or cow that

would cut hay, wheat, or even stocks of maize. François*
marveled at such a device and wondered if one could be
collectively purchased by the Charlesbourg farmers. The
boys were delighted with all the sights. Jean-François, the
family farmer, was the most interested in the show.

Charlesbourg - August 3, 1689:

At the same time their brothers were marveling at
modern farming, Jean-Baptiste* and Joseph were preparing
for their great adventure as they packed and readied to set
out on the overnight camping trip. As a perverse piece of
luck, young Marie-Anne now age four was feeling poorly
and Jeanne* had decided that the family would have to skip
mass at the cathedral. As a result, she relented to allow the
boys to stay out two nights but instructed them to be home
early Sunday morning.

They hiked into the Laurentian foothills and found
abundant small game. Both boys were skilled trackers and
hunters and enjoyed the procedure much more than the kill.
They did, however, acquire a good bit of small game. They
made camp the first night high in the foothills. The boys
had been well schooled by their fathers and took the lessons
seriously. They felt as much at home in the wild as they did
in their own beds.

The following morning they arose ready for another
full day. After a breakfast of pemmican and corn bread,
they set off. They had noticed interesting tracks and set off
in search of their owners. Before midday, Joseph stopped
abruptly and sniffed the air. No matter how hard he tried,

Jean-Baptiste* could not equal the Indian's sense of smell. He inquired, "Joseph, what is it?"

His friend replied, "I am not certain but let's proceed cautiously."

About an hour later, they arrived at a small overlook and below they could see what they were tracking. Both boys froze in their tracks. Joseph whispered, "What should we do?"

After some consideration, Jean-Baptiste* replied, "We should continue to follow, but we must stay behind. As we are traveling south and there is a good breeze in our face, we are decidedly upwind and at a clear advantage. We must hope that there are no more behind us and I fear we must leave our game." Both boys realized that leaving the game broke a cardinal rule as it left clear evidence of their trail, but after some discussion they decided that they had no choice and scattered the animals about as inconspicuously as possible, and continued ahead with hearts racing.

The boys spent the remainder of the day trailing their prey. They used all the skills they had been taught, strict silence, stay upwind, keep a safe distance and watch your back. Eventually their prey stopped for the night and Jean-Baptiste* and Joseph set a camp above with some view of the prey. They used no fire and kept watches while their prey slept. In the morning they continued and began to realize that their trail was leading them towards Charlesbourg.

<u>Montréal - Sunday August 5, 1689</u>:

When François* and Philippe and the three boys were returning to the fair for one more tour before returning home, they saw a large animated crowd in front of the cathedral. François* and Philippe went up to hear the conversation and they returned quickly to the boys. François* said, "It seems that the fair has been cancelled for the day and that we should be heading home without delay". In spite of the objections of the boys, the two men led them to quickly assemble their belongings and go to the canoe.

Chapter 8

<u>Charlesbourg - Sunday August 5, 1689, the same day:</u>

Jeanne* realized that this could be the quietest day of her life. The entire village without exception had parted for mass and the festival in Québec. The men and the older boys would not be home for a few days and the Jean-Baptiste* and Joseph were not yet home. Although they had promised to be home Sunday morning, she was not surprised that they were late and would probably arrive in the late afternoon with some excuse.

Marie-Anne was on the mend and playing with her older sister, brother Georges, and their youngest brother, the latest addition of the Allard family, Thomas, now age two. Jeanne* was using the quiet time to work on lessons with Marie. The Indian woman had expressed a desire to learn to read and write and was doing well, although they had not had much time to work on it.

As they discussed subtleties of spelling and pronunciation, Jeanne* raised her nose to the air. She arose and walked to the porch. She returned quickly saying. "I believe the Pageot barn is afire. I must go and release the animals. Watch the children."

She ran quickly to the next farm a short distance away. Fires in barns were common at this time of year when the hay was prone to setting itself on fire due to the heat caused by decay. Jeanne* realized there was little that she could do for the barn, but she needed to release the animals that were inside. As she approached the farm, she could see a blaze on the western side of the barn. She rushed to the door and opened it. The smoke was thick but she could see the two cows and the goats. She chased them out and as the last goat ran free she noticed that by her rushing out unarmed, she had made a disastrous error.

There was a small blaze on the south side of the barn as well. This fire had not started, it had been set! She carefully peered out of the door and saw five of them. She remembered the evil look of the man who had entered the ship many years ago through the cannon window. She recognized the fierce strip of hair down the center of his scalp. There was no doubt that they were Iroquois. She stopped for a second and thought of her brother and murmured, "Please God and André help me be strong and wise."

With that she soaked the front of her skirt in the water for the animals and put it over her head to protect her from the heat and smoke and waited. After enduring as long as she could, she again peered out. They were not in sight. She realized that they had likely not seen her but were now between her and her children. She crept out carefully.

Hiding behind a bush she could see at least seven. They were still occupied with the Pageot farm, which allowed her the opportunity to stay low and creep toward her house. Her heart racing as never before, she believed that she was clear of them and ran as fast as possible to the house. As she approached the door she saw three Indians toward the back of her house. She could not be certain that they had not seen her. Entering the house, she panicked when she realized it was empty.

Nothing appeared to have been disturbed; however she saw that someone had thrown flour on the surface of the table where she had been working with Marie. On closer inspection she saw writing in the flour done with a finger, CAVO. Her mind raced as she realized that Marie, who was not well versed in spelling, had meant 'caveau', and that hopefully she had realized the dilemma and taken the children to the caveau to hide. Jeanne* also realized that she would not be able to join them for fear of attracting the Indians to the hiding place and that it was up to her alone to defend her home and family.

She went to the hearth for her rifle but realized that one shot would alert the entire band. She searched the room for an alternative and saw André's neglected bow with a quiver with only five arrows. She took it and headed for the door, hoping Marie had taught her to shoot the weapon at least as well as she had taught Marie to spell. She looked outside and saw an opportunity to run behind a line of firewood that would give her cover between the house and the caveau.

Jeanne* waited for what seemed to be an eternity when two Indians appeared moving quickly towards her. She pulled out her first arrow and took careful aim at the first Indian who could be shot without immediately alerting the second. She waited as François* had taught her for the perfect shot. She took it and it hit the mark as the man fell silently. Jeanne*, realizing that she had killed a man, quickly crossed herself and let her fear of God lapse behind her fear for her family. The second man quickly saw his companion fall, but she had already taken aim and felled him as well.

Before she could recover, there were three more in front of her. She took her first shot quickly and it hit the mark. The second, although poorly aimed, also found its target. She rushed to get off the third and as expected from such a quick shot, it missed. When the third man realized she had no more arrows, he laughed an evil laugh and approached her slowly with his knife. As he jumped on her he had a terrible surprise. She had pulled her knife, the Christmas present from her husband, and stuck it expertly into the man's chest. With a scream, he covered her with his blood and fell limp.

Jeanne* retrieved the knife and fled to a bush closer to the caveau. Just as she began to think that there were no more, three Iroquois appeared walking dangerously close to the door of the caveau. Jeanne* noticed with panic that Marie had not concealed it well and it was only a matter of time before they realized that it was a door. Without another option she stood up and shouted at the savages, and like a mother partridge, she called the attention of the hunters to herself and away from her children.

Chapter 9

Covered with the last man's blood, she waved her knife and screamed at the Indians. She thought that if she could get them to give chase, she could run them away from the caveau and after they had killed her, they may not return to that area. She ran as fast as she could through a bramble to the Pageot property where the remains of the barn smoldered. Then she turned north and up the wheat field toward the forest. She managed to evade them almost to the forest line when she felt the hand of one on her dress.

He pulled her back and she turned to take a futile swing with her knife at the much stronger and now prepared savage. As she knew it was the end, she saw his evil face go blank. His grip loosened as he fell to his knees and then flat on his face. An arrow protruded from his back, expertly aimed just left of center to hit his heart. She saw a single bright red cardinal feather in the quill and realized this arrow could belong to only one person. The other two Indians who had been directly behind the first were now on their knees and soon equally dead.

Jeanne* looked up and shouted, "Jean-Baptiste*!" as she saw her son and Joseph cautiously approaching her. Just as she thought they were saved, four more Iroquois appeared from the forest. They took aim at the boys. Joseph was hit in the chest and fell quickly. Jean-Baptiste* reacted. He jumped quickly to the side but was hit in the shoulder. He fell momentarily, but arose and faced the men with his knife. Just as the first Indian was upon him, arrows again emerged from the trees. The first man fell immediately and the other three in very rapid succession.

Jeanne*'s elation was again short-lived as a new Indian appeared from the trees. She fought back her panic long enough to realize that he was not Iroquois, but an older Algonquin brave with long gray hair tied to a feather with a leather strap. The man went directly to Joseph. When Jeanne* arrived, he was expertly removing the arrow from his chest. He looked up at Jeanne* and said in excellent French, "Get pine tar quickly!"

Jeanne ran quickly to the closest pine tree and with her bloody knife scraped a handful of the sticky substance. When she returned, the man had turned Joseph on his side with the wound upward. Pale and his lips blue, Joseph was scarcely breathing. The man took the tar and blew into the boy's mouth. Air and blood bubbled out the wound and the man packed the tar in the wound and bound Joseph's chest with the bandana that the man had worn about his waist.

He propped Joseph's head up on a pack that he had carried. The boy began to breathe with some difficulty and his color improved. The man then went to Jean-Baptiste*. The arrow was only in the flesh. The man pushed the point out as Jean-Baptiste* let out a stifled cry and Jeanne* let out a great one. He then broke the arrow and removed both ends and bound the shoulder with another scarf.

The old Indian spoke again, "This is not grave. I believe your friend too will heal. Your father has taught you well to shoot the bow and how to have patience even under fear of death. You did well. You have saved your family and your village."

With that he stood and faced Jeanne* who now stood, dazed sobbing, and covered with blood. The man announced, "You must be Madame Allard, I am Henri."

Jeanne* and Henri brought the boys back to the house and Jeanne* went to fetch Marie and the small children from the caveau. Marie and young Marie Allard went to fetch water and ointments from the Indian camp. They cleaned the blood from Jeanne* and the boys and dressed the wounds. Soon both boys were sound asleep.

The others went to sit on the porch and Henri began his tale. "I have been three winters in the north country of the Huron, at the lake *Gitcheegumee.* I had started down to see my brother Anuk at his camp near *Trois Rivieres.* On my route I encountered some *coureur de bois* who had heard of planned Iroquois raids up the entire Saint-Laurent. I diverted my route to here, fearing that Charlesbourg would be an easy target as it is off the riverbank.

"This group had planned to attack before dawn. Fortunately they were a young band, more fierce than intelligent. Apparently the boys happened on them and trailed them for some time. Once their intentions were clear, the boys began to cause them trouble. Happily the boys were more intelligent than fierce. I believe they were able to ambush and kill the Iroquois one by one until they had removed more than half the band.

"The Iroquois finally left a few braves to fight the boys, who the Iroquois had supposed to be a larger group, and the remainder of the band made it here. However they arrived later than they had expected and were surprised to find the town deserted. They even chose the wrong place to start the first fire, being next to the only people in the village. Eventually the boys finished the group left behind and arrived here just in time to save you, and I arrived just in time to help finish."

Soon Marie noticed the Pageot wagon returning from town, she ran to give them the news and Catherine* Pageot said she would alert the other neighbors and ask them not to call at Allards until tomorrow.

As the sun set, they went into the house where Marie and young Marie had made a simple dinner. Jean-Baptiste* took some soup and Joseph continued to sleep fitfully. After dinner Henri said, "I believe my grandson will recover, Madame. You and the children should sleep and Marie and I will each stay on a porch to watch for any Iroquois stragglers."

He took Jeanne*'s gun from the fireplace and gave it to her, "Since you have no more arrows, keep this. Although I suspect it will be many years before the Iroquois come again to this house." And he gave his old wonderful laugh. Later in the night, young Marie Allard came out to sit with Marie. Many strong bonds had been formed this day.

Chapter 10

Charlesbourg - August 6, 1689:

The following morning, the entire community showed up at the Allard and Pageot farms bringing tools, food and burning curiosity. The men formed work parties to drag and bury the many dead Iroquois in a mass grave and clean up the damage at the Pageot barn. The burned wood was discarded, and all metal, nails, hinges etc. were rescued and readied for reuse. Plans were made to rebuild after mass in two weeks.

They collected twenty-five bodies in all including the twelve Jeanne* had killed or seen killed. Henri estimated that there were at least that many in the woods that had been killed by him or the boys. The ladies set up lunch and dinner tables around the yard and continually told Jeanne* to 'sit' although she kept jumping up to help. Joseph remained asleep and ran a fever, Marie* Renaud who was a sage-femme or midwife, brought herbal remedies for him.

Jean-Baptiste* was up and about and although his shoulder was sore, he was feeling fine. He soon found himself the center of attention as everyone gathered to hear his story.

"On the second day of our hunt, we encountered a fresh trail though the brush. It was easy to follow and at first we thought it was a caribou. As we eventually found tracks we realized it was a large band of moccasins in single file. It was odd for Indians to leave such a trail, so we followed it. Later in the day we saw them from an overlook. We were upwind and they were moving fast and without caution so they were easy to follow. We camped and held watches above them that night, and in the morning we realized that they were headed for Charlesbourg.

"When we crossed their camp, we realized that they had been drinking corn whiskey and that this would serve greatly to our advantage. We realized that we would likely be noticed if we tried to get ahead. We also realized that they were likely to get to the village when everyone was at mass and there would be no one to warn, well almost no one." He added looking up at his mother.

"We decided we would try to ambush them individually. As Joseph can move more quietly and quickly than I he would provide a diversion, and as I was the better aim, I would do the shooting. As I said, they were moving fast and in single file. Joseph would get the attention of the last man, and when he stopped, Joseph would briefly show himself. The man would try to shoot and I would shoot him from the other side of the trail. As they were excited and had been drinking, they always shot too soon and missed.

"Once the Iroquois was hit and the others were ahead, we would make certain he was dead, retrieve the arrow, and move the body off the trail and move forward. Eventually we realized that they were so careless and concentrating so much on what was ahead rather than behind, we stopped hiding the bodies and made better progress. We had removed more than twenty before they realized what we were doing.

"They made a stand to the rear, however they did not know who or where we were or how many. They made a few forays into the woods and we were able to kill another five. At that point they left a guard of six and moved on. Joseph moved quietly around their back and made a diversion. They all turned in unison, they were truly stupid and careless, and we were able to finish them off.

"By the time we made the village they had already arrived and we removed five more from behind before we saw them menacing my mother. This was the only time that we moved too quickly and of course were caught. When I was hit I thought we were finished as I estimated that there were at least five or ten more to our west. However it seems that Henri had arrived at the same time as we had and controlled that group as well as those that we had allowed to get in back of us. As my father says, this was not the day that God had chosen for us to die."

The audience sat dumbfounded at this fantastic tale that would become more fantastic each year for many years to come. Everyone hugged and congratulated the boy and lunch was served. The good news was that Joseph had begun to awaken and taken a small amount of broth.

Charlesbourg - August 12, 1689:

As François*, Philippe and the boys approached the western farms of Québec, they were hailed by a canoe. It was François*'s old shipmate, Guillaume* Renaud who had been sturgeon fishing with his three sons, Louis, Jean-Bernard, and Pierre*. Renaud quickly related the story of the raid and that the family was well, including Joseph who was on the mend. François* indicated that when they had heard of raids in Montreal, they had left in haste. He added further they had seen more than a few burned farms on the route home. With this they bid a quick goodbye and although they were now relieved at the news, they made more haste to shore and marched immediately up the Charlesbourg road to the farm.

Marie Allard saw them approaching the square and alerted the others who all came to the house for a happy and tearful reunion. François*'s elation was further heightened by the appearance of his old friend Henri. Renaud had neglected that part of the tale. Once they had settled, Jean-Baptiste* retold his tale which was beginning to grow already. This time Joseph was present to present his side as well. Young Marie took note that there seemed to be more dead Iroquois in the story this time but said nothing.

The family had dinner outside, as it was a beautiful evening but also to more easily accommodate the Indian family. Although their bond had already been strong, after this event it could never be stronger. François* gave a special grace thanking God for the continued safety of his family and friends in this wild place.

After dinner François* told his story. "On the morning of the fifth, the very day of your attack, we were alerted that there had been a terrible massacre south of the city of Montreal. As a result we left at once. It seems that it was the town of Lachine, which is south of the city. It sits on the wide portion of the Saint-Laurent that is called *Lac Saint-Louis* near the great rapids that as we have heard,

Champlain called 'La Chine' as he felt it was the route to China.

"It is now a town of about a several hundred inhabitants. One of its earliest citizens is Pierre* Gauthier. I had met him on two occasions. Apparently a large band of Iroquois swept down on the village at night. By some accounts there were as many as 1000.

"They burned the village and slaughtered the inhabitants who were butchered and scalped, men, women and children, as many as 400. Many more were taken as captives. I was told that my friend Gauthier and his wife Charlotte* Roussel-Gauthier have both disappeared. We heard that there had been many other raids up the coast and I regret to say that we saw more than a few burned farms on our return.

"I fear that we may expect more difficulties and everyone must be especially cautious. We must also see to it that the caveau is secure. It would seem that it was instrumental in our salvation this time.

Later in the evening Henri, Philippe, and François* sat and smoked on the porch. Henri and François reminisced of their early days. At the end of the evening, Henri announced, "If there is no objection, I believe I may stay a while with my son. I suppose some French company will not influence me too badly."

François* replied, "My old friend, nothing could please me more."

Charlesbourg - Sunday August 19, 1689:

After mass, instead of the usual picnic, the congregation gathered at the Pageot farm to raise a barn. Such events were becoming common and the procedure was streamlined. Those who had lumber left from tree clearing would bring it. The families with horses brought them and there were crews for setting the footings and the foundation, raising the superstructure and finishing the walls. Usually it could be finished the same day.

Thomas* Pageot helped where he could but as a tailor, he was not well versed in carpentry. Pageot had come to Québec as a very young man a few years before François*. He had come from the village of Mamers in the Perche region of Normandie where his father and grandfather had been tailors. He had worked several years as the tailor for the Jesuits at the seminary in the upper town.

After several years at the seminary, he decided to start a home of his own and obtained the farm next to François*. Two years later he married Catherine* Roy whose parents had come from Larochelle before 1660 with her three older siblings. Catherine* was born in Quebéc and was one of the first native Québécoise. At the time of the marriage, she was 16 years old and he was 33, but this was not unusual. Her native background made her stronger and more savvy of the wilderness than her husband.

In 1689 the Pageots had three children, Marie-Anne, 11 years, Jean-Baptiste, 7 years, and Anne-Elisabeth* 3.

Most of the farming was up to Catherine* so the enterprise was small, but the income from the tailor shop under the farmhouse was enough to keep them comfortable.

By late afternoon, the project was basically completed. Dinner was served and all the families began to return home. There remained only the Pageots and the Allards. Thomas* brought out a bottle of calvados and glasses. He said, "This is the finest drink I possess and I wish to propose a toast." The group all understood the half-joke, half-complement as it was the calvados made by François*. He continued, "To the Allard family, our neighbors and friends and now our saviors."

After the toast, Catherine* added, "I must confess that I always thought that Jeanne* was too French, too refined, and too educated to be a true pioneer. I now realize how very mistaken I was." And the two ladies embraced.

At this point little Anne-Elisabeth* age three came up to Jean-Baptiste* and said, "Baptiste*, you are my hero," and gave him a kiss on the cheek. Jean-Baptiste*'s face reddened and the families all laughed and after hugs all around they parted.

Chapter 11

<u>The Blue Goose Tavern, Charlesbourg - May 1694:</u>

Each year it had become more and more of a custom for the men of the village to gather in the evening at the tavern, especially on Saturday nights. They discussed local affairs and played cards, especially the traditional French game of 'euchre'. Wine and cider were being replaced by beer. Some of the tavern-owning colonists were from the Alsace region in the east of France and skilled in its fabrication.

François* was sitting with Jean* Poitevin (called Laviolette), Guillaume* Renaud, and Jacques Bedard. Tonight's topic was the recent dry spell. "If only we had a means of conserving excess water until it is needed," François* remarked, "We could avoid the poor crop years that these spells produce."

Bedard replied, "My father told me that in the south of France, there are 'aqueducts' which bring water from far away sources on demand. These were built many years ago however and require years of labor by many men."

François* returned, "Our region is not so dry as that of the French south, and the problem is only periodic. There must be a way."

Just then the door opened. It was difficult to ignore, as a strong north wind was howling this night. Three well dressed gentlemen entered. It was very unusual for people other than the local *habitants* to use this backwoods tavern.

The men knew one of the men but the other two were a mystery. They were younger and one had a thin moustache. He wore a large cap with a plume and a long black cape. The other was more plainly dressed. They came to the table and the older man announced, "Ah, Monsieur Allard, just the man we were searching."

François* replied, "*Bonsoir,* Monsieur Guyon." Denis Guyon was a well-known businessman. His father, Jean* Guyon, had come as one of the very first settlers from Perche. He was a stonemason and had become very wealthy. Denis dealt in furs and commodities.

Guyon continued, "Gentlemen, this is Monsieur Antoine Lamothe Sieur de Cadillac, and his assistant Pierre." The other men were introduced and Guyon continued, "Antoine is my son-in-law, having married my daughter Therese four years ago. He is in the service of his Majesty's army developing posts to support and protect the fur trade."

After the men were seated and Cadillac began, "When I first came to Acadie in 1683, I signed on to sail with Monsieur Guyon's brother, François, protecting our shores from the Dutch and British. Captain Guyon indicated that he had met Monsieur Allard at sea; he said that you were highly regarded by the captain and the crew."

François* remembered well his meeting with François Guyon. He was a privateer, or a pirate sailing under the protection of the French flag. François* replied, "Messieurs Renaud and Poitevin were both on that same voyage, we recall it well."

Cadillac continued, "It was through Captain Guyon that I had the happy occasion to visit the home of his brother and meet my future bride. The King has now ordered me to build a fort at the straits called Michilimackinac and I plan to leave before the year is out. My interest with you Monsieur Allard is that I have heard that you are expert in the fabrication of Calvados."

François* spoke cautiously, as the government was opposing local "grog shops" and other home made spirits which escaped tax. François had not been menaced as his operation was small and the colony was unable to find a better product. In addition, most of the high officials of both the government and the church were good customers. "The exact process is quite complicated. It is from an old family remedy."

Cadillac spoke up, "Have no fear, Monsieur, I have no interest in competing with you, as I understand it would be futile in any case. Rather I am interested for my own purposes in producing a simple distilled product from apples."

François* explained that it was little different than the fermenting and then distilling of any substance such as corn and gave a quick course on the basics. Cadillac seemed mildly interested, but Pierre produced a quill and paper and took detailed notes. At the conclusion the men stood and took their leave, but Cadillac added, "By the way, Monsieur Allard, I understand that you have a young son who has quite a reputation as an Indian slayer. I may have need of such a young man in my venture."

François* replied, "I'm afraid that his reputation has been a bit overstated. However he must speak for himself, his name is Jean-Baptiste*, he is now eighteen years." And with that the three men departed.

After they left, Bedard questioned, "Why would a man like that who can afford any manner of drink, be interested in the fabrication of cheap apple brandy?" The men shrugged and the euchre game recommenced.

Québec - June 1694:

Jeanne* and François* were standing in the square of the cathedral socializing with friends after mass. They were approached by a man in a large plumed hat with an attractive young lady on his arm. He held out his hand to François* and said, "Monsieur Allard, how wonderful to see you again."

François* responded by introducing Cadillac to Jeanne*. Cadillac responded, "Allow me to present my wonderful wife, Marie-Therese."

The Allards recognized Marie-Therese Guyon as the beautiful daughter of Denis Guyon. She was 23 years old, only one year older than their André. It was said that the marriage came with an enormous dowry from her rich father.

Cadillac continued, "As I indicated to you last month, his majesty is sending me on a project in the west and I wonder if your famous son would be able to accompany us. I would like to come speak with him but felt that I should again ask your permission."

François* responded, "As I have said, the boy is old enough for his own decisions. You are welcome to come and speak with him." And with that the couples took their leave.

Charlesbourg - The Following Week:

Jean-Baptiste* and Joseph labored under the blistering sun. There had been no rain for weeks and the crops were threatened with failure. François* had continued his plan to bring water to the crops and had had the boys digging a ditch from the pond in the northeast of the farm to the northern extent of the crops. He had hoped that they could convince the water to flow to the dry fields.

At this time, most of the fields of the Charlesbourg farms had been cleared in the areas near the square. Boundaries were poorly defined and the farmers had instituted the old French custom of the hedgerow. They agreed on the line and left a small line of brush and trees intact to maintain the boundary. The result was an easily discernible tree and shrub boundary between each slice of "pie" of the village. François* had begun to plan the future of the farms for his sons. He planned to divide the current parcel for some of the boys and had an option on an undeveloped track on the southeast of the square for the others.

The boys had been at the ditch project for a week. The combination of the difficult task and the constant sun was dampening their enthusiasm. Jean-Baptiste* was only spurred on by the thought of another hunting trip after the work was completed. He looked up and noticed two gentlemen approaching them.

The man with the plumed hat introduced himself as Antoine Lamothe le Sieur de Cadillac. His companion was a man named Pierre. Jean-Baptiste*'s father had told him that these men may come to talk and had alerted him to the nature of their business, but the boy did not share this information.

"We are to embark on an important mission for his majesty, a voyage far to the west to the land of the Hurons to make a post at a strait called Michilimackinac. I need a young man who is versed in the ways of the natives and good with a weapon to serve as my personal guard. What do you say, lad?"

Jean-Baptiste* replied, "I have interest, but would need the permission of my father. I would also suggest that we bring my friend," as he indicated Joseph.

Cadillac returned, "You mean this Indian lad?"

Jean-Baptiste* held his temper and replied, "He is more versed in the language of the Huron and the Iroquois than I and knows the ways of the wilderness better than I."

Cadillac thought to himself that this son of a respected *habitant* as well as his savage friend might be just what he needed and he agreed. "I will send Pierre in three days' time for your father's answer. We plan to leave by the end of the month."

With that, Cadillac turned on his heels and departed for his carriage.

That evening at dinner Jean-Baptiste* approached his father with the proposition. Jeanne* was skeptical but remained silent. François* said, "I fear that I will need your help if the drought does not break. I will think about it tonight."

That night in bed his wife told him, "I don't think I trust this man Cadillac, although he speaks for the king and has married into one of the fine families in the colony, he leaves me uneasy."

François* responded, "I don't trust him either, but this is the sort of thing that Baptiste* craves and it may be the occasion for him to decide if he is to be a woodsman or a farmer. If the drought breaks, I believe I will let him go."

Jean-Baptiste* was as enthusiastic of the project as he could be. Although he usually said only cursory prayers at night, that evening he prayed for rain. Late that night his prayers were answered and he awoke to a deluge that drenched the fields and even rose the pond level until a trickle of water appeared in François*'s ditch. In the morning François* held true to his word and gave his permission.

The next evening, François* and Jean-Baptiste* went to the Indian camp to discuss the plan. François* indicated that his wife was nervous about the affair, and Joseph spoke up, "Perhaps we could tell Monsieur Cadillac that my Pipi could come," using the French endearment for one's grandfather.

Old Henri gave this some thought and replied, "It is true that I have stayed my welcome here and have been thinking of returning to my people. I have lived in that area in camps of Algonquin, Huron and even on occasion, Iroquois. I could make certain that the boys are safe through the first part of the adventure."

François* said that he would discuss it with Pierre when he returned for the answer and the group broke up for bed.

The following morning Pierre arrived and François* gave him the proposition. He returned to Québec to discuss it with Cadillac. Cadillac thought carefully and then replied to his assistant, "Two savages is more than I had planned for, but if the man is experienced, we can use him to our advantage, and after that they are both expendable." The next day Pierre returned and sealed the agreement; the three men would depart in two weeks time.

The following day Jeanne* made an unusual mid-week walk to the chapel on the square. She entered the empty building lit only by the small windows. Although she had seen many of the great cathedrals of France during her trip from Artannes to Dieppe to come to the new world, she felt that God was closer to this rough building than anywhere else. She sat on the rough log pew in the front of the small chapel. The altar was a rough-hewn affair with a small cross carved in the front. Over it was a roughly carved crucifix and on her right was a painting of the Virgin Mary and on her left a painting of Saint Charles de Borromée with the rope around his neck.

She knelt in front of the Virgin and said a prayer only a mother could say for the safety of her son and his friends. Afterwards she walked about the square until she felt that the tears had cleared her eyes enough to return to her family.

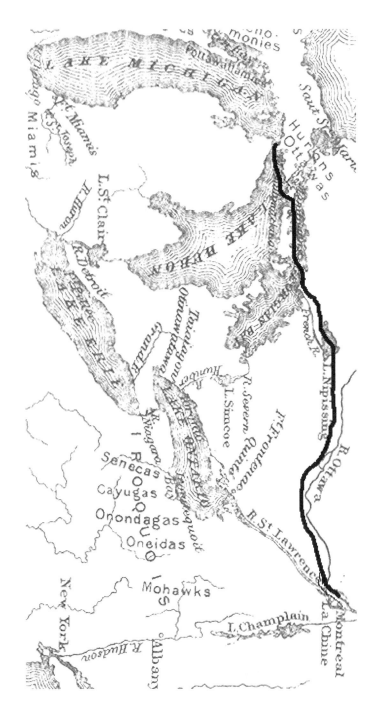

ROUTE TO MICHILIMACKINAC

Chapter 12

Québec - Early August 1694:

    The day of departure had arrived. Jean-Baptiste* and Joseph had raised their excitement to a fever pitch during the past few weeks. They were not only going to miss the drudgery of the harvest but were embarking on the wilderness trip of their dreams. The fact that Henri would accompany them was almost too much. The boys had bonded to the old man during the past few years and idolized him in every way. Jean-Baptiste* realized that his father had wanted him to stay and farm the land, but he had to see if this was his true destiny.

    Henri and the two boys met Cadillac's group at the foot of Port Royal. There were twelve canoes in all and about fifty men. There were ten other Indians and ten soldiers. The rest were French voyageurs most of whom were short and their shoulders as wide as they were tall. Joseph and Jean-Baptiste* recognized about half of the men. They were instructed by Pierre, "Baptiste*, you and your friend will travel with Monsieur Cadillac." Motioning to Henri he indicated, "You will come in my canoe." Henri grunted giving his best illiterate Indian imitation.

    They rounded Cap Diamant under the ledge of the Citadelle and headed south and west toward Montréal. Baptiste* was surprised by the speed of the boats. The two voyageurs in Cadillac's canoe paddled with an amazing force and efficiency and never showed the slightest hint of fatigue. The boys had to try as hard as they could to keep up. They made a brief stop at noon for pemmican, but they were told that midday stops would become rare, as time was important. Cadillac had predicted that it would take at least five weeks to make their destination.

They stopped to make camp just before dusk. As the days were growing shorter. They would have to make best use of the daylight. To set camp everyone had a task. The project went fast and would become much faster. A tent and table was set for Cadillac and the rest stayed out on the ground. Three fires were set for cooking. Dinner was basic and quick. Afterwards the men would smoke around the fire and tell tales and some would play simple instruments. A few men would be set as guards and they would rotate with others during the night.

Cadillac met with the boys for a short while. "Your primary task is as my personal guards. You are to sleep by my tent and keep both your guns and your bows at the ready. If a guard sounds the alarm, you must be ready to react. Aside from this you will be expected to aid in the paddling, portage and other work. I ask that you keep clear heads and do not drink. Particularly your Indian friend."

Jean-Baptiste* continued to be annoyed that Cadillac only referred to him by name and had a decidedly superior demeanor towards all the Indians, but Henri told him to expect this and not make anything of it. Later in the evening, Cadillac, Pierre, and the two head soldiers met in the tent to plan, drink and play cards.

The following morning, they were up before dawn, had a brief breakfast and were packed and ready to go.

Cadillac took the most time readying himself and the group waited until he emerged ready to depart. He seemed to enjoy this part of the voyage.

The weather was fine and they made Montréal in five days. Cadillac disappeared into town and Pierre took some of the men to complete their supplies and the rest of the men were allowed leave in the town for two days. The boys wanted to follow Henri, but he suggested they stay with the voyageurs and learn something.

The two days did indeed prove to be an education into sex, gambling, drinking, and fighting (including one death). When the group reconvened, Cadillac had added five more canoes with three voyageurs each and as many large barrels as they could hold. "Special supplies" was the great man's explanation.

They departed the following dawn. The boys were somewhat burdened by the effects of the various excesses of the previous nights. Jean-Baptiste* was happy to see that the voyageurs were perfectly accepting of Joseph. Interestingly, the Indians were equally as amicable.

They started by reaching and portaging the long Lachine rapids. The arduous task was the boys' introduction into what was to become a common activity. At the end of the portage they soon turned north into a smaller river. This was named for the Outaouais tribe whom the French called "Ottawa" and hence the "Ottawa River". Here the boys felt they were finally entering for their first time the true wilderness of Canada.

The river was much more narrow than the Saint-Laurent and the current was weak. The water was deep enough that there would be no portages for many days. The banks were true wilderness of cliffs or small beaches all followed by the densest of forest. There was no civilization except for a very rare cabin (often unoccupied or burned) or a small Indian camp. Occasionally the group would stop at one. As the Ottawa were Algonquin, they were generally hospitable. Henri became invaluable as he often knew the people and was much better accepted than the other Indians who were strangers. Cadillac became quite happy that he had brought the old man.

Six days out of Montréal they came to a natural harbor. There was a small Indian village and three cabins that represented a trading post used by the voyageurs. Henri told them that the French called it *Gatineau* but that now they had begun to call it Ottawa. The group stayed in the Indian camp and some friendly games broke out between the local Indians and the voyageurs. A favorite was pitting the strongest man of each group in a wrestling match without weapons. The French entry was a man called Esperance who was rather short but solid as an oak tree. The Ottawa entry was slightly taller and thinner but equally formidable in appearance. The battle was impressive. Jean-Baptiste* was certain that they would kill one another as they punched, slammed, bit and threw each other violently. In the end Esperance won but both men were beaten bloody.

Neither seemed to mind and they returned to the campfire as best friends. Later there was a similar battle but this time with teams of three with only one from each team fighting and the others trading places when they wished. The only rule was that the first combatant was required to "tag" the second before he could be replaced.

In the morning the party proceeded. The weather had again turned dry and the water was low and the forest dry. Jean-Baptiste* thought that had he been home, his father would again have him digging ditches. They reached a shallow spot in the river which would be their first long portage since Lachine. Due to the dry weather it was longer that usual and it took two full days of backbreaking work. The boys had become hardened to paddling all day but this was much worse as the canoes were filled with supplies and much of the terrain was difficult.

Following the portage there were two days of easy travel as the dry weather had made the current very feeble. At camp on the second night, the men announced that it was time to initiate the two boys. They would each have to fight one of the other men selected by the group. Jean-Baptiste* was to fight a man called simply le Roux for his thick red beard. He was not Esperance, but sturdy nonetheless. Joseph was to fight an Indian no less formidable in appearance.

Jean-Baptiste* went first. He cautiously circled with his opponent. Le Roux managed to land a body blow which knocked out every bit of Baptiste*'s air and then a blow to the head which truly caused the boy to see stars. Baptiste* decided he had to use his agility more and began to move more quickly. He did manage a body blow and one to the face, but he feared that he had hurt his hands more than Le Roux.

Le Roux made a quick move and grabbed Baptiste* from behind. He raised him in the air and slammed him to the ground. Jean-Baptiste* felt as though he had gone two feet into the ground but managed to rise. As he arose, he heard his father's word, "Patience." He ducked and weaved and waited for Le Roux to be careless. Finally Le Roux was and Jean-Baptiste* managed to land a blow to the man's midsection that actually sank in. Le Roux doubled over and Baptiste* gave him an uppercut. The man staggered and fell to the ground.

To Jean-Baptiste*'s dismay he got up, but he was disoriented. Jean-Baptiste* ran at him and hit his shoulder into the large man's midsection. The man folded over severely. Then Baptiste* landed one on the man's jaw. Le Roux's feet actually left the ground and he landed on his back. He arose, however, and spit out a bloody tooth. He held out his hand to the boy and said, "Enough." And with that Le Roux collapsed face first into the ground. The men all cheered and declared the match a draw. Baptiste* realized that this was prejudiced but was glad to be finished.

Joseph's match went much the same with the same outcome. Afterwards, Le Roux sat down next to the boys with a jug of liquor and said, "Pierre says you boys can have a taste tonight." After a while he said to both of them. "You both did well, you did not quit and that is what we wanted to see. You are now part of the group". Jean-Baptiste* could not think of a part that did not hurt other than maybe his hair, but he could not think of a time when he had felt better.

A few days later they came to a turn northward and a small westerly fork in the river. They were told that they would now leave the large river and take the stream until they were obliged to portage. Later in the day they hit that point and embarked on the most difficult portage yet. At the end they came to a large lake. Henri told them, "This lake is called Nipissing, and we will follow its south bank for two days until we reach the next river."

The boys had seen large wilderness lakes before but this was larger and wilder than anything they had seen. Every few hours they would see moose, caribou or bear drinking from the lake. Jean-Baptiste* began to wonder if he had died in the fight and this was heaven. On the third day they came to a small river. Henri said, "This called 'French River,' I do not know why. It leads to the lake of the Huron."

Two days and several short portages later they arrived at the bank of a lake with no opposite side. Henri explained, "This is the great bay of the lake of the Huron. We will go north between the mainland to the north and a great island called Manitoulin to the south. There will be no more portage." He added, "To go south one must follow the shore around south and again north out of the bay. This takes a few weeks. One can cross the bay west at this point. It only takes two or three days, but there is no land and if a storm arises, all are lost. The water in this bay can be as evil as that in the great lake of Gitcheegumee."

As predicted in two days they reached the wide opening into the north channel of the lake of the Huron. It was a magical place filled with high granite islands sometimes bare and sometimes with trees. It was filled with coves for camping and covered with blueberries, even this late in the year. A few days later they came to a narrows. Henri told them, "The Indian word for this place means 'little current'. At times the current is west, and other times east, depending on the weather." There was a small Indian camp here and they stopped for the night.

Jean*-Baptiste* began to reflect on the ease of his real job which was to protect Cadillac. He wondered if the need would ever occur. The following night Henri suggested to Pierre that because of the extended dry spell that the fires should be kept small and directly on the shore. Pierre dismissed him and said that Monsieur Cadillac preferred the camp in the woods for protection. Henri cautioned the boys to be vigilant for fire.

Two nights later the group camped on the north shore as usual. Late at night the wind came up from the south and the boys immediately sensed it. One of the fires had caught the wind and ignited an overlying tree. The following effect was mind-boggling. The surrounding forest took off immediately. There was pandemonium in the camp dragging the supplies to the lake. The boys managed to awaken Cadillac and lead him to safety and rescue most of his things. The men were forced to wade chest deep into the cold water to avoid the flames.

The sky lit up like day, the flames seemed a hundred feet high. Animals of all sorts began to seek refuge on the beach and in the water with the men often abandoning their usual reluctance to be near humans. Awful cries of many others filled the night. The heat was so intense that the men had to continually submerge to avoid roasting.

As day broke the wind swept the flames inland and the shore was left a smoldering cinder. The heat eventually abated to where the men could go ashore and assemble what was left of the supplies. Thanks to the early warning by the boys and the fact that Henri had warned the others to keep things close to shore, little of vital importance was lost. At midday they departed watching the flames in the distance and the great charred expanse on the shore. When Henri entered the canoe with Pierre he merely murmured, "Big fire."

Fortunately the south wind brought heavy rain and eventually the great fire died. However when the group reached the entrance to the northern shore of the lake proper two days later, the south wind was fierce. Henri told them that they would have to camp here until the wind and the waves died. The surf on the shore was incredible. Jean-Baptiste* had heard Guillaume* Renaud tell of the storms and waves of the Atlantic Ocean in his home on the coast of Normandie, and felt that he now understood.

Eventually the wind abated and the party progressed. In a few days Henri announced that they would arrive at Michilimackinac the next day. Six weeks from their departure and on the first day of autumn.

Chapter 13

The following day they followed the north shore until they could see the straits. This was not as narrow as Québec and other fort areas. The north and south shores were separated by about five miles. On a foggy morning, the other coast was not even visible. Cadillac considered his options. The south shore had higher ground but from the north one could see boats from either direction. In addition, there was some civilization in the form of the small mission of Saint-Ignace.

Actually, Cadillac considered this little advantage, as he regarded the Jesuits with the same attitude as the mosquitoes, an annoying but unavoidable fact of life in the new world. They landed on the north shore where they were greeted by the Mission Superior, Father Jean, who was most pleasant. Cadillac regarded him with only a hint of cordiality. The voyageurs set up the camp now with a makeshift tent for Cadillac who had lost his in the fire. That evening, Cadillac spoke to Pierre in private. "Here I have the two things that annoy me the most, the savages and now the 'black robes,'" referring to the Jesuits.

He continued, "At least I can make a profit from the savages. The only thing we could make of benefit from the Jesuits is a gourmet meal, if we were cannibals like these Indians." It was no secret that Cadillac, like his close friend, Frontenac, regarded the missionaries as nuisances that had more interest in the salvation of the savage souls than the commerce of the new world.

After a brief tour, the men commenced on construction. They began to clear an area to the east of the mission, trimming and hauling the trees to be used in construction of buildings. Cadillac's plan called for three structures, a home and office for himself, a storage warehouse, and a garrison for he soldiers. He told the men that Father Jacques Marquette founded the mission here in 1671. A small fort named Fort de Baude was then built in 1683, but there were not enough men to maintain it and it disappeared. He announced, "We will call this Michilimackinac for the strait." After a few days, the work was well under way and Cadillac called the boys and Henri, "We shall go with two soldiers and three voyageurs to explore these two large islands to the east and south."

The men assembled their essentials and paddled a short distance to the first island. It was a beautiful, high island with a high concentration of trees and a natural harbor protected by a smaller island no more than a large round rock. When they hiked to an overlook, Cadillac exclaimed, "This would be a wonderful lookout for a fort if the island were not so isolated; but it is something to consider for later. The Jesuit told me that the Indians refer to it as 'Mackinac', which I believe means turtle, or rat or something."

They spent the rest of the day exploring the island. Except for an impressive deer herd, it appeared uninhabited. The following day they headed south for the larger flatter island covered with white birch trees and a white sand beach. Cadillac declared, "I shall call this Bois Blanc for the white wood." On landing they realized that it was inhabited. Fortunately the Indians seemed to know Henri who went to speak with them and returned.

"This is a small Chippewa tribe. They are friendly, but speak no French. They say that they will welcome the trade."

On departing Cadillac muttered under his breath, "Speak no French, ignorant savages."

The following morning they returned to the post. Work was progressing, and Cadillac had the men move some things into the beginnings of their new homes. He was particularly interested in the large barrels that he had acquired in Montréal. The men loaded them into the new storehouse area. The boys were impressed at the weight. Joseph remarked, "Whatever they hold, it is tightly packed."

Henri rolled and spun one, "Liquid," he said, then he looked up and merely said, "Hum."

That evening, Cadillac approached Henri. "Tell me, Henri," using his name for the first time in the voyage. Is there a big chief of these local Indians? And how much does he control?"

Henri replied, "Big chief called Nanou." He stopped and picked up a stick and began to draw in the dirt. "Here Michigauma." He traced a large mitten, and then he traced a long thick finger coming close to the tip of the mitten, "We here." pointing to the small strait in between the two landmasses. Then he noted the area above the northern land. "Here Bay of Whitefish, good to eat, easy to catch. This leads to big lake Gitcheegumee."

He traced another landmass above the upper peninsula that extended north and east. "Here land of Huron, separated by *sault,* Indian word for long rapids and falls. Then the River of Sainte-Marie. Nanou's tribe lives between here and Sault of Sainte-Marie along all of Bay of Whitefish. Big tribe."

"Tell me, where can I find this chief to speak to?"

Henri replied, "Now he north, by bay. In winter he comes south to trade."

"Well, that's what I am interested in, his trade. Could you go find him and arrange a meeting?"

Henri replied, "I will take the boys, take eight or nine days."

"Will you take a canoe?"

"No, easier to hike. Long high portage on Sault of Sainte-Marie. Would have to lift a canoe the height of many men to get from level here to level of Gitcheegumee. Hard to get canoe through there."

Cadillac concluded, "Good, set out in the morning. I want to see this man as soon as possible."

Henri pointed out, "Maybe he not want to come."

Cadillac finished, "Tell him I have something that is certain to interest him greatly."

The following morning, Henri and the two boys headed north on foot. At first the boys thought that the walk through the incredibly dense forest would be impossible, but Henri found an Indian trail that led north with just enough room for hiking single file. As the day progressed, he showed the boys how to spot these well-hidden trails and by midday, they were making the directions themselves.

The walk was easy as there were few hills. There were many creeks and small lakes and a good deal of swampland, but the trails automatically skirted these. They passed occasional stone outcroppings that rose above the countryside. A tall thin such formation went above the tree line and provided a panorama of the area. Knowing that Algonquin frequently changed campsites, Jean-Baptiste* asked, "How will we find the camp of Nanou?"

The old man replied in the first good French he had used since leaving the Allard farm, "It will be no problem. I shall smell it." Toward evening it began to rain and as time progressed the rain became quite heavy. Henri chose to camp next to a small granite cliff with just enough overhang to keep them dry and allow a small fire as the nights were becoming cold. They had not brought or caught anything to cook so they settled for pemmican and water and were soon asleep. The following morning they repeated the evening meal and were quickly off. At mid morning Henri stopped abruptly and sniffed the air. He asked the boys if they sensed anything. Joseph sniffed and replied, "Indian, not Algonquin." Baptiste* would never get over his awe of Indian sense of smell.

They circled around and from a small overlook could see their discovery. A small band of about ten Iroquois was leading west. Henri motioned for silence and once they were far enough away he said, "Small group of Iroquois are common in this country. They are usually here for trade and mean no harm, but we will not test our luck with these numbers."

The following day, in early afternoon, Henri stopped and stated, "Nanou is just east of here." They made a turn and within 30 minutes they could see the camp. It was a larger camp than the boys had seen but similar in other ways to the camp of Anuk, Henri's brother. They proceeded cautiously until Henri saw a man with whom he was obviously acquainted. They spoke for a while in an odd Algonquin dialect. Henri then turned to the boys and said, "Nanou is out with a hunting party and due to return tonight. We will await him here." Indicating the man he said, "This is Wanou, the brother of Nanou."

The boys and the men nodded their heads in the typical Algonquin greeting as opposed to the French handshake. Wanou took them to a central fire pit in the camp where they waited and were brought food. Late in the afternoon, the hunting party returned with several deer and three caribou. Nanou greeted Henri and the boys and they were invited to dine. Afterwards the men sat and smoked and talked and Henri discussed the plan of Cadillac. Jean-Baptiste* realized that it would have been rude to do so before the meal.

Henri commenced, "We have come from Québec with a party of French. They plan to increase the trade at Michilimackinac. The leader is a man named Cadillac. I am not certain that he can be trusted, but he proposes great trade and seems to travel with the protection of the King of France himself."

Nanou replied, "I will go to see him. Nowadays we must wait for the various French voyageurs to trade. One central post would be of benefit. Tell him I will be there before the next moon."

With the business completed, the smoking continued and there was dancing and Indian singing that seemed to the French to be more like chanting. The boys finally went to their deerskin beds and were surprised to find two young maidens awaiting them. The following morning, Jean-Baptiste* thought that the wilderness life was looking even better.

At breakfast he asked Henri, "We are only in our third day and could be back at the post by day four or five. Why did you tell Cadillac it would be eight days?

Henri replied, "My business in this voyage is to show things to you boys. We will start today." And after breakfast they said goodbye to their hosts and headed west.

They followed the shore of Whitefish Bay, which was an enormous body of water by the boys' standards. At midday they arrived at a short cliff. Henri inspected it carefully and said, "Water is very deep here. This is a good place." He pulled out three fishing lines and baited each one and added a large weight. "The bottom is deep. Go all the way down and bob the line. When the fish bites, do not pull hard as you will lose the fish."

The boys began and each lost their first two fish by pulling too hard. Finally Joseph landed a silver fish about 18 inches in length. Henri showed the boys that the fish had a very soft small mouth and that the hook was easily pulled out. "It is easier to catch these with a net, but we will catch lunch and dinner." He was correct in that the boys landed another ten fish in the next hour. At one point Jean-Baptiste*'s line took off with great force. He felt as though he had caught a sturgeon, but when he fought the monster to the top, it was a dark gray unfamiliar fish about three feet in length.

Henri said, "This is the trout that lives in the deep lake. He is usually much deeper than this. He eats the whitefish and is dumb like the river trout, but much larger." When lunch was served, the boys found whitefish to be sweeter and more tender than any other fish.

After lunch they proceeded until the shoreline turned north. They continued north until evening when they reached a sharp point of land pointing straight north. To the east they looked over the whitefish bay, and to the west they saw the most endless water they could imagine. Henri sat down clearly having wisdom to impart, "Our ancestors called this Gitcheegumee to mean 'endless water'. In most places it has no bottom. The water has the same cold on the hottest or coldest days of the year. A man who drowns here never returns to the surface.

"It was said that there was no end to its boundaries but your grandmother," he said looking at Joseph, "and I walked around it. It took me more than one year to return to the place we started. On the northwest, there is a large magnificent island. The voyageurs call it the *Isle Royal*. It is filled with brown bear. It was there that your 'Mimi' was sent to her ancestors at the hands of such a magnificent beast. We will camp here tonight. If my weather sense is correct, tomorrow we will see something that few men have seen or will ever see."

85

Henri led the boys several hundred feet inland to make camp. Jean-Baptiste* asked, "Why can we not stay on the beach on such a nice night?"

Henri replied, "Perhaps by morning we shall see why."

As always, the Indian weather sense was good. A brief thunderstorm came through and the winds shifted violently to the north. Jean-Baptiste* heard crashing as though the rocks were falling, but he realized it was merely the sound of the great water.

At dawn they did indeed see the most remarkable sight. The waves were crashing ashore and coming a full 400 feet beyond where they had come the day before. The boys had marveled at the waves by Michilimackinac which, when they came from the south, were as big as houses, but these were as big as cathedrals. Rocks bigger than men were moved around like grains of sand.

Henri said, "A man would be crushed to death by these waves. I must tell you that I have truly seen them larger, but this is a good display. I suggest we sit here today and watch this wonder of nature and realize how much more powerful it is than man and civilization of any sort."

And so they did.

In the evening they set camp, and after eating, smoked a pipe. Henri announced, "You boys are now truly men and versed in the ways of the wild. When we return to camp I am going to leave and return to my people. My stay with the French has served its purpose. This man Cadillac is your leader and you are bound to abide with him during the voyage. He has hired you to protect him and you should do as good a job as you are able. However, I do not trust this man as he has no respect for the Indian ways, and I fear he has little regard for any man but himself. Be wary, keep your eyes open and watch out for each other." With that he went to his deerskin to sleep.

Chapter 14

When the three arrived back at Michilimackinac they were greeted by an anxious Cadillac. Henri reported that Nanou had indicated that he would come before the month was out. Henri advised him of his resignation, and Cadillac took it with indifference. Later he indicated to Pierre that he was glad that the old man would be gone by the time the other Indians arrived.

In two weeks' time, Nanou did appear with a small band of braves, most much younger than he. Cadillac was eager to do business and asked the boys to translate. Jean-Baptiste* said, "It might be best to talk after dinner with a pipe."
Cadillac smiled and replied, "Good idea, lad. The Indian way, put them at ease."

After dinner they met at the fire outside of Cadillac's tent. Pierre and two officers attended. Nanou brought three young braves, and Baptiste* and Joseph translated. Joseph spoke to the Indians and Jean-Baptiste* to the French. Cadillac thought there was a certain symmetry in this. He indicated that he was interested in consolidation of as much trading as possible at the post and assured the best deals. Nanou indicated that the Indians would have much interest if the deal was good and inquired as to the price and the nature of the payment.

Cadillac indicated to Pierre who opened one of the barrels brought from Montréal and gave a cup to each of the four Indians. Jean-Baptiste* began to see what was happening. After a while Nanou spoke, "I have a fear of this drink, I believe it corrupts the Indian ways. If you decide on more standard trade we may talk again." He thanked Cadillac for his hospitality and motioned to his braves and the entire band was gone in a matter of a few seconds.

Later Jean-Baptiste* said to Joseph, "I am glad that Nanou refused. Your grandfather would have greatly disapproved of trading liquor to the Indians."

At the same time in his tent, Cadillac announced to Pierre, "It has gone just as I planned. I felt the older man would not go for the deal. He is too much like that old Henri, too frozen in the old Indian ways; but the young ones saw it and I could see it in their eyes. They will be back and soon. My old friend, I see our real fortune on the horizon."

The younger braves did return, and as autumn progressed into winter, the pile of furs mounted and the collection of barrels slowly shrank.

Chapter 15

Northwestern Michigan - Early Winter 1694:

They were now three weeks into the excursion into the western part of the northern tip of the Michigauma Peninsula. Cadillac, Jean-Baptiste*, Joseph, and three voyageurs had been exploring the network of coves and bays that lined the shore. They had met a few Indian bands, and through the boys Cadillac had told them of the new trading post. He did not have to mention the brandy as the word had spread.

They had spent most of their time in a deep narrow bay running north and south. It was split by a long finger of land also running north. The autumn colors were still in the air when they left, but now the most of the leaves were brown and gold patterns on the water. There had been light snow that aided in tracking but not enough to hinder their progress.

Today they were paddling south, back in the big lake. There were two large islands on the horizon. Jean-Baptiste* said, "The last band we encountered told me that these islands are called *Manitou* as they appear to be bears."

Early in the afternoon they happened upon another harbor with a narrow entrance and a small bay. Cadillac ordered them ashore and suggested that they set camp and that the boys go search game for the evening meal, "Make it something better than squirrel," he commanded.

Jean-Baptiste* noticed a small river at the east end of the small bay. They landed there and began up the north shore of the river. They heard something ahead; Joseph sniffed and said, "Deer." Soon they saw it, and Jean-Baptiste* thought he had a good shot as it stood in front of a dense bramble. He shot too late and the deer bounded ahead. He was worried that he lost his arrow, but was surprised to see in sticking out of the bramble.

His arrows were easy to see. Ever since he began to make his own arrows as a young boy, he had always included one bright red cardinal feather at the end. He believed this brought him luck, and it also made it easier to find errant arrows. As he pulled on the arrow he was shocked that it was tightly stuck in something. As he cleared the bramble he saw a wooden wall, and not made of logs but cut wooden planks! He called Joseph and they began to uncover the wall. They began to realize that the wall was just between them and the river.

As the object took form, Jean-Baptiste* exclaimed, "It's not a wall, it's a boat! And a big boat. I am amazed we did not realize it was here but it is entirely covered with brambles." After some time they began to see the nature of the boat and Jean-Baptiste* shouted, "I know what this is." He remembered the tales his Aunt Madeleine had told about the grand inland sailing vessel that LaSalle had built but was lost at sea somewhere in the Great Lakes. "It is the Griffon!"

The boys managed to get on the deck. The boat was absent of any sign of men, but appeared to be ready to sail with all the lines and sails in place although badly worn from age. Joseph managed to pry open the hold and they had just enough remaining light to see the inside which was packed with beaver pelts, more that they had ever imagined.

Jean-Baptiste* whistled and said, "I believe Monsieur Cadillac will want to hear of this." And they abandoned the hunt to return to camp.

They returned to camp about nightfall. Cadillac was very excited at the tale and in spite of the darkness, he went with the boys and one voyageur by torchlight to see for himself. Once he estimated that they could be correct, he retuned to camp to scheme. In the morning the party took an inventory. At the end Cadillac announced, "You boys will stay to guard this find. Now that it is partially uncovered, anyone in the area may discover it. The rest of us will return to the post and began a convoy to bring in the furs. We will take as many as we can hold on this trip."

"It is imperative that none of you speak of this to anyone, now or in the future. There will be claims of ownership, and questions as if LaSalle had hid the boat himself. We must prevent the possible smearing of this great man's name, God rest his soul. The proceeds will go to the King as they should and help to build the post." They departed the following day.

Chapter 16

Two days later, the boys were exploring the area. They anticipated that the round trip to the post would take about four days and they were to use the time becoming familiar with the region. The river continued a short distance and opened onto a small inland lake. The lake was filled with fish and the woods with game. They began to build a store for the early winter as they realized that the gradual transport of the furs would last for many weeks.

That evening they climbed on to the deck to spend the night. At dusk they heard a commotion. Jean-Baptiste* looked out and to his shock, he saw that in spite of their hurried efforts to camouflage the boat, a group of seven men had discovered it. Hoping they had not been seen, he and Joseph scurried quickly into the hold.

Their hopes were quickly dashed as the men climbed aboard and one shouted. "I saw him right here, must be in the hold."

The boys realized they were trapped and although they could fight the men, the numbers were too great without the element of surprise. Jean-Baptiste* whispered, "I have an idea, give me most of your arrows." Without questioning, or understanding, Joseph handed over a handful of arrows. Baptiste* crawled to the side where he had noticed a chest. It was open and empty. He placed in most of his arrows as well as those of Joseph.

He had no sooner closed the chest when the hatch opened, a torch shown down and a man shouted in vulgar French, "Alright, come on out slowly."

The two boys came out slowly. The man continued, "Just you two?"

Trying to feign terror, which was not difficult to do, Baptiste* blurted out. "Yes sir, just us. My friend and I, he's Algonquin and speaks no French, ran off and have been living here. We found this boat and have been sleeping on the deck."

The man inspected the hold and returned. "Lads, I think this is our lucky day. There's more pelts here than we'll see in ten years." Returning to Jean-Baptiste*, he continued, "Who else knows about this?"

Appearing terrified, Baptiste* replied, "No one, sir. We just found it yesterday."

The man spoke to his companions, "Tie these two up."

Baptiste* then replied in his most terrified voice, "Please don't put us in the hold. It's terrible down there."

The man laughed, "Good idea, put them below, and lock the hold. Just take their arrows and knives."

One of the others grabbed the boys, "What about the bows."

The leader replied, "Bows ain't no good without arrows." And examining the quivers he added, "Looks like you two wasn't going to shoot much tonight," and he laughed as the boys were roughly tossed below and the hatch was shut.

One of the men addressed the leader, "Why don't we just shoot 'em?"

The reply, "Someone's got to unload this." And there was more laughter.

After the men dispersed, Jean-Baptiste* whispered, "It has worked better than I had hoped. There is a small hatch in the back. Late tonight one of us will crawl out. When they open the main hatch to begin unloading, the man outside will attack and with the diversion, the man inside can attack as well. We will have the surprise and may prevail."

Joseph agreed. "You are best shot and should be outside, and the first few minutes I can feign ignorance. It is simple to make Frenchmen fall for that."

Jean-Baptiste* crawled over to the chest and retrieved the arrows. In the total darkness, he missed one. Little did he know that it would next be touched three hundred years later by one of his many descendants.

Jean-Baptiste* cautiously left the boat at night. The men had been drinking heavily which made things easier and would aid them in the morning. He took a position just behind their camp and waited patiently.

Some time after dawn the men began to slowly stir. They went to the river to wash away the excess of the previous evening. They ate a quick camp breakfast and the leader rose and said, "Well, let's go get the boy and his red-skinned buddy to work. I'm anxious to be rich."

He and two other men climbed the deck and opened the hatch. The leader shouted in, "Time for you and your red-skinned girlfriend to get to work."

There was a moment of silence and then Joseph shouted something in Algonquin.

As the men's attention was drawn to the deck, Jean-Baptiste* moved silently and brought the first two men down easily. The third turned and fired his rifle, but as he was hurried, he missed. Baptiste* hit him directly in the heart. The fourth man tried to run but Baptiste* took slow and careful aim and brought him down easily.

On deck the first man looked in and Joseph shot him directly in the eye. He fell forward into the hold. The second man not realizing what had happened, followed him in. Having the advantage of being adapted to the dark, it was simple for Joseph to finish him as well. Taking stock of the situation, the leader, now the last man, jumped overboard and began running down the beach.

Joseph retrieved his own knife from one of the dead men and gave chase. The leader stumbled a short way from the boat. He turned to rise and saw Joseph approaching. He took his gun and shot quickly. He missed. He rose and pulled his knife. Joseph stood and waited. The man was much larger and stronger than the boy. He lunged at Joseph who sidestepped and let him stumble forward. The man came again and Joseph stepped aside and easily tripped him.

As the man tried to rise, Joseph grabbed him from the back and held him helpless. In perfect French he calmly said, "You should learn to aim more patiently." And with that he made a small nick in the man's neck which produced a great flow of blood. As the man weakened,

Joseph continued, "Know that you have been sent to Hell by a red-skinned girlfriend." As the man went limp, Joseph took his knife and with one skillful motion, removed his scalp. He raised the scalp and gave a brief yell before he threw it on the ground, sat and began to cry.

Jean-Baptiste* watched dumfounded from the edge of the clearing. He had never seen such anger from his friend, and realized that in spite of friendships, a great divide existed between these two cultures. He slowly approached his friend and sat silently by his side for some time. Eventually Joseph arose, cleaned his knife and said, "Let us clean this up."

Two days later Cadillac arrived with ten canoes. His men began the task of unloading the ship, filling the canoes and returning to the post to deposit them and quickly return for more. The task lasted past Christmas. The boys stayed at the boat to protect it. This time there was only hunting and exploring involved.

When the last of the furs had been unloaded, Cadillac ordered the men to strip the boat of all equipment, ropes, sails, etc. He then ordered them to take the canoes and pull it to a deep part of the big lake and sink it. As two voyageurs left the hold after chopping a large hole, one of them noticed the chest. "I think we had better leave it behind or we may go down with the ship." They departed quickly and the Griffon disappeared deep below the surface of Lake Michigan.

Chapter 17

Jean-Baptiste* and Joseph departed along with the last load of pelts. The lakeshore and bays were beginning to freeze and the north winds were brutal. The entire north of the Michigauma was covered with snow. Due to the ice floes, wind and waves, the voyage lasted five days rather than two.

After their arrival at the small post at Michilimackinac, winter descended with a vengeance. The boys realized that just as in Québec, the weather made for rugged living but also for a special type of hunting and the leisure time to do it. Their winter duties soon became hunting the region in the day procuring fresh game for the post and sleeping by Cadillac's tent at night to protect the great man.

The Indian trade remained brisk, each week one or two bands of young braves would arrive with their pelts and leave with a barrel of Cadillac's now famous apple brandy. Cadillac surveyed the situation and realized that he would run out of his awful brew before the ice broke. Fortunately he had sent Pierre to Montréal before the ice to insure that his people were making arrangements to produce as much of the awful stuff as possible. He knew that next years' trade would be even more profitable, and with the find of the Griffon, at the end of winter, he would possess the largest cache of pelts in the history of the new world.

Spring arrived much as it did in Québec. The weather changed abruptly, the maple sap ran, and the ice began to break and began its annual downstream voyage. As soon as possible, Cadillac began sending flotillas loaded with furs to Montréal and to return as soon as possible with more apple brandy.

Chapter 18

<u>Charlesbourg - spring 1695:</u>

François* Allard heard the bell and halted his plow which was being pulled by his magnificent Perchon stallion. The bell from the nearby Charlesbourg chapel was tolling the noon Angelus signaling a pause for prayer before the noon meal. He and his son Georges, who was guiding the horse, removed their hats and stood silently for a brief moment. They then headed toward the house. They were joined along the way by sons André, now twenty-two, Jean-François twenty, and Thomas now eight as well as their Indian tenant Philippe and his son Henri.

The family was extremely busy this spring on a number of fronts. They were expanding the current farm by adding another parcel on the square. André hoped to be married within the year and build a house and farm the expanded area. There would be some room for some of the brothers as well. François* was also considering obtaining more land in the region.

As they approached the house François* saw his old friend François Badeau approaching from the square. François* had worked for Badeau's mother when he arrived from France. Badeau was a well-known notary. The men greeted one another and Badeau said, "I have just returned from Montréal on business. I happened upon Monsieur Cadillac's man, Pierre. A most unusual fellow. He reported that Jean-Baptiste* and Joseph are well and highly regarded at the post for their work."

François* expressed his approval and Badeau continued, "An odd sort this Pierre. It seems that he has spent all fall and winter buying the dregs of apple crops and cider. He is buying enormous amounts and wants only poor quality and low price."

Francois* pondered and returned, "Some years ago, Cadillac asked me about the fabrication of Calvados, but for that one would only want the best apples and cider."

The two men shrugged it off and said good day.

Charlesbourg - November 7, 1695:

The harvest was over and the Allard family beginning the final preparations for winter. There was only tree clearing to be done, but they had great ambitions for clearing large areas from both farm sites. The sun was beginning to set as François* and the boys were heading to the house. Fall still hung in the air although many of the trees were now bare. As they approached the house they saw two men with packs approaching from the south. Georges recognized them first and shouted, "Baptiste* and Joseph!"

The young boys ran forward and jumped on the two adventurers, the rest came quickly and there was a fury of hugs, handshakes, and general pandemonium. Jeanne* and the girls came out on the porch and rushed in as soon as they realized what was happening. Eventually the family moved into the house and Henri ran to the Indian camp to fetch his mother. The two families gathered at the house and Marie and Jeanne* added food to expand the meal. After a lengthy grace by François*, the entire Allard family sat to dine together for the first time in almost two years.

After dinner the boys told the long tale of their adventure. They included all the high points with the exception of the Griffon. Although Jean-Baptiste* would have loved to tell this tale, he remained true to his word of secrecy with Monsieur Cadillac.

The following day the men fell in for a long day of tree cutting. The family operation had improved since the early days, and François* had acquired a long saw and with everyone helping and the immense contribution of Henri the Horse, they were able to clear many trees in a day.

Mid-morning the boys sat under a tree for a short rest. Jean-François started, "André, I believe it's time that you told our adventuring brother the news."

André looked up and said, "I would have told you last night but I didn't want to interrupt the adventure. It seems that I am to be married in two weeks."

Baptiste* smiled, "And who is the lucky mademoiselle?"

"Anne LeMarche."

Jean-Baptiste* was at first speechless but returned, "At least you are not robbing the cradle."

André returned, "She is the only girl in all of Québec who actually reads books."

The boys laughed and exchanged hugs and handshakes just as their father appeared with his "let us return to work" look.

As the work progressed, Jean-Baptiste* pondered this news. Anne LeMarche was four years André's senior and at 28 was old for a bride. Although marriages in the colony between young girls and older men were common, the opposite was rare. Anne's parents had come from France about 1650 and settled in Montréal. Her father was a master cabinet-maker and both he and her mother were educated. They had lived in Charlesbourg for many years.

Anne's mother died in 1680 when Anne was about 12 years old, and four years later Anne had entered in a contract of marriage with an older man, but it had been annulled for reasons that were unknown to Jean-Baptiste*. Anne lived with her father and cared for the younger children. He was not certain why she had not entered into another marriage thereafter. It was true that she was an intellectual like André and that was probably the reason. At least there would now be a little more room in the crowded boys' loft in the Allard farmhouse.

Once the trees were cleared on François*'s land, the group went over to André's new land and began the clearing process. The three older boys and Georges made a camp and stayed the night so they could work on the small farmhouse. Henri and Joseph joined them and as the big day approached, they had completed the task.

On November 22, 1695, the Allard family celebrated its first marriage between two Québecois natives. Both Jean-François and Jean-Baptiste* stood as witnesses. Jean-Baptiste* was pleasantly surprised that his brother had asked him to serve as best man. To no one's surprise, young Henri set up a camp at the newlywed's farm and some weeks later took a bride himself at the mission church in Beauport.

Winter of 1695-96 was colder than most. Jean-Baptiste* and Joseph spent as much time trapping and hunting as possible, but as spring approached, Baptiste* realized that he must now return to the drudgery of farming. He divided his time between helping his father and then helping André on his farm to the south. The farms prospered, but Jean-Baptiste* felt that he was merely biding his time praying for a new adventure.

Chapter 19

Versailles, France - Summer 1698:

Antoine Cadillac stood patiently in the splendid antechamber in the magnificent palace at Versailles. He had thoroughly enjoyed his stay in Paris. The capital was even more charming when one was indeed filthy rich. He did, however, object to the French custom of standing unless otherwise instructed while at court.

His exploits at Michilimackinac had been losing their allure. His brandy for fur scheme had been extremely successful and further aided by the acquisition of the furs from the Griffon. He had astounded the colony by arriving in Montréal in 1697 with a flotilla of canoes and 176,000 pounds of beaver pelts. However with the King's new edict that gave the government more control and hence more profit in the fur trade, along with the lengthy complaints by the blasted Jesuits regarding his use of brandy in trade and other activities had made him a bit of an embarrassment.

Never at a loss, Cadillac had hatched a new plan. To his amazement, he realized that not only would it greatly benefit him, but it would also benefit France herself. Finally an elegantly dressed servant opened the door and beckoned him into the much larger and even more opulent office. An elegant gentleman sat facing the door. Two functionaries behind him worked at trying to look busy and make the gentleman look more important. The servant announced, "Monsieur Antoine Lamothe Sieur de Cadillac."

The seated gentleman, in his fifties, arose and made a slight bow by comparison to the grand sweeping theatrical bow of Cadillac. Cadillac replied, "Count de Pontchartrain, how wonderful of you to receive me."

Count Jérome Phéyypeau de Pontchartrain was twenty-seven years older, but he looked every bit as dashing as he had when as Secretary of the Navy and Captain of the ship *Bon Roi Henri IV*, he rescued Jeanne* Anguille, now Allard, and the other *Filles du Roi* from the hands of renegade pirates. Now as Louis XIV's Minister of Finance, he was arguably the second most powerful man in the world; and it was widely accepted that in matters of the colonies, he spoke for the King himself.

"It is my pleasure, Monsieur Cadillac. Tell me, how is my dear old friend, Governor Frontenac? He must now be what, eighty years?"

Cadillac responded, "His health is failing of late but he sends his warmest regards and prays that you agree with his plan." Now it was actually Cadillac's plan, but he knew the warm relationship between the two great men and it would not hurt if Pontchartrain thought that it was from the Governor of Québec himself. In addition, Frontenac had to get Cadillac out of Michilimackinac to get the damned Jesuits off his back.

With a flourish, Cadillac rolled out a parchment map of New France. He proceeded, "At present the trade routes are spreading farther west and competition with the Dutch and English is becoming more fierce. We have some control at our post at Michilimackinac," he said pointing at the top of the Michigauma peninsula, which, on this map, looked like a heart, "which I have developed over the past three years. But the straits are wide and oftentimes the entire strait is not visible.

"The southern route past the great Niagara allows passage to most of the west. Past the *Lac du Chat*, which the natives call Erie for the Erieehronon tribe, is a series of two great rivers with a small lake in between which is named Sainte-Claire. Midway up the second river is a curve with a *détroit*, or narrow passage which is said to be a location with grand visibility. I, or rather the Governor proposes that I lead an expedition to build a fort and protect our interests from hostiles parties both European and native alike."

Pontchartrain regarded the map with interest when a man entered unannounced. Upon seeing him all four of the men in the room rose for a quick deep bow and a greeting in unison, "Your Majesty."

Louis XIV was fifty-five years of age, looking much older than the man who had kissed the hand of young Jeanne* Anguille many years before. He walked with a limp from a hunting accident but carried himself in a manner which left no doubt that he was King of the French Empire and the most powerful man in the world. Pontchartrain gave a short version of Cadillac's presentation and the King briefly studied the map.

He spoke, "The King of Spain is ill and will soon die without an heir. My grandson Philippe is his grandson as well and rightly in line for the throne. I expect significant resistance from King William and his English as well as the allies he could muster. I suspect this will involve a conflict in both the old and the new worlds." Gazing at Cadillac he said, "I believe your plan has great potential. Tell Governor Frontenac to make the arrangements." And with that he left the room and the business was quickly concluded.

Chapter 20

Beauport - November 5, 1698:

At the Beauport Chapel the second Allard marriage was taking place. Jean-François Allard was marrying Marie-Ursule Tardif. Her father Jacques had come from Rouen two years before François Allard, and her mother was a Fille du Roi from Chartres. The newlyweds had acquired a farm in Beauport in an area just east of Bourg-Royal. Anne's dowry included a tract of land adjacent to her father's, and the farmer in Jean-François could hardly wait to dig. Like him, Marie-Ursule was also anxious to start the farming life. Talk began on the subject of the prospects of Jean-Baptiste*, but he dismissed them out of hand declaring that he had no desire at this time for the married life. For now he was content to provide his service to the farm of his father or farms of his brothers as the need occurred, hoping that adventure would present itself.

Charlesbourg - Autumn, 1700:

Jean-Baptiste* and André sat in the Blue Goose Tavern each nursing a beer. They had been clearing trees all day from André's land. The three Allard farms were prospering. André had two young daughters and another birth due presently. Jean-François had had one son named Jean-Baptiste, but he had not survived his first year of life.

André looked up at his brother and said, "Baptiste* it is time that you settled down, take a girl and split my farm with me. That is the way father has planned it. We can help

each other. I can farm while you hunt." Jean-Baptiste*
knew that this tired old topic would come up this evening.

He replied, "I don't know André, I am simply not
ready, maybe next year."

At that moment the door opened and the cold north
wind gusted in, and with it brought a visitor. Jean-Baptiste*
recognized him immediately as Cadillac's man, Pierre.
Pierre saw Baptiste* and came straight away. After brief
introductions, he started, "Monsieur Cadillac has left his
post in the north and the King has ordered him south to start
a new post. It is to be at a narrows just beyond the lake of
the Erie. There is to be a large gathering of the tribes there
to discuss peace in the late summer and he wishes to be at
the strait by then. As relations with the Iroquois remain
poor, he will take the northern route to the lake of the
Huron. He has need of a personal guard who is familiar
with the voyage and has asked me to find you."

Jean-Baptiste knew his answer immediately but first
asked, "Is Joseph to come as well?"

Pierre replied indifferently, "If you wish to bring
him, yes."

Baptiste* rose to his feet and extended his hand and
said, "Then agreed." He knew that destiny had something
waiting for him.

Jean-Baptiste* continued his chores throughout the
Québec winter. With the breaking of the ice in spring, his
enthusiasm rose and on a day in early May 1701, he and
Joseph stood at the port of Montréal and assembled with
their new comrades. This was a larger group than had gone
to Michilimackinac. There were 200 men in all. Baptiste

recognized some as men who had accompanied them to Michilimackinac.

Now twenty-five years old, Baptiste* was no longer "the boy". Cadillac's deference to him caused the men to immediately afford him some respect. Cadillac met with his officers in the tavern the night before departure. As his personal guards, Jean-Baptiste* and Joseph were to be around Cadillac when possible so they too attended.

Cadillac put up a map of the region, and one of the two priests, Père Vaillant, gave a short blessing while Cadillac fidgeted. Cadillac then introduced his second in command, Alphonse de Tonti. De Tonti was the brother of Henri de Tonti who had built the Griffon for Lasalle. Like his brother he was of Italian heritage but raised and educated in Paris. Both Cadillac and de Tonti had elegant manners and engaging styles, but as Cadillac put people at ease (or off guard), de Tonti simply irritated them. Cadillac then mentioned the others. Baptiste* had already met one, Jacob de Marsac who he had judged to be an honest and forthright man and someone to trust. He also introduced them to a man named Chene who would be Cadillac's "official interpreter".

Cadillac then began, "Gentlemen, this is an expedition that is to assure France of her place as master of the new world." Motioning to the map he continued, "France currently holds claim to the lands west of the English colonies. However, the English and Dutch are coming in great numbers and can easily access the trade routes to the west through the Great Lakes from New York and other colonies. We have some control at Fort Frontenac built by LaSalle at the lake of the Ontario and at Michilimackinac, which I recently developed to the north. We shall pass by the now deserted Fort of Saint-Joseph where the Lake of the Huron meets the River of Sainte-Claire. This was developed by Monsieur de Tonti with Monsieur Duluth so Monsieur de Tonti's knowledge of the area will be valuable."

Looking at the map he continued, "We can easily see that the key location is here." And with great gusto he pointed to the narrows in the river south of Lake Sainte-Claire. "Whoever controls this strait, controls the future trade in the new world. His majesty in his wisdom is sending me to secure it. As a result of the current unsettled affairs with the Iroquois, we shall cross through the Ottawa River into the Lake of the Huron and then south. There is to be a meeting of the Indian tribes to discuss alliances by Lake Sainte-Claire this fall. Our new Governor thought that it might be safer for us to wait until after this meeting, but he has now agreed with his majesty.

" I suspect our voyage will take two months. We will take 25 canoes with 50 soldiers, 50 voyageurs, and 100 Indians." Then he added in an indifferent tone, "And two Jesuits." He took his glass. Jean-Baptiste* had noticed that he had abandoned Calvados as his preferred drink for Armagnac, a fine cognac from his native region of Gascony in France. "Gentlemen, to our success and the future of France."

Following the meeting the men stayed in the tavern like good Frenchmen. Jean-Baptiste* and Joseph met a few of the others. Joseph enjoyed a good reputation with the men. His French was perfect, and he dressed as Jean-Baptiste*. He had also showed himself to be a man of good character. Neither Baptiste* nor Joseph drank much alcohol as they felt it was their duty to Monsieur Cadillac to remain alert. Joseph also realized that like many native Canadians he did not handle liquor well.

De Marsac introduced them to two other officers, Louis Badeillac dit LaPlante and Vernon Grandmensil. The three men seemed to Baptiste* to be the 'brains' of the military unit. Marsac confided that the new Governor, who replaced the late Frontenac, was not fond of Cadillac and had opposed the mission; but Cadillac had gained the patronage of Pontchartrain while in France and no one had the courage to dispute him.

They talked a while with Cadillac's ever-present aide-de-camp Pierre and met a voyageur called simply "Grosse Pierre" who was the largest man they had ever seen, even larger than Pierre* Tremblay. He was reported to be the strongest man in all of Québec. As fistfights broke out, the French sign of the end of the meeting, Baptiste* and Joseph went to bed.

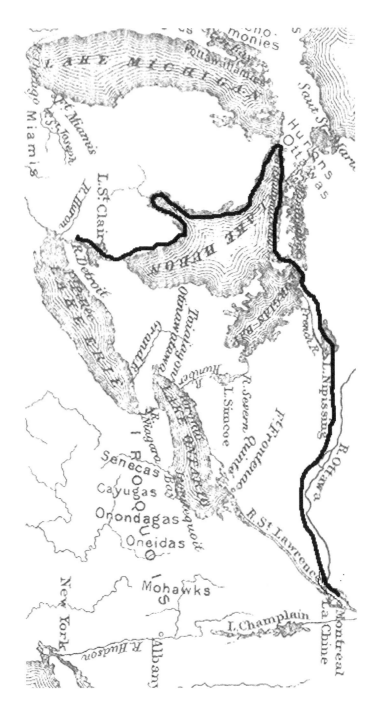

CADILLAC ROUTE TO DETROIT

Chapter 21

The group traveled quickly after leaving Montréal. The spring weather was fair and the water high. Trees burst with buds with birds and wild life abounding. The canoes traveled with extraordinary speed due to the large number of strong and experienced voyageurs and Indians. Jean-Baptiste* rode with Cadillac and Joseph with Tonti. They only paddled when one of the voyageurs or Indians needed a break. This was just as well as they could hardly keep pace with the others. The only child in the group was Cadillac's nine-year-old son, Antoine, who also rode in Cadillac's canoe.

It was a jovial group and they sang familiar voyageur songs endlessly.

> *Á la Claire fontaine*
> *M'en allant promener*
> *J'ai trouvé l'eau si belle*
> *Que je m'y suis baigné*

The voyage was truly idyllic. The weather was fine and the winds fair. The game was plentiful and the companionship warm. Jean-Baptiste* and Joseph's unusual relationship gave them an exceptional camaraderie with both the Indians and the French. They reached Lake

Nipissing in record time and then the French River and finally the great bay of the Lake of the Huron.

They chose the north shore to the North Channel and then onward to Michilimackinac where Cadillac stopped for supplies and to settle some accounts. Jean-Baptiste* and Joseph met a man they knew from their first trip named Biville who remarked, "I see the *Sieur* has again landed on his feet." Jean-Baptiste* said nothing but gave a questioning look and the man continued. "The Jesuits got on to his scheme of trading brandy to the Indians for furs. They found that the Indians preferred drinking to praying. They got word to Frontenac and he recalled Cadillac. We heard that he was to be sent back to France in irons, but I see he has again wound up on top."

Before they could question him about this, there was a call to depart. The entourage gathered and was quickly on its way. Again it was a perfect early summer day, bright sun, woods filled with flowers and birds, and the days almost endless. The singing of the voyageurs was endless.

> *Chante, rossignol, chante,*
> *Toi qui a le Coeur gai.*
> *Lui y a longtemps que je t'aime,*
> *Jamais je ne t'oblierai.*

Some days later they reached the large bay on the eastern coast of the Michigauma peninsula. The area that appeared like the cleft of the heart on Cadillac's map, or the web of the thumb on LaSalle's map. The winds were high so they decided to follow the longer route along the shore of the bay rather than risk the direct crossing. The water was quite shallow here, and long spits of sand projected into the bay. When they could see the southern shore of the bay they cut across to the eastern shore and continued north toward the tip of the peninsula.

They stopped to camp and encountered a band of Indians. Chene, Cadillac's official interpreter, spoke to them and returned to Cadillac, "They are an Algonquin speaking tribe called Saginaw. Their village is near here and they have invited us to stay."

Cadillac said, "Ask them if they have anything to trade."

Chene did and replied, "They have furs." Cadillac agreed and they hiked a short distance to the village.

It was a typical Algonquin village, very mobile with tents easily struck to move quickly. They sat by the fire and ate a meal of roasted game and later smoked. At that point the Indians produced a number of pelts and Cadillac produced some casks of brandy. A deal was struck and the evening continued with the crowd growing more enthusiastic with the brandy. As the evening wore on and the revelers retired, many of men from the troupe: soldiers, voyageurs, and Indians went with women of the village for the night.

In the morning they were awakened by a loud disturbance. It seemed that one of the officers had taken off with the daughter of the chief who did not take the news well. His braves had seized the officer. Cadillac went with Chene who was told that the group could leave but the officer must remain. Cadillac was considering the deal and his apparent lack of options when Joseph stepped forward and said something to the chief. After they had spoken alone for a while, Joseph returned and said, "He has agreed to allow all of us to leave if we do so at once." When asked what had transpired, he replied, "I explained what an important man Monsieur Cadillac was and that he stood for the King of France himself." Cadillac was quite content with this answer.

The men hastened to break camp and pushed off into the bay in a matter of minutes taking their now rescued but very frightened comrade. Later that night as they made camp now on the eastern shore of the thumb of Michigauma, Jean-Baptiste* asked Joseph what had actually occurred. Joseph replied quietly, "Last night the chief noticed the wampum I wear. As you know it is identical to that worn by my father, brother, and grandfather. Apparently he had met Henri years ago during his travels. I told him that my grandfather would consider it a great favor if he would release the man."

They both chuckled and Jean-Baptiste* said, "My father has said, 'sometimes it is as important who one knows as what one knows'."

A few days later they began to see the southern end of the lake of the Huron, which had taken them fully three weeks to traverse. From the lake the land was not as easily seen as it had been further north where the terrain was hilly. Here the terrain was very flat. The lake narrowed rapidly into a narrow river, very deep with an enormous current. The group quickly made camp on the western shore of the river where they found the ruined footings of a few buildings. As they surveyed the area, de Tonti said, "These are the ruins of old Fort Saint-Joseph. Duluth and I brought a few men to establish it in 1686. We did not have adequate numbers to protect and maintain it. So it was eventually abandoned."

Cadillac looked about and with his typical confidence stated, "We will be certain not to make that mistake this time." A few of the young Indians went to swim in the river and were carried far downstream in the treacherous current before they could make it to shore. Jean-Baptiste* and Joseph took a few of the voyageurs out in canoes and caught enough pickerel to feed the entire camp.

The following morning they headed south. The voyage was virtually effortless as the river carried a current as high as ten miles per hour in some places. There were a few islands along the way, and the forest was fairly dense although clearings appeared in marshy areas. The land was perfectly flat. Although it was seventy-five miles long, by the end of the day they came to the end of the river which broke into three channels cutting through marshland thick with cattails and bull rushes. Here they began to see signs of old and current Indian camps.

They took the south channel which seemed the widest and wove through the marsh until they entered a lake. It was fairly large but not nearly as large as the lake of the Huron and very shallow. Tonti explained "This is called the Lake of Sainte-Claire, as the French discovered it on her feast day. Our destination is in the southwest corner." They made their camp on a low marshy island near the end of the channel.

While making camp they encountered a band of Indians. Cadillac took Chene to speak with them. This time he also asked Joseph to come along. When they returned he reported, "They are an Algonquin tribe of Pottawatomi Indians. They have invited us to dinner." During the meal Jean-Baptiste* learned they called this place *Wah-pol* and it was a relatively permanent camp. They lived on fish and game birds. The men were given a delicious plate of smoked fish and duck preserved with salt much like a ham is cured. When Jean-Baptiste* asked about the salt, he was told that there were salt wells along the river just to the north.

The following morning they headed into the lake. They traversed the mouth of a large bay in the northern end of the lake until they came to the western shore and followed it south. Again the land was forested with marshy areas and a few large rivers draining into the lake. Again it was entirely flat. The southern half of the lake was a shallow bay with a sandy shore. It extended between a long point on the north and a wide point on the south. Cadillac sketched a map of the area where he called the bay *l'anse creuse* or the hollow cove, and wide point simply *la grosse pointe.*

They made camp at the southern end of *la grosse pointe.* Cadillac announced, "We shall make camp here near this *grand marais",* indicating the large marshy area near the opening of the river. "And tomorrow we shall explore our new home."

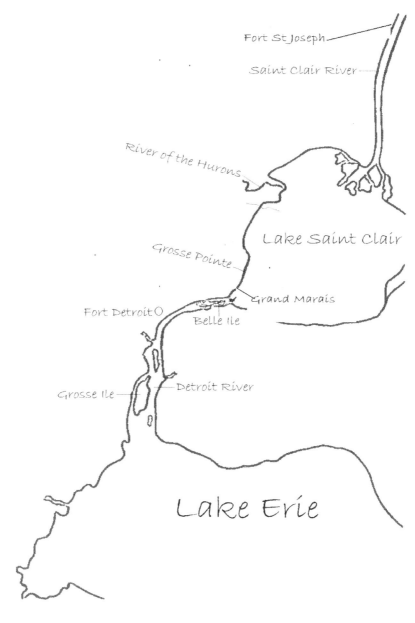

Détroit River Region 1704

Chapter 22

The next morning the group departed with great enthusiasm. It was a beautiful summer morning with the sun rising off the lake. The sky had a few puffs of white clouds and there was a fair breeze from the west making the lake dead calm. They held to the western shore of the lake which made a sharp right turn into the river and the western shore of the lake quickly became the northern bank of the river. A small island sat at the very entrance to the river and a short while after they encountered an oblong island lined with weeping willow trees that gave it a most beautiful appearance on this bright morning. Cadillac noted the islands on his map and wrote *belle isle* to distinguish the latter.

A short distance after, it appeared that the river ended up ahead, but as they progressed they realized it was making another sharp turn to the left. At the center of the turn, the river was most narrow, the land on the southeast was low and the land on the northwest somewhat higher providing an ideal perch for protection. In addition, one could see long stretches of the river in each direction from this point.

Without even double-checking his maps Cadillac exclaimed, "This is it! This is our *détroit*." Using the French term for a narrow strait. "We shall proceed to explore the end of the river and tomorrow we will land and begin to build. The southern portion of the river was longer and wider. Jean-Baptiste* noticed a number of streams and a few rivers emptying into it. There were a few small islands and a large low island with few trees on the eastern shore and then a large wide island that almost filled the river. It was heavily forested. Cadillac simply noted this as *la grosse isle* on his map.

They eventually came to the lake of the Erie which was another impressive expanse of water. At this point Cadillac turned the group around and landed on a sandy beach of the *grosse isle* to camp for the night.

The Detroit River - July 24, 1701:

They arose before dawn and were in sight of their destination just as the sun rose over the *belle isle*. They landed on a sandy beach just east of the prominence and began to unload. Père Vaillant, the priest, approached Cadillac, "Monsieur, the first thing we must do is set a stone for the church."

Cadillac regarded the man in the black robe and replied, "Father, I believe we should name our church Sainte-Anne for the patron saint of New France and mother of the Virgin. I believe her feast day is in two days. I believe that will be the best day. I am going to explore the vicinity. Why don't you take Grosse Pierre and search for an appropriate stone?"

The priest wanted to protest but had realized he was no match for Cadillac so he agreed. With that, Cadillac left de Tonti and Pierre in charge of unloading and he took Jean-Baptiste*, Jacob de Marsac and a few other men to explore the area.

The ground was higher and better drained here than it had been in their marshy camp on the *grosse pointe.* There were several small clearings indicative of old Indian villages and a network of Indian trails which Jean-Baptiste* was able to find making exploration easier. They were able to cover a surprisingly large area in one day. There was a river to the west of the proposed camp, and soil throughout was good and also quite flat.

That evening when they returned to the camp Cadillac told de Tonti and the officers. "This area is perfect, not only for a post and a fort and a church; but here we will build a great city in the wilderness!"

The following day the building began in earnest. Cadillac laid out a fenced area to be enclosed by stockades with a grand lookout of the river. Inside he laid out locations for the church, a garrison for the soldiers, and a warehouse. There was also room for houses for him, de Tonti and some others. There would be enough room for the entire group to sleep inside the walls at night.

The work progressed rapidly. Many of the men had been with Cadillac at Michilimackinac or with LaSalle when he built Fort Frontenac near Niagara; and they knew the drill. Some cut and prepared wood, some hauled and some assembled. Jean-Baptiste* and Joseph lent a hand when possible but were usually occupied hunting or exploring for or with Cadillac.

<u>The Detroit River - July 26, 1701:</u>

As promised, Cadillac used this day to dedicate the church. Grosse Pierre had acquired an enormous piece of pink granite and dragged it to the site. Anyone who had seen this feat would never have words with Grosse Pierre. The two Jesuits, Père Vaillant and Père Dehalle said a few prayers and blessed the stone.

At that point Cadillac jumped on to the stone and addressed the group. "By the grace of Almighty God, I claim these lands for his majesty the King of France, and today on her feast day, I dedicate this church to the patron saint of New France, Sainte-Anne." Unexpectedly he added, "And I hereby christen this fort and village, *Fort Pontchartrain du Détroit*! It is here I shall build a city in the wilderness." He then planted the fleur-de-lis the flag of France, and so a new city with a new name was born. The priest said a short mass and construction continued.

During the next few days, Cadillac sent out parties to explore the region and give word to local natives that the fort was being built and he wished to meet with them all to establish peace, trade and mutual protection.

A few days later a French canoe appeared upstream, and two voyageurs landed the craft and walked up to the fort. Jean-Baptiste* immediately recognized one as Joseph Parent from his childhood in Charlesbourg. They were greeted by Pierre and taken to Cadillac who knew the men from Michilimackinac. Parent's companion was Pierre Roy. Joseph Parent began his explanation, "We have been trapping and hunting this area for the past three years. Our main camp is at the stream north of here across from the island. We usually make it back to Montréal in the spring for the market and to see my family."

Cadillac inquired about the local Indians. Parent replied, "There are lots of tribes, this being kind of a trade crossroads. Down to the south there's the Miami, they come from the Maumee River in the lake of the Erie. Then there's Pottawatomi, and across the river the Ottawa and Huron. To the north it's the Fox and the Wolf tribes. They're both a little strange and unpredictable. All and all, the natives are pretty friendly to us. Trouble is, they don't always see eye to eye with one another and there's always some disagreement or other going on.

"I'll tell you, if anyone can get all these boys to play together, it'll be you Cadillac." Jean-Baptiste* startled at the familiarity, he had never heard anyone speak so informally to Cadillac. However the man seemed to take it in stride.

Cadillac then asked him about the beautiful island to the north, "I've named it *belle isle.*" he said.

Parent replied, "Well, we call it something else. You'll see why. Tell you what, let us take Jean-Baptiste* and Joseph here over there tomorrow and we'll bring back something real special. Anyway, we'll be around from time to time, and we'll spread the word to the locals. If you need us, just holler." And they took their leave.

Later that evening as Joseph and Jean-Baptiste* sat outside their small tent by the beginnings of Cadillac's house, Parent and Roy stopped for a visit. Joseph Parent was the son of Pierre* Parent and Jeanne* Badeau who lived a few farms from the Allards. Jeanne* Badeau was the daughter of Anne* Ardouin-Badeau, François* Allard's first employer in Quèbec. As a young boy Jean-Baptiste* had idolized Joseph Parent who was only six years older than Jean-Baptiste* but always seemed older, bigger, stronger and more skilled than his age.

He had shown no inclination to farming and had left early for the backcountry. He was, however, honest and always kind, at least when he didn't feel the need to kill you. Like most voyageurs he was married to a girl in Montréal and had a few children by her. Jean-Baptiste* also knew that he had at least three others by various Indian women in Michilimackinac.

"How are my mother and the others?" he asked. Jean-Baptiste* replied that they were well when he left. Parent's father Pierre* had died three years earlier. He asked, "How about the three boys?" Referring to his brothers, the famous triplets.

Jean-Baptiste* indicated that they were fine and had all married five years ago.

Joseph Parent continued, "I always knew you would be the Allard boy to take to the wild. Even when you was little. Your brothers were too serious about learning and farming." Addressing Joseph he said, "I learned more about the back country from your grandfather Henri than all the rest. He was the best."

With that he arose and said, "Be ready at dawn, and you better bring your rifles."

At dawn the next day the four men took Parent's canoe on the short trip upstream to the *belle isle*. After

127

landing, they hiked into the interior and came on a small clearing connected by two trails that looked like Indian trails but more heavily worn. Parent indicated the men get behind the brush and he made a high squealing noise. They waited a short while before hearing an enormous crashing through the trail. A giant beast came lumbering down the trail. Before Jean-Baptiste* realized what it was, Parent had brought it down with a shot to the head.

They approached the beast as Jean-Baptiste* realized what it was. He had seen the rare wild boar in Québec but never so huge. Parent commented, "It's hard to bring one of these down with an arrow before he takes you down."

The men took turns until each had taken a boar. They then gutted them and dragged them to the beach. At over 500 pounds each, they would supply a good meal for the camp. Before departing Parent and Roy gave Jean-Baptiste* and Joseph a tour of the island. About two miles long, less than one mile wide, and crossed by streams and ponds, it was as beautiful an island from the inside as the outside.

When they presented Cadillac with the catch, Parent stated, "Now you see why we call it *Isle aux couchons*." And it would remain the 'island of the pigs' for a century before reclaiming Cadillac's name, 'Belle Isle'.

Chapter 23

Fort Pontchartrain du Détroit - September 1701;

As autumn arrived and the weather turned cooler, Cadillac's village was taking form. The stockade was almost completed, the church and garrison roofed, and most of the other buildings nearing conclusion. The land outside which had been cleared for lumber was being prepared for crops in the spring.

A number of small Indian bands had visited, and most expressed interest, and some planned to return before winter. One afternoon the call of alert came from a watchtower of the stockade. Cadillac rushed up with Jean-Baptiste* and Joseph behind as was their job. He questioned the watch guard who merely responded, "Indians." Cadillac looked puzzled as Indian visits had become common. The man continued, "Look sir, many Indians."

Cadillac looked over and saw hundreds of Indians descending slowly on the fort. Joseph said, "From their hair they are Huron. It appears to be a peaceful group."

Cadillac took the risk and walked outside the gates flanked by the two men. A man who appeared to be the leader made a sign of welcome and the women began bringing gifts of fur, pots and other items, laying them at Cadillac's feet. After some ceremony, he invited the chief and his entourage inside the walls. The men sat and talked. Joseph's position in Cadillac's eyes was again elevated as he realized Joseph was much more fluent in Huron than his official man, Chene.

Cadillac proposed that he would provide land for the tribe in exchange for rent, trade and mutual alliance. The chief agreed and a two-day festival commenced in and outside the fort. Eventually the Huron moved to their land on the opposite shore. As the next two months progressed, more and more tribes came in numbers. By winter there were Huron and Ottawa villages on the opposite shore; Pottawatomi and Miami to the south; and Fox and *Loup* or Wolf to the north. As the snow fell, there were approximately 6,000 Indians at Fort Pontchartrain du Détroit. Cadillac's vision of a city in the wilderness was already coming to pass.

As the winter progressed, Jean-Baptiste* and Joseph did some hunting and exploring, but much of their time was spent communicating between the various tribes and Cadillac. The many dialects made it difficult. Sometimes they would use other Indians from the group who understood an unusual dialect but knew no French. They would translate for Jean-Baptiste* and Joseph who would in turn translate for Cadillac.

In early winter they received word from Québec that a peace had been signed in Montréal between the French and the Iroquois agreeing to open up the passage through Niagara. Cadillac told de Tonti this would allow them to send for their families as soon as the winter broke. What they did not know was that Mesdames Cadillac and de Tonti had heard about the peace in late summer and had made their own plans.

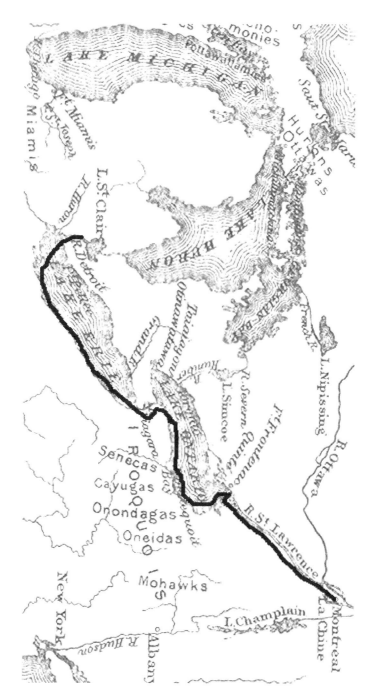

ROUTE OF MADAME CADILLAC TO DETROIT

Chapter 24

Fort Frontenac, Lake of the Ontario - April 1702:

Marie-Therese Guyon-Cadillac watched out the window of her cabin. Spring was indeed here, the snow and ice were almost gone and the birds were singing. The past seven months had been difficult to say the least. Sometimes adventurous, sometimes frightening and now very boring. Hopefully Monsieur Reaume would return with some news today. There was a knock at the door and it was indeed Robert* Reaume.

Reaume was slightly larger than most Frenchmen, not heavy but remarkably solid. He was probably handsome if he ever cleaned up and certainly the strongest man Marie-Therese had ever met. His icy blue eyes betrayed his French-Atlantic heritage. He was generally silent, never smiled, and in the past seven months, she had found him kind, sensitive, honest and honorable almost to a fault.

"They have indeed returned. Trottier and his Indians have returned, Madame Tonti is with them and apparently unharmed."

She replied, "How wonderful! Where have they been and whatever have they been doing?"

He responded, "I am told they had detoured into the back country to rescue an injured boy who has subsequently died. They were, however, caught in the early blizzard and forced to winter at an Indian camp in the north of the lake."

"Do you find this story credible?"

"Madame, my job is not to judge truth. It is to protect you and your son and deliver you safely to your husband at the *détroit du Lac Erie*. Your father is paying me well for this and due to this misadventure I will now collect four times the amount. Rest assured I will do my job."

They went outdoors and she saw Marie-Anne. They rushed to each other and embraced in happy tears. Madame Cadillac sobbed, "Oh my dear! I was so frightened. I feared you had perished, or worse."

Marie-Anne responded calmly, "I was actually quite well cared for. I was able to play Indian princess for the winter, and I did have Monsieur Trottier to amuse me."

Marie-Anne Picote de Bellestre-Tonti was the wife of Alphonse Tonti, Cadillac's right hand man. She had disappeared seven months ago when she and Madame Cadillac had been traveling to the straits of Lake Erie where their husbands were building a fort. Madame Tonti had been traveling in a canoe with her brother's new brother-in-law, Joseph Trottier. Trottier's canoe had detoured at the head of the Lake of the Ontario on a mysterious errand. When they failed to return, Monsieur Reaume had taken Madame Cadillac and her son in his canoe to Fort Frontenac. An early blizzard caused them to end their voyage for winter at the fort. Marie-Therese had been overwhelmed with fear for her friend but was now greatly relieved.

The voyage had been arranged at the end of the summer by Joseph Trottier as soon as word arrived of a new peace with the Iroquois which made travel though the

Niagara possible. Marie-Therese's father Denis Guyon and René Cuillerier, a relative of Marie-Anne Tonti, had financed the voyage. Both men were rich Québec fur merchants. Joseph Trottier was handsome and charming enough, but Madame Cadillac thought him a bit of a rascal and was suspicious of this disappearance with her friend.

That evening when the women were alone in the cabin they were able to compare stories.

"Marie-Anne, whatever occurred? We saw Trottier stop to talk with a band of Indians in two canoes and soon you disappeared. I have been worried nearly to death."

Madame Tonti replied, "My dear, it was the most fascinating adventure. We were following you down the lake when Joseph caught sight of the two Indian canoes. They hailed us and he proceeded to them. They spoke hurriedly in Algonquin. I could not follow it, but Joseph later told me that there was an injured French boy nearby and we were to detour a short while to help.

"We went a ways down the shore and landed. We then hiked an hour to a clearing. There were four ferocious looking voyageurs I did not recognize and a young boy who had been injured in a fall. He was gravely injured, and we decided it best to carry him to a nearby Indian camp. I nursed the boy through the night, but alas, he died in the morning. Trottier had gone with the others and did not return for two more days. He told me that the weather was to turn bad and we would again spend the night. Indeed there was a terrible blizzard as you know, and further travel was out of the question. We spent the next seven months in the camp and proceeded only three days ago."

Marie-Therese was aghast. "Dear lord! Were you not frightened out of your mind?"

"At first I was uneasy, but the Indian women were quite kind. One spoke a little French. Joseph left occasionally on 'errands' but he was most kind and very charming. There was also a handsome Indian brave who kept me company when Trottier was off in the woods."

Marie-Therese looked at her friend in disbelief. "My dear Madame Tonti, I trust there was no impropriety at this savage place."

Marie-Anne giggled and simply replied, "Marie-Therese, you are such a prude."

Marie-Therese returned curtly, "We leave tomorrow and I trust there will be no more diversions and your conduct will be beyond reproach, especially in front of my son." And with that they went to their beds.

Marie-Therese had a room adjoining a smaller room where her son Jacques stayed with an Indian nurse. She went in to say good night. The boy sat on his bed playing with a wooden gun he received for his seventh birthday, which had been spent at Fort Frontenac. Marie-Therese sat on the bed, "Tomorrow we shall begin the last part of our voyage, I hope in three weeks' time we will see your father and your brother, Antoine."

"Mama, will papa's fort be like Frontenac?"

"Soon it shall, but it is quite new and things just being built. Are you excited?"

"Yes mama, I can not wait to see papa."

"I'm sure that he and your brother will be equally as pleased." She kissed the lad and went to her room.

The next morning the canoes departed, following the southern shores of the lake of the Ontario which at this time was frequently referred to as Lake Frontenac. The weather was cool but the women and young Jacques had furs to lie on and cover with keeping them quite comfortable. Marie-Therese and Jacques rode with Robert* Reaume and an Indian. Marie-Anne rode with Joseph Trottier, and one other voyageur. A third canoe held two Indians and two voyageurs. By mid-day they passed the place where they had parted ways in the fall. Reaume told Marie Therese, "Two men in a light canoe were dispatched this morning to announce your arrival. They should arrive a few days before us."

The Niagara River - Late April 1702:

On the fourth day of the trip they arrived at a river heading south. The current was fierce. Reaume told Marie-Therese that they would paddle as far in as possible and then begin the difficult portage. Soon it sounded like distant thunder and Marie-Therese wondered how this could be on such a clear day. She then realized that it was not thunder but water. They began to see what appeared to be fog but was actually mist from the falls. When the current became too strong, they landed.

Reaume had told them that this would be the worst part of the trip. Even the women were asked to carry some packs. The terrain was slippery and constantly going up. In late afternoon they stopped to camp. The woman were exhausted. Marie-Therese could hardly believe the loads the men were carrying under these conditions. Even Robert* Reaume began to show signs of fatigue.

The next four days were even worse. The women wondered if it would ever end. The fifth day proved even steeper, but just as they thought they were surely going to perish, the terrain began to level out and by late afternoon it was flat. After a brief rest. Reaume arose and said to the ladies, "Come with me and bring the boy." They began on a trail to the north accompanied by Reaume's Indian companion. "Now you may have your reward."

After a short while they came to a clearing. The sound of the falls had been present for the entire portage, but it was now deafening. As they came across the clearing, the falls came into sight. Marie-Therese had heard stories of this fabled place since she was a little girl, but nothing had prepared her for this. The most ridiculous sounding exaggerations were nothing compared to the reality. The falls stretched for almost a mile across and the force and speed of the water was beyond belief. The river below could be seen in the distance, but a magnificent cloud of mist covered the area below.

Reaume picked up a log and flung it into the water. It disappeared over the edge in lightning speed. Marie-Therese grabbed Jacques' coat and held on to him with all her strength. They stood for a long while in absolute awe when Reaume broke the silence, "We had better go if we are to be back at camp by dark." And they reluctantly turned away.

The following day the walk continued although the terrain was much flatter. Reaume explained, "We must portage far enough south to be out of the strongest currents. Many men have been lost by putting in too soon."

Indeed when they put in later in the afternoon the current was still extremely strong, but the able voyageurs were able to make good progress.

The Lake of the Erie - May 1702:

Robert* Reaume stopped to make camp on a sandy beach. It was their second night on the north shore of the Lake of the Erie, a beautiful clear night and not too cold. Reaume estimated that they were only a few days from their destination. The sun set over the western shore at a point that he estimated to be the exact location of Cadillac's fort. As was his habit, Reaume awoke just before dawn. He was preparing the fire for morning as the sun rose over the eastern shore. The misadventures of Joseph Trottier had cost Reaume an entire winter's trading, but he was not angry. The payment promised in such an event would more than cover his losses.

As the others began to stir, he startled at a very faint but definite crack of a twig. He looked immediately to Anaki, his Indian companion who had also sensed it. They cautioned the others to come close and remain silent. The men went to ready their rifles when the shouting began. A group of braves with Iroquois hair fashion had fallen upon them. One of the voyageurs and one of the Indians from the third canoe had fallen to arrows. The men discharged their weapons, and three or four Iroquois fell silent.

The fighting went quickly to hand-to-hand with knives and hatchets. As Reaume finished his attacker, he saw young Jacques being taken by a nearby foe. He adroitly fell on the man releasing the boy and began a new skirmish. Jacques rushed to the arms of his mother who was immediately menaced by a particularly large Indian standing with a large bloody knife. The other men were all occupied and unable to come to their aid. Marie-Therese gave a shrill shriek and the man looked surprised and fell in front of her. As he fell, she saw an arrow in his back. Even in the excitement, she could not miss the bright red feather.

Three new Frenchmen appeared from the forest and as quickly as they had come, the Indians were gone with the exception of the few that lay dead in the sand.

Reaume looked up and shouted, "Parent!" and the two men embraced. He thought that the two younger men looked familiar but could not immediately place them. The group regained their order, the men pulled the dead bodies into the woods and returned to their preparations. Marie-Therese could never cease to marvel at how quickly things could go from violence to tranquility in this savage country.

As they sat to eat Reaume exclaimed, "François* Allard's boy, the one they call the Iroquois slayer."

Jean-Baptiste* blushed and introduced himself and Joseph. He then went on to explain, "Monsieur Cadillac received word of your impending arrival a few days ago. We were sent to scout the shore and advise him of the exact time of your arrival so that he could arrange a ceremony. Last night we saw your fire and camped west of here not wanting to startle you in the darkness. As we proceeded in this morning we saw the attack, landed just west of here and circled inland."

Reaume replied with voyageur bravado, "Well, you saved us the trouble of killing a few more Iroquois."

Marie-Therese added, "You saved my boy and me and I am entirely grateful, Monsieur Allard. I can only think what those savages would have done with us women."

Parent replied, "I doubt they would have harmed you. They would have likely taken you to the fort and ransomed you to your husbands. Captives for ransom seems to be gaining favor with the natives."

The group continued together and two nights later arrived at the mouth of the river of the Erie. At dawn Jean-Baptiste*, Joseph, and Parent left early so they could give Cadillac some advance notice. The others headed north up the river a short time after and by afternoon they could see smoke from the settlement.

Cadillac's village had grown remarkably in the first few months. The sand beach rose to a steep bank on which stood the large, imposing wooden stockade with watchtower platforms, the most southern of which flew a large fleur-de-lis flag. Inside the walls stood a small church, a barracks, a warehouse and several houses. The land outside the walls was cleared and being prepared for planting. Indian camps filled the countryside on both sides of the river.

Cadillac had a dock built off the beach, which allowed the canoes to unload without beaching. He and Tonti stood on the dock in full regalia. Behind him was a small group of soldiers including a drum and a bugle. Further back were several voyageurs and Indians. As the ladies landed, the crowd cheered and the small 'band' played. Cadillac bowed with a theatrical swoop of his plumed hat and announced, "Welcome to Fort Pontchartrain du Détroit." The couples embraced and entered the walls for "a tour of the city".

The early fort had several buildings. Entry was on the east wall facing the river. To the rear on the west wall were two long houses for Cadillac and Tonti. The Church of Sainte-Anne and the priests' house stood along the northern wall while the magazine and barracks were on the south along with a smaller gate. On the eastern side by the main gate were fourteen cabins of varying sizes. Marie-Therese was astounded at the size of the infant fort and the number of people and amount of activity. Particularly amazing was the number and variety of Indians completely interspersed in the activity of the city.

That evening the couples had private conversations of the events of the past winter.

"It was quite bizarre," started Marie-Therese, "We were headed for the Niagara when the Trottier canoe took off to go with these two other canoes. They seemed to indicate we should wait which we did. When they had not returned in two days, Monsieur Reaume thought it best if we returned to Frontenac. Thank the lord that we did. The snow descended and in two more days' time we were stranded. The captain at the fort made us most comfortable and the women did all they could to make our stay bearable, but it was quite boring, and Antoine, I did miss you so."

Cadillac responded, "My reports of Monsieur Reaume are all good. Fortunately you were in good hands. Trottier, however, seems to be another matter."

Marie-Therese added, "Marie-Anne seemed to have no regrets, but sometimes I wonder about the woman."

Cadillac went on, "I have always found the women from these Parisian families somewhat bold. Her husband as well is odd. Quite arrogant and does not relate well to the men. I feel at times he is jealous of my position."

In the Tonti home a similar conversation ensued. Marie-Anne said, "The winter in the Indian camp was hard but rather interesting. Monsieur Trottier was quite kind."

Tonti had always suspected that his wife had an unfaithful tendency. His Italian heritage made this seem acceptable, but he resented Cadillac's attitude that "his" wife would never stray. He replied, "Cadillac is often quite insufferable. He acts as though everything rises and falls on him, and that all the problems are my problem. His idea to name the fort, Pontchartrain is just too self-serving. I only wish I could expose him for what he is."

"Whatever do you mean, Alphonse?"

"I am certain that the man is a fraud. He simply overwhelms people and they don't realize that half the time he doesn't know what he is talking about."

In the tent of Joseph and Jean-Baptiste* just outside the houses a third conversation was taking place. Joseph Parent and Robert* Reaume had come to smoke and talk. Parent began, "What do you suppose was the detour of Trottier?"

Reaume thought and with a candor he reserved for other voyageurs, he said, "I have always felt the man was a rascal. He realized we were in prime territory where there has been almost no French trade for three years as a result of the Iroquois. I believe he detoured to trade for the winter and that he has a great store of furs on the Ontario which he will retrieve on the way home. He had better be careful as the law has become very strict concerning trade without license. I plan to leave in the morning with Anaki; I wish to avoid returning with Trottier with or without his furs. I have a family and a farm to tend and hope to be out next winter trading again, **with** a license"

Chapter 24

<u>Québec - June 1702:</u>

As the city grew, some events became commonplace, but there was always great excitement when a boat arrived from France. As was the custom the harbormaster circulated the dock announcing any thing that may have arrived for a particular colonist.
François* Allard was in the crowd with his son André. They had come to town for supplies and had waited to watch the ship unload. François* was surprised to hear his name called and he stepped forward. The harbormaster regarded the letter and said, "Looks pretty important."

François* looked at the back and it carried the seal of the Bishop of Tours. He told, André, "We had better let your mother open this."

Back in Charlesbourg, they rushed to the farmhouse where Jeanne* was laboring in the kitchen with the two girls assisting. François* delivered the envelope which she looked at while she was seated and then broke the seal.

April, 1702

My Dearest Sister Jeanne*,

I hope that this letter finds you and your wonderful family well in your wilderness paradise. Your brothers and sisters are well. Michel has assumed the duties of father's farm and businesses and is doing well. My own work at the archdiocese keeps me fully occupied. The reason for my letter is to inform you of circumstances in Europe that may affect you even in your far away home.

Charles II, King of Spain died this winter without an heir. The grandson of our King Louis XIV, Philippe the Grand Dauphin, has a rightful claim to the throne of Spain by way of his mother. King William of England and his daughter, Anne, who he has named as his heir, have announced that they will not allow the French to have control of Spain and are gathering allies throughout Europe. I fear that another European war may be upon us.

My fear for you is that the consolidation with Spain would unite the French and Spanish Colonies in the Americas, and I see that England will do what it can to stop that. I fear that a good deal of the fighting will be on your soil between New England and New France.

As always I will continue to hold you in my prayers.

Your loving brother,
André Anguille, Bishop of Tours

As Jeanne* finished the letter, her husband said, "I suppose this will also mean resumption of hostilities with the Iroquois."

Jeanne* put the letter in a basket in which she kept all such letters and turned to her husband, "Why must men always fight? Why must there always be war?"

François* returned sadly, "Only God himself knows, we can only pray that some day cooler heads will lead the people."

The village had grown greatly in its first two years. The fields were now cultivated and barns had been built outside of the walls to house crops and animals. Many more Indians had arrived and Cadillac's vision of a hub of trade for the region was showing promise as was the fort's potential to secure the trade routes. This had only been somewhat thwarted by increasing hostilities in the east with the English and the Iroquois. As a result, Québec had recalled several of Cadillac's troops.

Jean-Baptiste* reported to Cadillac after making his morning rounds in the Indian villages to the north. "There seems to be some unrest between some of the tribes, particularly one group of Huron."

Cadillac replied blaming this on the inefficiency of Tonti as well as his lack of men. "Keep me advised," which was always his response. On his way out Jean-Baptiste* encountered Joseph Parent.

"Pierre Roy and I plan a trip to Montréal before the bad weather. Perhaps you and Joseph would care to accompany us." Jean-Baptiste* had been considering how routine this adventure had become and said that he would discuss it with Joseph.

That evening, Joseph awoke and shook Jean-Baptiste*. "Baptiste*, I smell fire much hotter that a campfire."

Jean-Baptiste* could never fathom how his friend could smell how hot a fire was, but knowing to trust the Indian's amazing sense of smell, he arose quickly. They skirted the periphery and saw flames in the barn on the southeast corner. As they rushed to sound the alarm, Jean-Baptiste* felt certain he also saw fire in the barn to the west. They alerted the sentry and sounded the alarm. Within minutes the village had turned out for the fire drill. They had contained a few small fires with buckets of water from the river, but this blaze was obviously too large and far along. In addition, strong wind from the south pushed the flames along fiercely.

Joseph and Jean-Baptiste* left to make sure the rest of the town was alerted and evacuated and soon they all watched helplessly as Cadillac's dream turned to ashes. The only good fortune was a rainsquall that hit suddenly after midnight. It doused the fire but by this time a large segment of the city inside the walls had been gutted.

At daylight they inspected the damages. The fire had been deliberately set and there were witnesses who had seen suspicious looking Huron around the barns at nightfall. Cadillac addressed the citizens and soldiers. "We must begin at once to rebuild." He and Tonti began to organize work crews. He came to Jean-Baptiste* and said, "I need you to travel quickly to Québec and alert the Governor that I require more men urgently. Make ready and I will prepare documents." Jean-Baptiste* was relieved that he would not have to announce to the great man that the evening before he and Joseph had made plans to leave.

So having witnessed the birth and near early death of the great city in the wilderness, Jean-Baptiste* and Joseph made their way south with Parent and Pierre Roy. That evening at the campfire on the north shore of Erie, Parent proposed, "I wouldn't be at all surprised if the Huron were put up by Tonti on this fire. There is no doubt that he dislikes Cadillac greatly and I have heard that Cadillac sent word to Montréal accusing Tonti's wife's friend, Joseph Trottier, of illegal trade. At any rate, we may try the trade up at Gitcheegumee this winter."

The voyage to Montréal was quite rapid compared to the voyage to Détroit. Not only did they travel light but also with the current they virtually flew. Even the portage at Niagara was downhill. The fall colors were at their height and brilliance was everywhere. Parent took Joseph and Jean-Baptiste* to the falls. They were reminded of the night they spent on the shores of Gitcheegumee with old Henri watching the storm. Sometimes the force of nature is unbelievable.

They reached Montréal in only four weeks, and unloaded in Lachine after portaging the rapids, where they encountered Robert* Reaume.

"I spent a whole week this spring in court for Monsieur Trottier," he told them. "The law did get wind of his shenanigans, I think, by way of Cadillac. At any rate they fined him and put him in jail overnight. Nothing compared to the money he got for the furs. But that's what happens if you got rich friends."

Jean-Baptiste* and Joseph left the voyageurs to gossip and make winter plans as they went to the government building to report to the captain. He in turn sent them in a canoe with two soldiers to see the Governor in Québec. The soldiers were hardly the paddlers that Parent and Roy were and they made much slower time down the Saint-Laurent. It was good to see familiar country again although the waterway was considerably more populated than just less than three years before.

In Québec they went straight to the Governor's house. Louis-Hector de Callière had been in Québec only four years. He disliked the country and compared to the immensely popular Frontenac before him, the country did not much like him. Happily he had just received word that he was blessedly being recalled to Paris. He had met Cadillac once and found him arrogant and altogether disagreeable.

The men delivered their papers from Cadillac and stood while Callière perused them. "Tell me, lads, how do you find this man, Cadillac?"

Remembering what his mother had taught him, Jean-Baptiste* responded, "He is a strong and determined leader, sir."

"And what do you make of this place, *le détroit du lac Erie*?"

"It is certainly strategically placed, sir, I believe it will some day be a great city in the wilderness as Monsieur Cadillac says."

Callière would have liked nothing better than to tell the arrogant ass, Cadillac, to paddle himself back to Michilimackinac, but he recalled that Cadillac was well regarded by Pontchartrain, and Callière wanted nothing to impede his rapid escape to Paris so he bit his tongue and said, "I will supply everything he wants and at once. You may return with my reply."

149

At this Jean-Baptiste* replied, "I am sorry, your Excellency, but my friend and I are going to return to our families in Charlesbourg."

"No matter I will send it with the military dispatch. Thank you and good day, gentlemen." As the men turned to leave he muttered under his breath, "Smart lads."

Before leaving the city the boys decided to walk by the harbor. They might be able to catch a ride across the river. In the square Jean-Baptiste* was surprised to see his sister, Marie Allard, with two young woman. He called and as they closed in on each other, he realized one of the women was his young sister Marie-Anne, now a young lady, but he was puzzled by the third. She looked vaguely familiar but much more beautiful than any young woman he knew.

In a teasing fashion he asked them how three young single girls found themselves on the streets of Québec in midweek. Marie replied, "If only you ever stayed at home, you would be more *au courant*. As it is, I am now married five months."

Astonished, Jean-Baptiste* questioned, "To whom?"

"Why to Charles Villeneuve, of course."

He thought quickly. Villeneuve was the son of the older sister of Anne LeMarche who had married André. As he recalled Charles had been around the Allard house quite a lot, but Baptiste* thought it was to see Jean-François.

She added, "We are still living at home but plan to move to Bourg-Royal soon. We have a farm adjacent to the new one of André and Anne. They were able to acquire a large tract of land next to Anne's father and will eventually include Anne's father's land and we will split it. It is extremely large."

Marie-Anne added, "Georges is going to settle the farm by Papa that André had initially planned to occupy. In fact he is in town with us."

Jean-Baptiste* returned his stare to the beautiful unknown, and asked, "And you are…"

Marie-Anne answered, "Baptiste*, how rude, you remember my friend Anne-Elizabeth*."

Jean-Baptiste*'s face reddened and his jaw dropped, and he thought, "Anne-Elizabeth* Pageot? This beautiful woman was Marie-Anne's irritating little friend from next-door?"

Sensing, as beautiful women can, that she was finally at the advantage of this boy she had loved from afar since childhood, Anne-Elizabeth* said demurely, "Why Monsieur Allard, certainly you remember the day I brazenly kissed you after your famous triumph over the Iroquois."

Before Baptiste* could gather his wits, his brother Georges was upon them. Now twenty-three, he was as tall as Jean-Baptiste*. "Well, if it is not the returned Indian slayer." Poking Joseph he said, "No offense, Joseph." The group laughed and they decided to sit under a tree and catch up on this wonderful day full of autumn color. Baptiste* could not take his eyes off Anne-Elizabeth*, and the attention was not lost on her.

Eventually Georges rose and suggested they be on their way. They loaded the canoe and pushed off into the fading fall daylight.

Chapter 25

<u>Charlesbourg - That Evening:</u>

As the group crossed the Charlesbourg Square, they saw their father returning from the fields with Thomas in tow. Thomas, now sixteen, was almost as tall as his father and taller than any of his brothers. He rushed to greet Jean-Baptiste* as soon as he recognized him. François* came along more slowly. Now 64, he had a mild limp and a stoop in his posture although he still said he could outwork any of his sons. He gave his son a vigorous hug, shook his hand, and the group headed in for dinner.

Jeanne* was the most excited and fawned shamelessly over her well-traveled son. Soon the door opened, it was Charles Villeneuve, Marie's new husband. He was working daily at their farm next to André Allard in Bourg-Royal. He and Marie were temporarily living with the Allards until their new house was ready. Charles was two years younger than his bride but a serious man and avid farmer.

François* said grace and Jean-Baptiste* told the short version of his adventure. He was then brought up on family news. André and Anne were well settled on the farm in Bourg-Royal. One year after they had moved close to François* and Jeanne*, he was able to obtain a large parcel in Bourg-Royal and they decided to move again and give the Charlesbourg farm to Georges. They now had four children. As it happened the farm was next to the large farm of Charles's father, who had given them the section next to André.

Jean-François and Marie-Ursule were living on his farm in Beauport. As expected his farm was a great success, and he already had plans for expansion. Marie-Ursule had suffered some poor health. Her first two children died at birth, but a third, named Jean-Baptiste after his uncle, was prospering at age one year.

When a lull appeared in the conversation, Marie-Anne said, "Mama, you should have seen Baptiste*'s face when he saw Anne-Elizabeth*. He looked like a fox after a chicken."

The group laughed, and in spite of his deep tan, Jean-Baptiste* turned bright red.

His mother replied, "Well Baptiste*, if you have eyes for that girl, you had better move quickly. I predict she will not remain available for long. I might add that a shave and haircut might not hurt either."

This was the first comment about Jean-Baptiste*'s backwoods appearance. His hair was almost to his waist and tied in back. He had a thick full beard and his skin was a dark red-brown.

That evening François* and Jean-Baptiste* sat on the porch and smoked. François* began with the obvious, "What do you propose now that you have returned?"

"I believe I should like to stay and try my hand at farming. I have had my adventures in the back woods, and although I love it, I am not certain that it is my true destiny."

"I don't suppose this has anything to do with this girl next-door?"

Jean-Baptiste* blushed again, "I have given it some thought, but it certainly is premature."

His father continued, "I truly believe that to be a good family man, a man must farm. Although it is done, I don't see how a voyageur can give proper consideration to both his family and his work. Also if you don't mind some other advice, it would not do well to leave a woman as beautiful as that alone for the entire winter in a country filled with Frenchmen."

His son chuckled and arose, "As always, good advice. Now I have a matter with my mother."

On his way in, he ran into Marie and Charles. Marie said, "We have come to say good night. Charles must rise early and we are sleeping in the girls' loft while Marie-Anne sleeps in the parlor." She gave her brother a sly grin as she led her husband up the ladder.

As he entered the room, Jeanne* sat by the oil lamp with a book. She was now 56 years old and her hair was almost entirely gray. "Mama, I wonder if you could give me some assistance with the scissors."

She looked up, "Why Baptiste*, I believe this is the first time you have taken my advice on such a matter since you were five years old." She arose and went to work.

At breakfast Marie-Anne was the first to see him, squealing, "Marie, look at Baptiste*, he looks like a dandy."

When the laughter and jokes subsided, Jeanne* looked at her handiwork. As the two older boys resembled their father, she had not realized how much Jean-Baptiste* resembled her own brother. "Son, if you were in a cleric's collar, I would swear you were your uncle André." And a small tear ran down her cheek.

Jean-Baptiste* stayed to help Georges and his father. Philippe and Joseph came up and the men talked awhile about the adventure in Détroit as it was now being called. The Indian family had enjoyed a similar discussion at dinner. Today they started to bring in the corn. Joseph and Jean-Baptiste* quickly fell back into the procedure and the work progressed well. François* had bought a second horse, a mare and it was pregnant. He hadn't said anything but he planned to give the new horse to André and Charles. His weathered old Perchon, Henri the horse, although well along in years was still of great use.

That evening after work Jean-Baptiste* loitered about the square waiting for his brother-in-law. The men spoke for a while and then went together to the house to dinner. At dinner Jean-Baptiste* asked François* if he could go with Charles to see André in the morning.

"I've done without you for most of your adult life. I don't see why I cannot tomorrow."

The following morning André was delighted to see his brother. They went in to see Anne and meet his four children, Marie-Catherine age 7, Marie-Genevieve age 5, Jacques age 3, and Pierre-André age 1. André demonstrated the additions to the house since he had moved in. Then they toured the farm. Indeed there was a sizable place to the west, which was from Charles' father. The two men were also working this land and building a house for Charles and

Marie. "The work on the house is slow because of the farming. Once the harvest is in, we will complete it." André announced, "You know, Baptiste*, there is considerable land here and it goes north all the way to the mountains. I always thought that we would work well together."

"I will give it some thought."

Just then, Joseph's brother Henri appeared ready for work. He and his wife had moved with André and built a camp on the land. Jean-Baptiste* said, "I'll leave you boys to your work and walk down to Beauport to see Jean-François."

When he arrived at his brother's farm, he was quite impressed. It had the look of a much more mature operation. Jean-François employed two Indians and two hired Frenchmen. He had several acres cleared and a large house and barn. "We have worked very hard here and I have been fortunate enough to hire help and double my profits." He invited Jean-Baptiste* inside. His wife Marie-Ursule was thin and pale. She held an infant who was robust in contrast. Jean-François announced, "And here is your namesake, the new Jean-Baptiste Allard."

They visited for a while before Jean-Baptiste* left to walk home with his thoughts.

The next day was Sunday and beautiful fall weather still held. The Charlesbourg Chapel had been lengthened and now had room for almost two hundred parishioners. In addition there were now two services. As was tradition in good weather, a picnic was held after the last mass. A great many neighbors came to see the returning woodsman. Jean-Baptiste* was reunited with many old friends and the parents in the neighborhood. All stopped by with a pleasant comment or piece of advice or both.

Jean-Baptiste* surveyed the crowd until he saw what he was interested in. He walked over to where his sister Marie-Anne was talking to Anne-Elizabeth* Pageot and three young men. Anne-Elizabeth* saw him approach and broke out of the group to greet him. "Why here is Marie-Anne's woodsman brother." Then addressing Jean-Baptiste*, "Baptiste*, what happened to the great outdoor beard?" And she looked at him with her soft brown eyes and swept her hand over his smooth chin sending tingles into several parts of his anatomy.

One of the other men asked Anne-Elizabeth* if she was ready to go eat, to which she replied, "Why we can't be rude to Baptiste*." And she took his arm and led him to dine. Normally Jean-Baptiste* was very quiet around woman, but he found a new fluency that had previously escaped him. After an altogether pleasant afternoon, he walked her back to her house and said good day.

On his way home he talked to himself, "Why are you thinking about women? First you need to see what to do with your life. Besides what would this beautiful girl want with someone with no job, no farm, and no plans? You'd better keep women out of your mind for a while."

That night Jean-Baptiste* discussed his future with his father. "I think I would do well if I moved down by André. You and the two boys can handle this place and expand it when they are ready. I feel I might be able to better consider my options with him."

François* responded, "I knew that you have never been committed to farming, but as I have said I believe it is the only suitable life for a family man. If this is what you want, you certainly have my blessing."

The following morning he left. The men were able to work more hours on the house for Charles and Marie, and soon it was finished. Joseph came with him and the two men set up an Indian style camp on the property.

"I can scarcely believe that I have my own home," said Marie Allard on their moving day. She was already pregnant and showing with her first child and more than ready to leave her parents' home. Her brothers and sister helped them get settled with a few rudimentary pieces of furniture.

Chapter 26

The fall chores were completed and they were settling in for winter. Joseph and Jean-Baptiste* were making winter hunting plans when a caller came to André's. It was a man named Jacques Dugué, who had been an officer in Cadillac's regiment in Détroit and had recently been called back to Québec. He met with the men, "Many of us from the outposts have been called back to help protect the towns from an anticipated escalation of hostilities from the English and Iroquois. We have asked to revitalize and expand the local militias."

Local militias had always been a fixture, but they had been poorly organized and mainly provided a prospect for some of the men to take off occasionally to hunt, shoot and drink. He continued, "We are asking every able bodied man of fighting age to join. I have been requested to ask Jean-Baptiste* and Joseph to lead the Charlesbourg unit. You both have some military experience with Monsieur Cadillac. Jean-Baptiste* could organize the Frenchmen and Joseph could help include the Indians."

Directing himself to Joseph he said, "I have learned locally that you are held in exceptional regard by the local citizens, French and native alike, and should be ideal. We will meet Sunday after mass in the Chapel." And with that he took his leave.

That evening at dinner they discussed it with the two wives. Marie said, "I hate to have to see you do this, especially André and Charles who can't hit a crow with a gun." After some laughter, Anne LeMarche-Allard joined in. "I heard in the square that there have been attempted raids already in Trois Rivieres and Montréal. I suppose it is necessary to protect our families."

That Sunday all the young men gathered to hear Lieutenant Dugué speak. "Men, there have already have been organized raids by combined English and Iroquois forces along the Saint-Laurent. Farms have been burned and captives have been taken to the English forts. I am told that the Dutch and English mean to use this war to take over the French trade routes and allow English colonial expansion into the French territory of Louisiana west of the current English colonies. I fear we will be significantly outnumbered and will have to count heavily on militias. We will organize the group to meet and train weekly and to have a notification system so that we can be called to arms when necessary. The nature of the situation makes it imperative that we are ready at all times and at a moments' notice."

The men met and trained each Sunday after the picnic. They had an active group of twenty-five Frenchmen and as many as twenty Indians. Some of the older men like François* would come occasionally but were only expected to fight if the need arose. Jean-Baptiste* and Joseph shared their wisdom of shooting, maneuvering and using Indian trails. One morning just before Christmas, an alert arrived. Dugué wrote that a party of Iroquois and English was headed their way. His intelligence said they had crossed north of *Ile d'Orleans* and planned to approach Beauport and Charlesbourg from the north.

They met at the church and marched toward this area hoping to meet the Beauport militia but had little idea of what to expect or what to do. Rather than march, Jean-Baptiste* and Joseph led the men single file thru the Indian trails, traveling more like Algonquin than soldiers. As they approached the north of Beauport, they actually found the Beauport contingency, which was about the same size and make-up and included Jean-François Allard.

They decided to camp in the area, send scouts and wait. It was only the first morning when Joseph and another man returned to camp with word that they had seen a small camp four miles to the north. It consisted of some soldiers, some Iroquois and other men, probably the English counterpart of their own group. The sizes of the groups were apparently comparable. The men organized and headed cautiously in that direction. An hour later Jean-Baptiste* ordered a halt. "They seem to be approaching in mass. We should split into three groups, leave one group here in their way and send the other two around the sides to surprise them from the rear."

Joseph took one group, his brother Henri took the second, and Jean-Baptiste* stayed in front. He could see them easily. They were actually marching and coming straight for them. He had never actually seen an English soldier before, but it was true that they wore red coats. Amazed, Jean-Baptiste* said, "Why a blind man could track these people."

As they approached he gave the order and they attacked from behind the forest. They fired some shots and some arrows and the enemy returned their fire. The two flanks converged and general pandemonium broke loose.

The enemy abandoned their plan, and even a few of their weapons and ran in full retreat. Jean-Baptiste* chuckled, "Well I guess we have our first victory. I wonder if they'll stop or run all the way back to New York."

On inspection they seemed to have prisoners. None of the French group was injured with the exception of Pierre* Renaud who had tripped and broken his new pipe. There was, however, a wounded soldier in red, and a British colonist. A dark black man was tending them as they approached the trio. Fortunately, Jean-Baptiste*'s intelligent brother André spoke some English. He reported to the group, "The English soldier, an officer named Johnson, appears to be badly shot. The colonist is named Jacob* Thomas and is not bad off. The black man apparently belongs to the officer and is unharmed. He is called simply Tom."

The group's brief military education had not included prisoners, so the men decided to take them to Jean-Baptiste*'s camp. Pierre* Renaud summoned his mother, Marie* de la Mare-Renaud, was a mid-wife. She attended the officer and reported he would probably not last the night. Indeed he was dead in the morning and the men buried him but kept his uniform.

Jacob* Thomas was injured in the arm. Marie dressed it and said it would heal. He told them that he was a poor colonist, "I moved to western Massachusetts three years ago. There is such immigration that good land is scarce and particularly scarce for a man with no fortune. Just as in England, the rich have taken the best land and in enormous quantities. As a result, large tracts of prime land lie fallow for the lord of the manor to chase the fox with his hounds, and the common man has no access to land where he may scrape out a living. I joined the militia as a way to eat and bide my time. To tell the truth, I have no desire to return home."

The black man Tom was the slave of the officer. Apparently he was born on a farm in the southern colonies. His parents had been taken from Africa. He had been purchased by Captain Johnson as a personal attendant. Jean-Baptiste* had heard of slaves in Canada, but had never actually seen one. There were a few dark people in the colony from the Island of Martinique, but none that he knew from Africa and none so black. Tom had a definite interest in not returning.

When Jean-Baptiste* reported to Dugué the next day, the Lieutenant said, "Good work, however I fear the next time may not be so simple." He also had no idea what to do with the 'prisoners' so the camp of Joseph and Baptiste* now had two more workers.

Charlesbourg - Sunday March 30, 1704:

Spring was arriving and the ice was just beginning to break. At mass the priest announced that Lieutenant Dugué wished to address the congregation afterward. "Friends, we have received news of the largest raid to date on the English colonies. Combined military and colonial forces with the aid of Abenaki Indians raided the town of Deerfield in western Massachusetts. The village was largely burned and a large number of people were killed or taken hostage to Montréal. This may signal greater hostilities in the near future. The militia must be ready to act on a moment's notice."

Following mass, Jean-Baptiste* ate with Anne-Elizabeth* Pageot who looked even more beautiful in the winter air. He reported to her about the new camp mates, "Monsieur Thomas is very energetic and has picked up much French. I believe he wants to stay in Québec. Tom is the strongest man I have ever seen and cannot seem to accept the fact that he is no longer 'owned'. In fact there they are now." As it happened, Jacob Thomas came to America by way of Ireland and was originally Catholic. He had joined the Protestant church in the colonies but was happy to return to his old faith. The two men came over and made polite conversation in their rudimentary French and took their leave to return to the camp.

Jean-Baptiste* continued to tell Anne-Elizabeth* about his plans for the farm. "I hope to be in a position in a year or so to build a house and maybe start a family."

She responded, "I am in no great hurry. My mother, as you know, was wed before she was fifteen years old. It was the custom then, but she feels it was too young. I plan to wait, maybe even to age twenty."

This news greatly lifted Jean-Baptiste*'s spirits and he decided he could start thinking again about women.

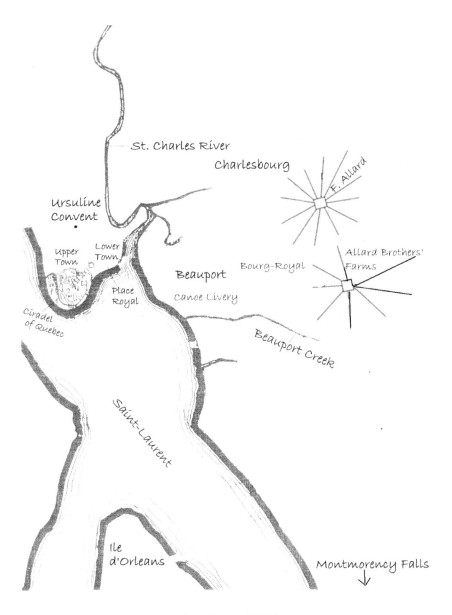

Québec 1704

Chapter 27

<u>Bourg-Royal - November 1704:</u>

Jean-Baptiste* looked up from his carpentry at the clear blue sky over the fading colors of autumn. The summer of 1704 had been the best in memory. Fine weather and steady rain provided everyone with record crops, even Jean-Baptiste*. The three new Allard farms occupied the northeast corner of the Bourg-Royal 'pie'. Although Bourg-Royal was now part of Charlesbourg, it retained its old name to avoid confusion with the similar pie-shaped development of the original Charlesbourg just next to it.

His brother André's farm was the farthest west of the Allard farms, just east of the farm of André's father-in-law. Next came the farm of his sister, Marie Allard-Villeneuve and her husband Charles. She had delivered their first daughter, Marguerite, in the late summer. The most easterly farm was that of Jean-Baptiste*. His farm had grown much faster than anticipated due to the addition of his two old prisoners and now friends, Jacob* Thomas and the ex-slave, Tom. Both men had proved to be excellent friends and capable farmers, especially Tom who was almost as strong as Grosse Pierre in Détroit.

Both men had learned basic French quickly. Jean-Baptiste* was surprised that Tom learned even more easily than Jacob*. Both men had been well accepted in the community and were now members of the local militia, which fortunately had enjoyed a quiet summer. Currently all four men lived in the Indian camp that Joseph and Jean-

Baptiste* had built. Because of the extra help, much more land had been cleared and cultivated and now the house that he had not expected to build until next year was almost finished. He realized that he was approaching the point when he could truly consider taking a wife.

He continued to see Anne-Elizabeth* Pageot at every opportunity and always at church on Sunday. He was beginning to regard going to mass with the enthusiasm that he had once only held for hunting and fishing trips. As he placed his final board of the day he heard, "Baptiste*, I wondered if you would care to join us for dinner this evening?"

It was Anne LeMarche-Allard, his sister-in-law. There was little deciding to do, as the fare at the men's camp was decidedly basic. He stood and smiled and simply replied, "Delighted."

He gathered his tools and ran the short way to the camp to clean up. The other three men had gone hunting for pheasant after the farm work was done. The fact that Jean-Baptiste* chose to stay and work on the house showed how much of a farmer he had become. He then walked north passing in front of his sister's house and over to André's.

As he entered the house, the four children, who were always pleased to see their favorite uncle, mobbed him. Especially enthusiastic was the oldest boy, Jacques, who although not yet five, had accompanied Jean-Baptiste* on short forays into the forest to hunt. Anne and the two girls were working in the kitchen and his brother André sat reading a book to the youngest, Pierre-André, who was not yet three.

Jokingly, Jean-Baptiste* said, "Just what this family needs, another intellectual."
His brother arose and gave him a very French handshake just as Anne called the brood to dinner.

André said grace and the dishes were passed. Anne's mother was from La Fleche in the Touraine region of France. Her cooking was very similar to that of their own mother and Jean-Baptiste* always loved it. Anne started the conversation, "Well, Baptiste*, it looks as though your house is taking form."

"Yes, in fact now that the harvest is in, André, Charles, Joseph, Jacob, Henri and Tom are going to help next week, and we should be finished by the time to start clearing trees."

"Are your 'boy-friends' going to move in with you?"

"No, I think they are happiest at the camp."

"Don't tell me you are going to live alone, or does this mean you might consider a wife."

Jean-Baptiste* blushed and wavered and Anne jumped in, "Jean-Baptiste* Allard, If you don't ask that girl now, you are going to lose her. She is talented, intelligent and perfect in every way, not to mention the most beautiful girl in all Québec, and for reasons none of us understand, she adores you. Don't expect me to make your dinner for the rest of your life."

Just as he formulated a response, he was saved by young Jacques, "Uncle Baptiste*, may I come and help build your house?"

Relieved his uncle replied, "But of course, *mon petit,* we could not do without you."

The conversation fell to the usual and after dinner, Jean-Baptiste* took his leave and returned to the camp.

The men had returned, and ten large colorful birds were hanging from a tree while Tom was roasting two others on a stick.

Baptiste* said, "Looks as though you found a few small birds without me."

Joseph returned, "We did well. Tom shot five with arrows."

Jean-Baptiste* replied, "Tom, I think you are more Indian than African."

The ex-slave replied, "I only hope I can take the winter like one."

Tom had never been north of South Carolina in the winter and was already complaining about the cold. Jean-Baptiste* sat down next to Jacob* Thomas who was being unusually quiet, "Pheasant get your tongue."

Their English friend replied, "I'm still marveling at my new home. Here I sit living with a Negro, an Indian, and a Frenchman; and they are now the best friends I have ever had. I'm living in an 'enemy' community which has accepted me better then my own people ever have. The French government is not sending more rich people to push the poor into the frontier. In fact it, seems they don't care much what people do here."

Jean-Baptiste* arose and headed for the tent he shared with Joseph, "I hope you are planning on helping your new friend finish his house this week," and went in and under his deerskin for the night.

Québec- December 25 1704:

Jean-Baptiste* escorted his mother out of the Cathedral after Christmas mass. Jeanne* looked up and said, "Without doubt this is the most beautiful Christmas I have ever seen." The sky was perfectly clear, there was a scant foot of new white snow on the ground. The temperature was almost balmy and there was no wind. The warm 1704 had continued and the river had hardly started to form ice. Most of the families of the north shore had come by cart and forded the Charles River, but some of the more hardy, like Jean-Baptiste*, had come by canoe a feat never heard of at Christmas in Québec.

They stood in the square and visited with friends and neighbors while Jean-Baptiste* searched the crowd. As soon as he saw her, he excused himself and walked over where she stood with her parents and younger brother, another Jean-Baptiste. As he approached, Thomas* Pageot stepped forward and greeted him. "Jean-Baptiste*, *Joyeux Noel,* how wonderful to see you. I hear that your new farm is prospering."

"As well as can be expected, sir, I have managed to finish and move into the house."

Jean-Baptiste* had lived his entire life next door to this man and had always had a warm relationship, but as time now progressed, he began to live in fear of the old tailor. Greetings and small talk were exchanged before he and Anne-Elizabeth* managed to be off alone as had been their habit of late.

She began with the obvious, "What a spectacular day."

He agreed and wished her Merry Christmas. She then produced a small object wrapped in paper. "This is for you."

He unwrapped it and was astonished; it was a small military compass. She continued, "A man gave it to my father in exchange for work. Of course, he has little use for it."

Jean-Baptiste* would have told his friends that he had little use for it as well as a true backwoodsman did not need a compass. However, there had been many times that he would have dearly loved to have one. "Why it is wonderful, much too fine, I can hardly accept it." Then reaching into his pocket he produced his own package, "Here, this is for you, but it is really nothing."

She opened it and it was a small heart carved from oak on a small leather strap to be worn as a necklace. "Nothing, why it is only the most beautiful thing I have ever seen," and looking quickly in the direction of her father, she gave him a quick kiss on the cheek.

Just then someone cleared their throat from behind them. They both startled and turned to see Marie-Anne Allard. She smiled, "Don't worry, no one else saw it." She continued, "Jean-Baptiste*, why don't you give Anne-Elizabeth* and me a ride home in your canoe. It is the most perfect day. I'll go ask her father. He will never say no to me." And without waiting for a reply she was off.

She soon returned with his approval and they departed. The trip across the Saint-Laurent was truly wonderful. The weather had been so warm that there were still geese flying south. They landed and began to walk to Charlesbourg. About halfway there, Jean-Baptiste*'s sister announced, "I have work at home, so I'm going to run along ahead." And off she went.

As they proceeded, Jean-Baptiste* realized that his entire family was into matchmaking. He decided it was now or never. He reached down and clumsily took Anne-Elizabeth*'s hand. She squeezed his and they continued on, "Did I tell you my house is now finished and I have moved in?"

"Yes, you did mention it," she said thinking to herself, "Maybe ten times."

"The thing is, it is very lonely." And then it just came out, "Anne-Elizabeth* Pageot, will you marry me?"

They stopped and she looked up with her wonderful warm brown eyes, "A fine lady like me with a backwoodsman turned farmer?"

"You are correct. I don't know what I was thinking."

"Jean-Baptiste* Allard, I have been waiting all my life for this question," and throwing her arms around him, "Of course, I will marry you. I would go to the convent before I settled for anyone else." And with that she gave him a kiss, as he had never had a kiss.

They sat on a nearby log as she continued, "Let's do it as soon as possible. Come to see my father and we will read the banns and can wed by the end of January."

His heart racing, he said, "I'll come see him today."

"No, it would be more proper Sunday after mass. I will say I have invited you to dinner."

So they agreed and proceeded home hand and hand. Jean-Baptiste* went directly to André's and announced the news. His brother and sister were delighted. Anne asserted her role as a French wife of the community. "We shall have to see to making your house livable. Marie and I will start tomorrow. We shall take care of everything."

The following Sunday Jean-Baptiste* Allard headed for the Pageot farm. The famous Iroquois slayer of Charlesbourg who had faced Indian raids, wolves, mountain lions and bears, the fire of Détroit and the pirate voyageurs at *Le Griffon* was paralyzed with fear.

After enduring dinner he found himself alone with Thomas* Pageot. "Sir, did I tell you that my farmhouse is completed?"
"Yes, Baptiste*, I believe you did."
"Did I tell you how well the farm is doing?"
"As I recall."
"Well, did I …"
"Jean-Baptiste*, do you wish to marry my daughter?"
"Well, yes sir, in fact…"
"Well, thank God, lad, I've known forever that she would never have anyone else. Let's see if I have any of your father's Calvados."

As the old tailor arose and went to the cupboard, he called out, "Catherine*, Anne-Elizabeth*, come here and bring four glasses, Monsieur Allard has finally come to take you off my hands."
As the group took their glasses he said, "Your father is the finest man I have known and the best friend and neighbor. I have prayed for this day, *Santé!*"

They drank and hugged and sat to discuss. Jean-Baptiste* finding his tongue said, "If we announce the banns, we could wed by the end of the month."

Pageot replied, "I shall need two months. Let us say the end of February."

Jean-Baptiste* looked puzzled and Pageot continued, "If a girl has a tailor for a father, there is only one advantage and I plan to give it to Anne-Elizabeth*." And with that a date was set and the evening ended.

During the ensuing weeks, the other women in Jean-Baptiste*'s life descended on his house. In this situation there is only one recourse for a Frenchman; he went hunting. When he returned, his house had been transformed. Anne had summoned her father. Even though he was in his eighties, the old Jean LeMarche remained a skilled cabinetmaker. He had made basic furniture and even a great bed similar to the one he had made for Jean-Baptiste*'s father many years before. His sister and sister-in-law had added quilts and details that made it look like a real home. Jean-Baptiste* was overwhelmed. "I don't know how I can thank you."

His sister-in-law responded, "Just don't back out."

The next Sunday at mass he told Anne-Elizabeth* all about it. "I can hardly wait to see it," she said, and the next week she found an opportunity. Just after Jean-Baptiste* had returned from his chores, there was a knock at the door. He was more than surprised to see his future bride.

"I simply couldn't wait. Don't worry, no one saw me come." And she hurried inside. He gave her the tour and she said, "It is almost too perfect." And with that she threw her arms around him, and they shared a very long kiss. The kiss led to a rage of pent up passion, and an hour later they awoke on the bed realizing they had broken one of the community's prime rules (at least one of the most public rules).

She jumped up and quickly dressed and said, "We should see no more of each other until the wedding except for the most public places like mass." And she ran rapidly out the door. The next few weeks were agony for Jean-Baptiste*.

Chapter 28

Charlesbourg Chapel - February 23, 1705:

It wasn't until his wedding day that Jean-Baptiste* realized why his new father-in-law wanted to postpone the wedding an extra month. Girls in Québec were traditionally married in a plain white dress that was used for most occasions. Anne-Elizabeth*, however, appeared in a beautiful wedding gown suited for a much richer girl. "There are few advantages of a tailor father," announced Thomas* Pageot, "And this is one."

Jean-François stood as best man for his brother and the event took place on this crisp clear winter day. Following the ceremony there was a grand wedding dinner by Charlesbourg standards. Eventually the couple took their leave and were transported to their new home by André in a cart with the new horse. Alone at last, the new couple were able to release the passion that they had built up without the urgency and hurry of their first experience a few weeks before. As Jean-Baptiste* began to fall asleep, he felt a calm and satisfaction that life was good.

His calm was soon interrupted by banging and shouting at the door. He rose quickly to find his brother André.

"Dugué has just sent the alarm. There is a raid headed for Beauport. We must leave at once."

Jean-Baptiste* quickly dressed and took his gun and bow and quickly informed his frightened young bride. As the two men ran from the house, André explained. "Some hours ago there was a raid at Sainte-Anne. The group broke through the militia there and burned farms. We are to intercept them at Beauport. The others have gone ahead."

When they reached Beauport, they could hear the fighting and see at least one barn fire. Jean-Baptiste* found Joseph who explained, "They are in the woods. We have been holding them but are starting to lose men and ground. They are working from a much better cover."

Surveying the situation, Jean-Baptiste* replied, "We must draw them out. I will take one group to the south and you take another to the north. André will lead a retreat toward Beauport."

As André sounded retreat a large group of Iroquois with a few English pursued. Once they were out of their cover, Joseph and Jean-Baptiste* attacked from behind. Baptiste* was pleasantly surprised that the ruse worked. The back half of the group turned and soon realized they were surrounded. The fighting lasted all night until the enemy group relented and fled. At daylight they inspected the damage. There were two damaged farms and four dead French and three Algonquin. There were at least twenty dead English and Iroquois. More than a few falling to red-feathered arrows.

As they returned home the following afternoon, the rest of the village was taking shelter in the church. Jean-Baptiste* and André announced the all clear and the group gathered for a replay of the battle. As Jean-Baptiste* escorted his bride back home, she said, "It is certain that no one will ever forget our wedding night."

On return they decided to forgo the day's chores and spent the rest of the day and night enjoying each other.

<u>Charlesbourg - Early November 1707:</u>

During the past three years, the Jean-Baptiste* Allard farm had prospered along with the others. Crops had been good and times relatively tranquil. There were still raids but none as severe as the one of the wedding night. The family group had built a sturdy network of caveaux for security.

Joseph had taken a wife. She was the métis daughter of an Algonquin woman and a French trapper. More interestingly, Tom, the ex-slave, had married her twin sister. The two couples had remained at the Indian camp originally, but eventually built a rudimentary house for both families. It represented a combination of *habitant maison* and Indian camp, "One must not become too French," joked Joseph in his perfect French. To become slightly more French, both families decided to take the family name of the girls' father, *de Baptiste.*

Jacob* Thomas had married the illegitimate daughter of the voyageur Pierre Roy. They had acquired a farm in a new area just north of Bourg-Royal and were respected members of the French community. Although the church frowned upon *enfants naturelles,* or illegitimate children, they were accepted much better into French society than into the English counterpart.

On this beautiful warm November afternoon, Anne-Elizabeth* and her sisters-in-law, Marie and Anne, sat on the porch taking a break from a day of putting up preserves for the winter. The yard was filled with young children.

André and Anne's three youngest, Jacques age seven, Pierre-André age five and Thomas age two. Marie and Charles Villeneuve's, Marguerite age three and Marie-Charlotte age one. Along side was Jean-Baptiste* and Anne-Elizabeth*'s first, François, almost two.

On the porch, Marie nursed the newborn Michelle-Françoise, and Anne-Elizabeth* was large with her next child. André's two oldest girls, Catherine and Genevieve, helped the women. Across the square a gray-haired man proceeded toward the house rapidly but with a decided limp. The children recognized him and ran to mob their Pipi. As François* made his way through the melee, he called to the ladies and asked where the men where. Anne-Elizabeth* responded that they would soon be in from the barn and he should sit and visit.

Soon the three men returned and joined the group on the porch. François* began, "The Governor has decided to hold the Community Council meeting at Montréal in respect for its enlarging population and due to the fact that it has suffered the most from attacks and needs its men to stay close. I was wondering, Baptiste*, if you could accompany me."

The Community Council was a early forerunner of self-government. Each community elected a representative to meet locally each month and discuss common issues and have the ear, if not the accord, of the government. Each year at the completion of the harvest, they met in Québec. This year as François* had indicated, it would for the first time be in Montréal. Jean-Baptiste* agreed and they made plans. In two days they were pushing their light canoe into the Saint-Laurent. Due to the lack of equipment, and the slow current of autumn, the trip was quicker than usual.

Montréal - November 1707:

The town was teeming with people. Montréal had grown to nearly the size of Québec but it remained much rougher and a true frontier town. It had developed into the true center of the fur trade. François* and Jean-Baptiste* met many old friends in the square. They were headed toward the inn for dinner and a possible room when a loud bell began to sound rapidly without stopping.

Everyone knew that this signaled a possible attack on the city and encouraged those not dealing in defense to take shelter inside the city's stockade. The two men made their way with several others. The stockade area was large, holding the fort, many businesses and some homes. It sat on an overlook of the Saint-Laurent and the harbor. Once inside, the gates were closed and the men made way to a tavern. The room was crowded but they saw a table in the corner with only a young frightened woman and a small child. François* approached her, "Do you mind if we share your table."

"No sir, in fact I wish you would. You seem to be gentlemen and this room looks to be full of rough sorts."

As they sat she continued, "I came to town for supplies for my husband. He is a shoemaker, and we have a shop and farm just outside of town. It looks as though we shall not get out of here tonight. This is our first child, Marie-Elizabeth. She is two we call her Louise as Marie-Elizabeth is also my name in Québec."

Noticing that she spoke French with a British accent much like Jacob* Thomas, Jean-Baptiste* asked, "What do you mean by 'my name in Québec?'"

The young woman looked up, and started to speak, but stopped before saying, "I'm afraid it's a terribly long story."

François* replied, "I believe you said we have all night."

With that, the young woman gazed out the window for a moment, beginning, "I came to Québec from New England where my name was Elisabeth. Now in Québec my baptized name is Marie-Elizabeth."

"And how was it that you came to Québec?"

"I was born in 1683 in Northampton, Massachusetts, a town on the frontier of the English colonies. My mother's name was Sarah* Webb. Her father came from England as a very young boy in 1620 to Boston with his father Richard* and his grandfather Sir Alexander*. Alexander* was a noble who came from a town named Stratford in Warwickshire in England to escape the evil King Charles. The family had a great deal of wealth."

Looking puzzled, Jean-Baptiste* asked, "If you were wealthy, such a move seems odd."

"Unfortunately my grandfather lost his wealth due to poor business dealings. He made his way as a blacksmith and an innkeeper. Eventually he settled in Connecticut where my mother was born. She married a man named Zachariah Field. They moved to Northampton in Massachusetts where he farmed. Later they moved to Deerfield, and even farther into the frontier of

Massachusetts. As this was the furthest outpost, it was prone to Indian attacks. In one such attack, my mother's first husband perished. She later married my father, Robert* Price, a colonist who had come to America. He had traveled as far as Deerfield because he was poor, and land was hard to find for such men inside the region of true civilization.

"I was the middle of five children with two older sisters and two younger brothers. My older sister Mary was pious and perfect, I was always a bit of a rebel, never conforming to the norms of our strict Protestant community.

"There was a young man just my age in the community with whom I was a friend from early childhood. He was the son of an Indian woman and a colonial woodsman who had arrived in Deerfield where she died during his birth and the father disappeared. Joshua Stevens, who was our neighbor and a good Christian man, took the orphan and raised him as his own. He even convinced the minister to baptize him Andrew and gave him his own family name, Stevens.

"Andrew was as kind, gentle, and Christian a man as had ever lived. When a young boy, he worked for the church and only did good. He was well regarded by all. We were friends and became lovers. Against the will of all, I was able to convince the minister to marry us, as Andrew was indeed a member of the church."

"Did you come to Canada to escape persecution?"

"No, however the community did turn against us. They felt it was improper because of his Indian heritage. This hypocrisy only made me more determined. To their credit, my parents consented although they truly did not understand. We lived in their home but still became outcasts in our own community. We lived there until the winter of 1704.

"On the night of February 28, 1704, a raid such as had never been seen descended on our village. French woodsmen and soldiers along with over one hundred Abenaki Indians came upon us. Because of previous raids, the town was protected by a stockade. However, the snow was so deep it had drifted up to the top of the walls and the enemy merely walked across.

"As was our plan, we took refuge in the fortified meetinghouse, but it was to no avail. The burning and killing lasted through the night and in the end, the entire village was either dead, run off or captive. I have been told that of the 298 inhabitants that occupied the village, 50 were dead, 137 escaped and 111 were captured. Among the dead were my own mother Sarah* and older sister Mary as well as my beloved husband Andrew. My younger brother Samuel and I were among the captives."

Becoming very intent on the story, Jean-Baptiste* asked, "Whatever became of you?"

"We were locked in the meetinghouse until the Indians entered and supplied us with Indian slippers for walking in deep snow, and we were forced to march north. The snow was waist deep and the terrain was difficult. Those who were too young or too old or could not keep pace were murdered or left to perish from the cold. We traveled as many as 35 miles a day and marched for many days.

"We were beaten mercilessly and endured unimaginable hardships and physical insults. On the ninth day we were separated into groups and proceeded on our separate ways. I never saw any of the other groups after this. To my good fortune, an older Abenaki man took pity on me. He was a curious man with a crippled leg; in spite of this he was quite agile. He found I spoke some of my husband's native language and this allowed us some communication. When he learned of my marriage to Andrew, he became friendly and helped my brother Samuel and me to survive. He would bring us food, helped us remain warm and warned us when trouble was about to occur.

"We traveled many more terrible days until we reached an Indian camp near Montréal. My friend warned us this would be a terrible event but reassured us he would help when he could. On the outside of the village we were forced to strip naked and were painted red. We were then driven forward as the Indians beat us with sticks and chased us into tents where we were to become the slaves of the owners. My friend herded us into his tent where he gave us clothes and food."

Now on the edge of his seat, Jean-Baptiste* blurted, "How did you escape?"

"The next day he took us to the Ursuline convent in Montréal where he sold us to the nuns. The sisters took pity on us and showed us every kindness. Were it not for this crippled Indian man, I fear our fate would have been the worst nightmare. The nuns took us in and nursed us, instructed us in French and restored us to health. There was a wonderful priest, Father Meriel, who helped us greatly. Of the other groups, some were never heard from again. Many more were ransomed back to their homes. Some, such as the young daughter of the minister preferred to remain with the Indians and adopt their ways."

With a quizzical look, François* asked, "Why did you not return home?"

"I had no reason to return as my mother and husband were dead and I was an outcast, so I elected to remain with the sisters. I was instructed in religion and converted by Father Mereil. Eventually I met a young French colonist who had recently come from Limoges. He and I were married by Father Mereil and now live in Montréal where my husband works as a shoemaker. I am content in my new home and comfortable that the French, although not without their faults, do not share the same level of hypocrisy as my native Englishmen. As you see, we now have our first child and hope for many more."

As François* and Jean-Baptiste* commented on her remarkable story, she suddenly interjected, "I almost forgot the most unusual part. As my Abenaki benefactor left me at the convent, he told me his own story. He said that as a young boy he was rescued by a white man on an island far to the east of here. He had been hunting with his father when he was crushed beneath a tree and was dying until his father happened upon this Frenchman who helped him save the boy's life and his leg which did become crippled.

186

"Then the most curious thing. He said his father gave the man a precious wampum for luck, and the man gave him a strange necklace with a medallion. He said that the man said it was for good luck, and my benefactor said that it had indeed brought him good fortune. He then removed it and gave it to me, saying perhaps it would work to my good fortune."

With that she removed an old leather strap with a medallion from her neck and showed it to François*. As he took it into his hand, he felt a strange but familiar sensation he had not felt since he was a young man. He looked down at his father's old medallion in amazement.

The young lady remarked, "Why, sir, you appear as though you have seen a ghost."

François* replied, "Indeed, madam, I believe I have." He paused before continuing, "I came to Québec from Normandie as a young man, now forty-one years ago. When we reached the Saint-Laurent, we eventually stopped at a large island. I was sent with a hunting party for game but stumbled and lost my way. In searching for my companions I came upon an Indian man who was trying to free a young boy from beneath a fallen tree. I assisted the man and we splinted the boy's badly broken leg.

"The man then took an intricate wooden wampum from around his neck and gave it to me, I still have half of it." He produced his half of the old charm and showed it to the young lady, "I did not know how to react. I had a medallion, which had been given to me by my father upon my departure from France. Legend had that it had been passed down through the men of my family since the time of Jeanne d'Arc. There is no question that this is the same medallion." And he handed it back.

The young woman looked at it turning it in her hands. "I often get a strange sensation when I handle this. I always knew it was something extraordinary. It has indeed brought me good fortune, and it seems certain, Monsieur, that I am now to return it to its rightful owner. I cannot overestimate my gratitude for what it has done for me and my family." She kissed the medallion softly and handed it back to François* who placed it at long last back around his neck.

As rays of sunlight began to shine through the tavern window, the all-clear bell began to sound. The group in the tavern began to leave. As he stood, Jean-Baptiste* asked the young woman her name. She replied, "Marie-Elizabeth* Fourneau. My husband is Jean* Fourneau, but in the odd fashion of the French, he is called Brindamour. In Massachusetts I was Elisabeth* Price." She arose and left to return to her husband.

The raid had been minor, and the life of the town returned rapidly as was the fashion in this wild frontier place. The council met for two days, and the members then parted for their farms. On the second night of their return voyage, while the men sat at their fire on the bank of the Saint-Laurent, Jean-Baptiste* questioned his father, "Why do you only have half of the Indian wampum?"

The older man looked out into the distance and began, "On the voyage from France I was asked to help care for a young woman who had fallen gravely ill, a beautiful young woman from Paris. As she recovered I fell madly in love with her. She also confessed the same feelings toward me. At the end of the voyage we realized our situations would make any prospects impossible. The wampum Separated into two pieces and when we parted, I gave one to her.

"I saw her some years later in Montréal where she lived with her new husband and children. I never saw her again and do not even know if she still lives. I thought that I would never love another woman until the day I met your mother."

The following morning François* returned to this conversation, "I have long considered to which of you boys I would give the wampum. I suppose that after the Iroquois raid when you were young, I knew it would be you. The return of my father's medallion under these circumstance seems to ordain it." He put the wampum and the medallion around his son's neck. Jean-Baptiste* was startled at the strange sensation he felt when the old metal coin touched his chest.

Chapter 29

Charlesbourg, The Blue Goose Tavern and In- Early Spring 1710:

Jean-Baptiste* sat with André, Jean-François, and Charles Villeneuve along with Joseph and Tom de Baptiste, the ex-slave, discussing the upcoming planting. The families had continued to grow, Jean-Baptiste* now had three sons, François, four years, Thomas, two years, and Jean-Baptiste Jr., six months. André's brood had grown to six and was to be seven any day. Charles had five mouths to feed, and Jean-François four.

Their brother Georges had married in the winter to the young sister of Anne-Elizabeth*, Marie-Marguerite Pageot. Georges had moved two years earlier to the farm on the southeast corner of the Charlesbourg Square. Where he maintained a small working farm although he was more interested in business, rapidly becoming Charlesbourg's leading businessman.

When a voyageur enters a tavern, the door truly 'bursts' open. At that moment the door to the Blue Goose burst open leaving no doubt what sort of man was to enter. Into the room swaggered Pierre Roy who had in tow his son-in-law Jacob* Thomas and his partner Joseph Parent. The three men quickly joined the table and Pierre Roy ordered a round of drinks in the true fashion of a voyageur desperate to turn cash into liquor as quickly as possible.

Roy quickly made reference to the fact his family was in danger of becoming respectable as a result of Monsieur Thomas. He slapped the poor Englishman on the back with a gale of laughter while spitting an enormous brown wad onto the floor. Joseph Parent brought the conversation under control explaining they were forced to come to Québec to obtain trading licenses for the upcoming season. "Government is more determined than ever to dissuade the poor man from dealing in fur." Changing the subject he referred to Jean-Baptiste*, "Do you know your old patron Cadillac is moving south?"

Jean-Baptiste* replied in the negative so Parent continued, "It seems the government could no longer abide his swindling and trading liquor to the natives. The King 'promoted' him to Governor of Louisiana. He is to leave this season. I can tell you he is not content on the issue." Then using his best voyageur rhetoric, "We have been there twice and I can tell you the south of Louisiana is the true ass-hole of the world. It is all swamp and the climate is unlivable for a Frenchman. I am surprised that Cadillac has not called you, Jean-Baptiste*, I think you are the only person he truly trusts.

"At any rate Détroit continues to develop, I have even moved my family down from Montréal. We have a farm just north of the fort by the creek. Pierre lives on the grounds with his current Indian woman."

As Pierre ordered the fourth round of drinks, the men took their leave hoping that they were still sober enough to find their way home.

Chapter 30

<u>Beauport - February 1711</u>:

Every few years some pestilence visited the colony. The winter of 1711 it was measles. Because the disease was common in France, most people had been affected as children, survived and developed immunity. However in Québec most of the native Indian and French had not been so fortunate. The colonists had learned a terrible lesson from the experience of the Huron who had been infected by the Jesuits and almost eradicated from the earth.

It was important to isolate the ill and use those previously exposed to nurse the sick. The disease began as a cough and sore throat, progressing to the telltale rash and high fever. Children frequently survived if the fever quickly broke, but if they developed neck and headaches and convulsions, they usually perished. A great many of affected adults would thus succumb and die, although a great number of herbs and remedies were applied. The careful observer would realize that isolation of the ill and the original state of health of the patient were the only things that truly mattered.

A large number of families in Beauport were affected, including the home of Jean-François Allard. Jeanne* went immediately to help both her son and the other neighbors. Measles had struck the Anguille home in France when she was extremely young. Her brothers André and Michel were quite ill but recovered. Jeanne*'s mother told her that she had a 'light case' and recovered quickly because of her very young age. Marie Tardiff-Allard told her mother-in-law that she too had had a light case as an infant.

Jean-Baptiste, age 10, was the first to start to cough; as he developed the rash Marie-Charlotte, age 9, was next then in age order Jacques, age 5, and Pierre-Noel, age 3. All four were confined to bed while their mother and grandmother cared for them ladling chicken soup with herbs down their sore throats while coating their necks with goose grease before wrapping their necks with a woolen sock.

Jean-François was banished to an unaffected neighbor's house and Jeanne* made daily rounds to several of the surrounding farms. The vigil lasted weeks while the men went to the churchyard for the ghoulish job of digging graves in the frozen ground to quickly accept the dead.

The three boys proceeded as expected for their age. Their rashes became severe, their fevers spiked, but in the end broke and they improved. Marie-Charlotte, on the other hand, would not improve. She could not be convinced to eat more than a few sips of tea or soup. Every night her fever spiked but it always returned the next day. Her mother and grandmother tried every known remedy. They prayed, burned candles and incense, and bathed her in cold water when her fever became severe.

They covered her with goose grease and filled her with herb potions. After two weeks she began to complain of the feared head and neck aches. She seemed to have small convulsions, although she was always a girl prone to fainting. Then one night her fever rose to terrible levels. They bathed her in cold water and alcohol. They both knelt praying by her bedside as she convulsed with rigors. They both fell asleep with their heads on the girl's bed.

In the morning when the light began to stream through the small window, they both awoke with a start and saw the girl sitting bolt upright looking at them. She started immediately, "Mimi, I would like some soup please."

The two women were overtaken with joy, clearly the crisis had passed and the Allard family had been spared. Two days later she was almost back to normal. The crisis seemed to have left the village so Jeanne* made her way back to Charlesbourg.

At home things were returned to normal. She fell into bed and slept through the next day. She only awoke once with a short spell of coughing. The following day she got on with her chores but the cough and heaviness in her throat continued. When she knew no one was watching, she even took a drink of François*'s Calvados with honey as it often soothed a sore throat. Two days later when she went to comb her hair in her small looking glass she saw it and she knew.

A few red specks spread along her forehead. Jeanne* and her contemporaries were unaware that mild cases of measles in the very young although providing some resistance did not give life-long immunity. Two days later she was bed ridden. She made Thomas leave the house but François* would not leave. He stayed by her side and tended her in every desperate way he could, but on the 12th of March 1711, the rebellious and beautiful girl of privilege who had followed her destiny to the wilderness closed her eyes for the final time.

The following day she was blessed and quickly buried in an unmarked grave in Charlesbourg's Saint-Charles de Borromée cemetery, near her infant daughter, Marie-Renée, who had been put there to rest eighteen years earlier. That Sunday there was an enormous outpouring of the community at the mass at the chapel including many of the *Filles du Roi* who had shared her adventure.

Speaking after the service was the unlikely Madeleine de Roybon, "She was all the wonderful things that I could never be. She was kind, brave and generous to a fault. She gave her entire being to her family and her destiny. She was truly a mother of this great new world."

Five days later, Georges Allard's wife of just one year, Marie-Marguerite Pageot, died after only four days of the disease, leaving Georges and their infant daughter Marie-Françoise.

Four weeks later, Jeanne's daughter-in-law, Marie Tardiff-Allard, experienced the same symptoms and one week later she was placed in a similar hastily dug grave, leaving her husband and four young children. In one month's time this disease of children had left the Allard clan with three widowed husbands.

Two days later, François* Allard left for a private trip to the north. That night as he sat at his fire with a late spring snow falling, he contemplated his life past, present, and yet to come. Eventually he fell asleep. When he awoke in the dark covered by a thin coat of snow on his deerskin, he looked across the fire to see his old friend, Henri smoking his pipe.

The old man looked to François* and said, "And when they die, their spirit goes to join the spirits of their ancestors, and they continue to hunt the spirits of the brave animals with whom they shared their life on earth. What is so naïve about that, my old friend?"

In the morning, François* returned home.

Chapter 31

Louisiana - June 1, 1711:

The heat was becoming oppressive, not as oppressive as it would be in a month, but bad enough. Jean-Baptiste le Moyne de Bienville sloshed along through the marshy terrain. It really was a beautiful place, but sometimes the swamp, mosquitoes, and heat could be a bit much. He thought back to his boyhood days in Normandie and its wonderful weather.

Although he and his brother Pierre had been born in Montréal, their rich merchant father had sent them back to his home in France to be educated. Considering the winters in Québec and the summers in Louisiana, he wondered why his father had come at all. Actually he realized it was the lure of fortunes to be made by those with close ties to the crown. He also realized that he, like his father and brother, relished the adventure.

His father had arranged to have his older brother, Pierre le Moyen d'Iberville named governor of the new colony in Louisiana, and although the task was difficult, he was succeeding. He saw his brother approaching; the locals as well as the public officials had taken to referring to the two men as simply *Iberville* and *Bienville* referring to the small fiefdoms in Québec which they each controlled. Iberville began, "Well, it is certainly official. He is to arrive from France at any time. I am told he is the most arrogant and irritating man to ever draw breath. He apparently has traded liquor with the natives wherever he has been. He was sent here only to remove him from Détroit."

His brother returned, "Even though he is to officially replace you as governor, I hope you will still remain truly in charge."

Iberville countered, "I have just received word from Monsieur Crozat who is beginning to fear for his investment. He has sent men to Québec to form a party who will help us to that end. We can only hope that he knows his business."

Charlesbourg - The Blue Goose Inn and Tavern, The same day:

As tragedy struck suddenly in Québec, recovery was equally swift. The Allard boys and friends sat around the table discussing prospects for the future. Jean-François, realizing that an intact family was necessary for survival, had already made plans to marry young Genevieve Dauphin at the end of the harvest.

André was writing and calculating, "We can see how well Jean-François has done with only two cows. If we could add more, the profits would grow greatly."

Jean-Baptiste* replied, "The problem is money, the only way we can raise it is by our hard labor and time. I fear we must be patient."

At that moment the door burst open and in walked Joseph Parent with Pierre Roy and a slightly older man they did not recognize. They came straight to the Allard table and Joseph Parent began, *"Bonsoir, mes amis."* Then

198

looking to the stranger he said, "Saint-Aubin, these are some of the Allard boys. As I told you, their father began life in Québec working for my grandmother, and my father's family lived by theirs in Charlesbourg." Then looking to the table he added, "Jean-Baptiste*, we need to have a word with you and Joseph in private."

Joseph and Jean-Baptiste* rose and headed to an isolated table at the end of the establishment. When seated, the older man spoke, "My name is Jean* Casse, however, everyone calls me Saint-Aubin after my home in the region of Bordeaux. I have been sent to seek you men out by a Monsieur Antoine Crozat, a very wealthy gentleman with considerable interests both in France and New France. Monsieur Crozat has invested an enormous amount of wealth in the settlement at Louisiana, and is sending men to protect his interests."

Jean-Baptiste* interrupted, "How could this possibly concern us?"

Parent entered the conversation, "It seems your old patron, Antoine Lamothe Sieur de Cadillac, has been appointed governor of Louisiana."

Jean* Casse dit Saint-Aubin continued, "I came to Québec around 1700 with the military. I was made an officer in Cadillac's regiment and sent to Détroit in 1707. I am now officially retired and live with my family in Détroit on a farm just by that of Monsieur Parent. During my duty with Cadillac, we related well; however, it was clear to me as to others that he was a bit of a scoundrel and always driven at base by self interest.

"In 1710, Pontchartrain was forced to call Cadillac back to France due to the difficulties he had caused in Détroit as well as in Paris. Cadillac was appointed Governor of Louisiana and is sailing from France with his family. They should arrive any time. The current Governor is a Pierre de Moyne, called *Iberville,* who has been there for some time and is truly responsible for the settlement. His brother, Jean-Baptiste, called *Bienville,* is also there. Both men are competent and loyal to the crown. It is hoped that Iberville will retain most of his duties, although he cannot be pleased by the arrival of Cadillac.

"The King considers this territory, like the settlement in Détroit, to be critical to maintain France's hold on the territories west of the English colonies; and Monsieur Crozat is very concerned in the safety of his investment. Monsieur Parent has told me you men are of the highest character. We do not expect you to do anything deceitful.

"Apparently Cadillac has indicated there is no one whom he trusts as you two. We ask that you join a few men there to protect the interests of the King and Crozat. You will act as guards and scouts. We feel that if you are with this party, it will be easier for them to work with Cadillac."

Jean-Baptiste* thought for a while and looked at Joseph. He then replied, "Monsieur Saint-Aubin, I appreciate the confidence, but I cannot see how we would be of much use. In addition we are no longer voyageurs but farmers and have families and a busy farm to run that can scarcely function without us."

Saint- Aubin replied, "You would be paid."

Without much enthusiasm, Jean-Baptiste* said, "Just how much."

Saint-Aubin reached across and handed him a folded sheet of paper, "This much is guaranteed, one-half on departure and the rest on return, with bonuses for any extra time or particular difficulties."

Jean-Baptiste* was a good card player and could keep his thoughts inside. He thought he did a reasonable job here, but the number on the paper almost stopped his heart. Without much change in his straight face he handed the paper to Joseph. Both men knew that Joseph could not read numbers but the effect was good. He unfolded the paper and looked at it. Although he could not read numbers, he knew that the longer the figure, the higher the number and this seemed quite a long figure. He merely grunted.

Baptiste said, "We will have to talk to our families, but it is possible that something could be arranged."

Saint-Aubin continued, "I will return in two days for your answer. If we could leave by the end of the week, you could possibly be back next year in time to plant. You will also need to bring two other men whom you trust." The two men arose, collected Pierre Roy, who was regaling the others with his endless tales of the back country, and left.

Joseph and Jean-Baptiste* returned to their table and relayed the nature of the meeting. André was first to ask, "How much would they pay you?"

Jean-Baptiste* handed him the paper and replied, "I think you can began to look for cows, and I think I am going to order a round of drinks."

That night the families met to discuss the prospect. Anne-Elizabeth* was obviously worried by the prospect of being left for the winter, even though she realized she would have the help of the extended families. André started, "With the money mentioned we can easily hire four or more extra men." With a laugh he added, "One real farmer could easily replace both Baptiste* and Joseph."

Jean-Baptiste* returned, "Don't be so confident, perhaps I shall take the money and build a mansion on the Grande Allée and become a baron."

André became serious, "In truth we can hire the needed help and buy all the improvements and livestock we had planned for the next ten years at one time. Seriously, Baptiste*, I know you and Joseph are fine backwoodsmen, but why such an obscene amount of money? Surely you would have done it for less than a third that sum."

His brother replied, "I am not certain, but tomorrow morning I will try to find out why. In addition, I believe we should take Tom de Baptiste as our third man. He is strong and a capable paddler, but more important he has lived in the south. I also wish to see Monsieur Cadillac's reaction to a black ex-slave. In addition I believe Jacob* Thomas will serve a good fourth. He has become capable in the wild and we may find a need for his excellent English."

Anne added, "Anne-Elizabeth*, we will all care for one another, I will send one of the older girls to live with you for the duration, and you can all come to our place if there is danger."

The following morning Jean-Baptiste* headed to his father's house. François*, Philippe and Thomas were hard at the planting, his sister Marie-Anne was still at home and serving as woman of the house. Jean-Baptiste* discussed the project with his father who was equally surprised at the nature of the offer.

Jean-Baptiste* said, "I think I will walk across the square to the Parent farm, I suspect Joseph will have stopped for a visit."

The old farm of Pierre* Parent had grown. Both Pierre* and Jeanne* Badeau had died, but there were several farms on the old homestead belonging to various Parent children and their families. Currently Jean-Baptiste*'s boyhood friends Jean and Joseph (another Joseph, as it was not unusual for large families to have more than one child with the same surname), were residing. They were two of the famous triplets, and had married two Belanger sisters and lived here together.

Jean-Baptiste* saw Marie-Françoise Belanger-Parent on the porch and enquired into the whereabouts of the older Joseph. She replied simply, "Around the back."

Jean-Baptiste* went to the back of the yard where Joseph lay snoring under a deerskin on the ground.

"Well, Monsieur Parent, I see you have all the comforts of home."

"It seems the Belanger sisters believe a man must bathe twice a year to be fit for inside. I tell you, Baptiste*, I don't know what Québec is coming to. I can't wait to get back to the river."

Jean-Baptiste* sat down and began to look for his friend's read on the situation.

Parent started, "You know, Baptiste*, I was equally astounded at the offer. I believe they made it so that you could not refuse, and frankly I don't believe that they will let you refuse. Someone has led this Monsieur Crozat to believe that you and Joseph are indispensable in this mission. As to the amount, I have heard that Crozat has invested almost one million livres in this Louisiana project."

Jean-Baptiste* almost fell over. This was more money than he had ever envisioned existed in the entire world. He asked Parent about Tom and Jacob* Thomas, and Parent replied, "Probably a good choice. There are black people in Louisiana, mostly run off from English plantations, and the English speaker may be of great help. Cadillac may be surprised, but I think it will not be a problem." With that, Jean-Baptiste* returned to get as much squared away as possible on his farm in the next few days.

The following afternoon, Jean* Saint-Aubin arrived at the Allard farm with Joseph Parent. Jean-Baptiste* confirmed that they would go and they agreed on Tom and Jacob* Thomas as the extra men. Saint-Aubin concluded, "We shall meet at dawn the day after tomorrow at the canoe livery on the Beauport Coast. You need only your clothes and weapons, we shall travel as lightly as possible."

Parent added, "We will use light canoes, and all men are experienced paddlers. We shall kill our food as we go and travel hard. I believe we can reach Louisiana between four and five weeks." Jean-Baptiste* was surprised at the figure as it had taken them five weeks just to reach Michilimackinac which was less than half the distance.
Saint-Aubin then handed a package to Jean-Baptiste*, "This is the down payment. As agreed the rest shall be paid at the end of the voyage."

Baptiste* went directly to André's and delivered the package. They opened it and were overwhelmed that they were looking upon more money than they thought they could accumulate in their collective lifetimes. The following evening the collective families gathered for a farewell dinner on the lawn of Jean-Baptiste*'s farm. That evening as they lay in bed after a long bout of passion, Anne-Elizabeth* turned to her husband, "I know that voyageur wives live with this routinely, but you have never been absent for more than a few days during our entire six years of marriage. Please be prudent."

Jean-Baptiste* replied, "I am always prudent and I have Joseph to watch my back. We do not expect hostilities, and although they may seem to be rascals, Joseph Parent and Pierre Roy are the most experienced backwoodsmen and are always cautious foremost. I promise that I shall return and we shall be rich as lords."

"I truly don't care about the money, but it will make life easier for us and the children as well as the other families."

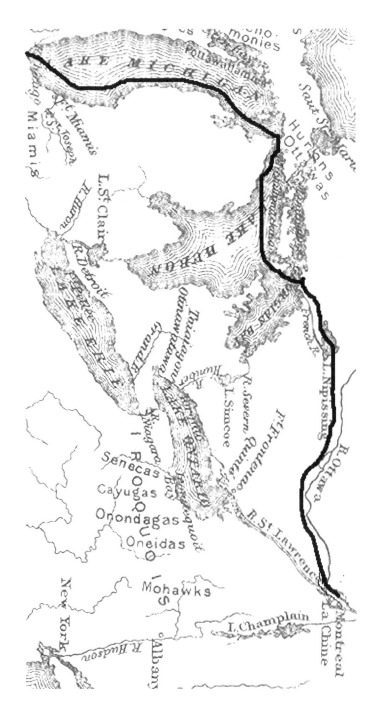

ROUTE TO LOUISIANA NORTHERN PART

Chapter 32

The following morning the four men arrived at the Beauport shore just as the sun began to show over Mount Sainte-Anne to the north and east. The canoe livery was an area reserved for canoes of the farmers and other residents who lived inland. Where it had started as the occasional overturned canoe, it was now a veritable field of such crafts, each carefully marked to note its owner. As François* had learned from Henri many years ago, canoe theft was considered the most dishonorable of crimes.

They saw their friends but there was someone they had not expected. It was a man named Laforest who worked at the mill in Montmorency. As they were formally introduced, Parent explained that Jean* Laforest had married the daughter of Joseph Parent's oldest sister, Marie*. Laforest lived north of Beauport at Sainte-Anne and farmed but also worked the mill.

Saint-Aubin explained, "We are bringing Monsieur Laforest for his expertise in mill work and construction. He will share it in Louisiana, and later, he and I will travel to Détroit where he will do the same."

Parent added, "We shall leave forthwith. Joseph, Jean-Baptiste*, Laforest and Saint-Aubin will take Saint-Aubin's larger canoe. Pierre and I shall take Tom and Monsieur Thomas and instruct them in voyageur paddling." He put his arms on the two men's shoulders and said, "My friends, by the time we reach the French River, you shall be as accomplished as any voyageur in Canada." Then addressing the rest he said, "We will pick up a few supplies and the rest of our group in Montréal. I hope to be there in three days time. Let us not dally. As they pushed off, Jean-Baptiste* looked at Joseph wondering what magic they would use against the late spring current.

Montréal - June 8, 1711:

Indeed the men landed three days later in Montreal, and as they pulled ashore in front of the fort, Parent announced, "Our stay here will be brief."

No sooner had he spoken than a group of men headed by Robert* Reaume greeted them. Reaume was accompanied by his son Nicolas*, only 13 but quite large, and who had already accompanied his father on trading trips. They introduced two other men, Joseph Gauthier who was about Jean-Baptiste*'s age, and Michel Charbonneau who was in his forties and a contemporary of Joseph Parent. Rounding out the group was Grosse Pierre whom the men knew from their voyage to Détroit. All men were experienced voyageurs and all had been to Détroit at the time of Cadillac.

In addition there were six Indians, two Algonquin and four Huron. After a quick introduction, the men launched canoes and proceeded rapidly. The first portage at the Lachine rapids was incredible. Due to the light weight of the canoes and the strength of the group, they virtually ran the path. Two men could easily carry each canoe. At intervals they traded chores and managed to maintain the pace.

As they put in below the rapids they began what Parent said would be their daily pace. Each stroke was timed, measured, and executed perfectly, swiftly, and with all available strength. As the trip progressed, Parent moved the men about as chessman, finding where each would work the most effectively. He kept Tom de Baptiste and Jacob* Thomas with Pierre Roy and himself. They learned very quickly. The speed of the crafts was amazing. They overtook other voyageurs along the route who were traveling with the customary canoes and loads and would pass them and leave them out of sight in a matter of one half hour.

Immediately after the rapids, they turned north up the Ottawa River. They were at Gatineau by afternoon where the new post was now called 'Ottawa' and well beyond it when they stopped for the night. Jean-Baptiste* and Joseph, who thought the trip from Québec had been grueling, were sore everywhere. Tom and Jacob*, who had been meticulously instructed in form, were surprisingly less sore.

As became routine, upon landing one group set camp and another went to the brush to hunt game. Jean-Baptiste* and Joseph were invariably in this group. When game was plentiful, it would be prepared so that it could be used for the next night or nights as the amount allowed.

The first evening after eating, Jean* Saint-Aubin called the men together, "As you know, each of you has been chosen for this voyage for your knowledge of travel as well as a good relationship with Monsieur Cadillac. When we arrive we will have been ostensibly sent to aid in his first year as Governor to develop the fort and post. We will be met by agents of Monsieur Antoine Crozat sailing from

France to Louisiana with Cadillac and his family. They may have already arrived.

"As I have told each of you, I have been assured that none of us will be expected to do anything deceitful or unlawful. We are merely to help Monsieur Cadillac build a successful venture that will aid the investment of Monsieur Crozat. In addition I have been told the King has deemed that this outpost and the entire Mississippi River Basin are essential to the crown's holdings in North America and control of unbridled English expansion.

"I realize each of you is familiar with some of the others, but I propose that each evening one of you introduce yourself to the group and tell a little about your life and experiences in outposts especially those with Monsieur Cadillac. If you don't mind, we shall begin tonight with myself.

"I was born in the village of Saint-Aubin de Blaye in the Bordeaux region of France in the year 1659. My name is actually Jean* Casse, but no one uses that any longer and my family is destined to remain 'Saint-Aubin' after the village of my birth. My father's family owns a vineyard and winery which has been in the family for many years. Not being interested in the wine business, I left it to my older brothers and went to a military school in the nearby city of Bordeaux where I became an officer and served with the company d'Aloigny in the town of Etauliers.

"In 1701 our company was sent to Québec where I served until I was transferred to Monsieur Cadillac's regiment in Détroit, serving with him until his recall to

France in 1710. I married Marie-Louise Gauthier, a native of Québec. Her father was a navigator from Larochelle. Her mother, also from Larochelle, came as a *Fille du Roi*. I still have ties to the military but am also a farmer. We have a long farm in Détroit between the fort and the farm of Monsieur Parent on the eastern edge of the city, and we now have three young children, Jean-Baptiste, Pierre*, and Marie-Anne.

"I have had very close dealings with Monsieur Cadillac. I have found him to be generally self-serving, however, he generally finds a way for the best interests of the project to coincide with his best interests. If there are no questions, we have a big day with an early start tomorrow."

The following day was another of swift travel, for the high water of late spring made it unnecessary to portage and hence saved more time. They were beyond the turn from north to west of the Ottawa River by the end of the day. After eating, another story was heard.

"My name is Joseph Gauthier. I was born in Montréal in 1672. My father was Pierre* Gauthier who came from the Larochelle region in France. My mother was Charlotte* Roussel who came from Normandie as a *Fille du Roi*. They moved to Lachine when I was young and established the first farm in the town on the bank of the rapids. In 1689 the Iroquois raided Lachine, The village was burned, and many people taken or massacred. Both of my parents were taken. My oldest brother, Jean*, was 20 years old at the time. I was second oldest at 17. We managed to place the younger children with friends and the following year my brother left to be a voyageur.

"Some years later my father returned. He had been held captive and slave for many years, but one day he found the opportunity to run away. He had never seen my mother after the night of the massacre and assumed she was killed at that time or soon after. He has henceforth been called *Sanguingoria*, which is an odd combination of French and Indian and refers to one whose throat has been cut.

"Soon after he returned, I married a widow named Clemence Jarry. She is older than I but did not object that I, too, wished to follow the life of my brother. I have been to Michilimackinac and Détroit, and I have worked both places with Monsieur Cadillac. He has always seemed a capable leader, but in truth I would trust him no further than I could throw Grosse Pierre.

"My brother, Jean* Gauthier, is a very experienced voyageur; he has been farther north than Gitcheegumee, farther west than the Mississippi and to Louisiana and beyond. Indeed all the way to *La Jonquière* on the Saskatchewan River. He now lives with his Indian wife and family at the mission in Kaskaskia. We will stop there and he will also accompany us."

The following day they paddled hard until early afternoon when the river finally became impassable. They began the long portage to Lake Nipissing. Jean-Baptiste*, Joseph and Tom took the opportunity to hunt along the way. The portagers made the bank of Lake Nipissing long before dark. About an hour later, the hunters arrived exhausted from dragging a large caribou. Jean-Baptiste* announced, "We will eat well for the next few nights."

A small trading post on the northeast corner of the lake was called simply, North Bay. One old trapper in residence joined them for the feast, and explained the deserted nature of the post. "The Iroquois have been active of late, often times with some English friends. We had several Huron living here up until a few weeks ago when word came that the rascals of the Five-Nations Iroquois were raiding the Huron villages at the end of the French River and on the Manitoulin Island. So they left and I ain't heard from them since."

After a grand feast of roasted caribou, it was time for another personal history. "My name is Michel Charbonneau, born in Montréal in 1666. My father, Oliver* Charbonneau, was born in Larochelle. His first two wives died in France. His third wife was my mother, Marie-Marguerite* Garnier. She married my father in Larochelle three years before they came to Canada. They sailed with my mother's three sisters, two of whom came with their husbands. My oldest sister, Anne* Charbonneau, was barely two when they came.

"During the year 1659, the religious wars were active in the region and at this time Catholics were persecuted. Jeanne Mance and Marguerite Bourgeoys themselves financed the voyage to help Catholics escape to Canada. The voyage was terrible and the plague broke out. All the children save my sister died on this voyage. The families moved directly to Montréal while it was still called *Ville-Marie*. My father was among the first residents of the city.

"I married Marguerite Denoyon in 1692. Her family was much harmed by the Iroquois. Her mother orphaned at their hand at the age of one and her first husband killed in the first year of their marriage. We now live in Montréal. My older brother, Joseph Charbonneau, is also a voyageur, and we have worked together since before 1700. We both were in Détroit in the early days of Cadillac and knew him well. I was never bothered by his shenanigans as I always felt that I understood and anticipated what he was up to. I also agree that in spite of himself, his projects tend to succeed."

The following morning as they set off into Lake Nipissing, Joseph Parent announced, "We are entering the fine calm weather of summer. If it holds, we may risk crossing the lake of the Huron directly. I have other good news. It is possible from this point on we shall have only one portage of note and that is at the very end of the voyage." The group flew across the 25 miles of Lake Nipissing to the opening to the French River where they began their first downstream current.

They made the end of the French River by nightfall where they found a small Huron village, deserted and partially burned. As they walked through it, Pierre Roy commented, "Even the Indian cultures cannot always abide one another." Jean-Baptiste* thought this was the first truly serious thing he had ever heard the voyageur say. At the end of dinner it was time for Roy to tell his story.

"I don't know when I was born or where my father was born, or truly who he was, although I have been told that his name was Roy. He was a voyageur to whom my lonely mother was attracted one cold winter night. Her own voyageur husband was off trading when this man took shelter in her house. He left the next day and I appeared some months later. The priests called me *enfant naturel,* and were kind enough to baptize me. My mother's husband had little use for me except to help with the hard labor. At the age of ten I took off to the woods.

"I was given refuge at an Algonquin camp and traveled with them for two years. learning the ways of the wild and the ways and language of the Algonquin. Later I again went off on my own and landed with a band of Huron who continued my education until one night I was taken on an Iroquois raid. I spent three years with the Mohawk at Lake Champlain and learned a great deal more.

"One day I found the opportunity to depart and ran into this Joseph Parent, and I've been keeping him out of trouble ever since. I've had four Indian wives, two Algonquin and two Huron. I have a few children and in fact Monsieur Thomas here has tried to make me respectable by marrying of my daughters."

He paused to think and then continued, "You know the cultures of the Indians are at least as varied as the Europeans. When we see a raid such as this one here, we forget that the Five-Nation Iroquois are the same tribe as the Huron. Indeed they have many similarities. They are settled, that is to say that their villages are relatively permanent and their lodgings are also permanent. They have a social and, I guess, political way that is quite advanced.

"In my experience, the Five Nations are quite advanced, their society is rigidly regulated, but all members have a true voice in the government, much more so than the French or English. They are very fierce yet very protective within their society. The Huron have a similar way but are not so rigid or protective. We all know the terrible stories of the early days of the Jesuits when the black-robes came and the Huron welcomed them and tried to learn their ways. Their reward was near annihilation. True it was from disease and not violence, but the Huron have come to accept it and although most no longer welcome the black-robes, they have forgiven them. The Five-Nations would have ended the French in America for all time.

"The Algonquin are quite different, in many ways much more primitive. They are nomads. Their villages are temporary and their lodgings more so. They move with the hunt and have little use for farming or raising animals. Their culture and regulations are also much more simple and less rigid. The French frequently complain they are thieves, as some of the less civilized bands will take what they need, but the French don't understand Algonquin do not view this as theft, for personal ownership is not an important part of their culture.

"Well, I guess I've said my piece. Oh, and Cadillac, I would never turn my back on him. He has less civilization then any Indian I know." No one in the group would ever regard Pierre Roy in the same manner again.

The following morning, they entered the great bay of the Lake of the Huron. The sky was clear, and the bay was as flat as a mirror. Parent suggested that rather than skirt the north shore, they make a straight shot across to the southern tip of the Manitoulin Island. Which would take them across seventy miles of unprotected water that could become treacherous in a storm, but Parent had consulted with Joseph and the other Indians about the weather and they all agreed it was likely to stay fair. The prize would be cutting a full day off the journey.

They were out of sight of land for most of the day. Jean-Baptiste* had not confessed he was the owner of a military compass. He did check it from time to time, amazed on the continued accuracy of Parent's course. As the weather remained fair, they arrived at the island in mid afternoon.

Chapter 33

They landed at the site of the Huron village. Many Indians were working on some charred buildings still smoldering. Parent spoke to one of the men who indicated there had been a raid in the evening from Iroquois and a few English. Although they had chased them off, some damage had been inflicted. They invited the men to spend the night. Parent relayed the news adding, "They have also indicated we may be in for a very interesting evening." Looking at Baptiste*, he said, "Perhaps the most interesting of our lives."

Soon they saw a group of Huron, both men and women, walking down the beach toward the village. A small old man with a large staff was leading them. Joseph Gauthier gasped, "Can that be who I think it is?"

Parent replied softly, "Yes, Soaring Eagle, he still lives."

Jean-Baptiste* had heard about this old sage of the Huron but he had come to believe that it was merely a legend.

The old man and his entourage came into the camp and spoke with the chief, who came to Parent and said, "The great chief will indeed stay with us tonight, and he wants to meet each of your party individually."

The men gathered to meet the old chief who first came to Jean* Saint-Aubin. The old chief was as withered as anyone Jean-Baptiste* had ever seen, stooped over but still quite agile. He looked into Saint-Aubin's eyes and said in perfect French, "You are the leader but not a voyageur, a soldier but no longer a soldier."

Jean* was taken aback by the accuracy of the statement. He gave a cursory explanation of their voyage. The old man continued, "You are welcome. Anything that discourages the spread of the English is welcome."

He then went on to each of the voyageurs in turn, Parent, Pierre Roy, Grosse Pierre, Gauthier, Charbonneau, and Robert* Reaume, greeting each as if he knew them well, even occasionally asking about their fathers. Later some of the men admitted they had never before met the old chief and were baffled he knew so much about them. When he came to young Nicolas* Reaume, he asked nothing but simply stated, "Your father is a good man and true, mold yourself after him."

When he came to Jean* Laforest, he said, "Not a voyageur but a builder and worker." Laforest explained he was along to build mills. The old Man continued, "I prefer the ax and the stone, but your mills do seem to do the job as well, but not so eloquently."

When he looked at Jacob* Thomas he said in English, "What does an English farmer do with this group?" Dumbfounded, Jacob* gave a brief history of his journey, and the old man replied, "You are wise to stay with these men. They are better stewards of the earth than your former people."

To Tom he said, "How does a slave from Africa find the good fortune to bring him to this group?" Tom gave a brief history of his story and the old man replied, "In your

219

good fortune, never forget the plight of your people. Your life's work and the life's work of your sons and daughters should always be to strive to see them freed from this unworthy bondage."

When he came to Joseph, he looked at his wampum and said, "Could you be the seed of my great friend Henri?" Joseph applied in the affirmative and the old man continued, "Henri and I shared a fire for many nights. He was a great and wise man. Emulate your grandfather and you too shall be great and wise."

At the end he came to Jean-Baptiste*. Looking at his wampum he said, "You do not look to be Abenaki." After Jean-Baptiste* explained the story of the wampum, the old man replied, "You must be the son of François* Allard of whom Henri often spoke. I believe Henri helped your father to become a great and wise man. Then what is this?" as he took the Allard medallion in his hand.

Immediately his face went blank. He was silent for a long while, then his eyes became very intent. Jean-Baptiste* felt as though the old man was looking into his soul. Finally he spoke, "Rarely have I seen an object with this magic. I see visions through the ages. I see great wars of men in armor on horseback. I see a young girl being burned by evil men for their own purpose. I see a great voyage and a great family that spreads across the land, I see…" He let go the medallion which hit Jean-Baptiste*'s chest feeling like a hot poker.

Jean-Baptiste* asked, "What do you see?"

After a while the old man replied, "Great tragedy, but I may be wrong. I am only a man who has lived too long."

220

With that he returned to his entourage. Later Jean-Baptiste* realized he had an image of the medallion burned into his chest.

That night after dinner the men sat and smoked with the Indians. Finally Soaring Eagle appeared ready to speak. He began in flawless French, "I was born a great many winters ago. As my father was a chief, it was assumed that I too would be one. As tradition had it, my mother was given this staff. She had been instructed to make a notch at the first snow of each winter. When I was old enough, it became my job. In this fashion, the tribe knows how many winters the chief has seen. I have not counted these myself for many years but my daughters tell me that there are now one hundred and seventeen notches." With a chuckle he added, "Of course, in the years that I chased the women, I may have neglected a notch or two."

Jean-Baptiste* did the math in his head and realized that this man walked the earth before Champlain ever saw Canada. The old chief continued, "A man or woman can be born with the gift of intelligence, the ability to solve puzzles and learn how to read and write. However, to be wise, the man or woman must regard all things about them. Wisdom comes from experience and observation, and wisdom is related to age. Do not fail to learn what you can from those who have gone before you. Then continue to observe and pass your wisdom on to the future.

"Yesterday evening we had an encounter with the Iroquois. Unfortunately men died and we now mourn them. In truth, the Huron are also Iroquois and we are brothers, however, we have always had differences. Indeed all men who walk the earth are brothers, but there are always differences and disagreements, be they land, hunting rights, women, or nothing at all. When I was young, battles were different. It is true that there was some killing, but not as today. The goal then was counting *coups,* to use the French word. If a man touched or hit the opponent, it was a sign of strength and victory. It has always put me in mind of our game of *Ah-kee,* or Lacrosse as the French call it, a boy's game to prove superiority.

"Battles were much the same but with more of the passion of youth. The white man considers the battle differently. His goal is to inflict harm on his opponent, yes even death. Any man's death diminishes the others. It proves nothing and brings nothing to the solution. I now fear greatly when I see the Indian accepting this barbaric practice of the European. The Indian as all men should mourn all the dead regardless of allegiances.

"I was a young man when my people saw the first white men. At first we did not know what to think, but we welcomed them cautiously as we would any tribe. As I grow older, I must say I fear the white man more. I fear this burning need to kill his fellow man, which is contrary to all the principles of my people. More than this I fear his concept of religion.

"As you may not know, there is no Indian word, neither Algonquin or Iroquois, for religion. Indians are spiritual people, more spiritual, I believe, than the Europeans. We know a higher power; we worship the things that are good in our lives. We have a moral code that dictates good will to man and nature. But it is always here," he said as he lay his hand on his heart. "And it is for each man to discover. For each man it is different but it is not wrong that he may differ with his brother on the question of his own spirituality. However it should never alter his regard of his brother, and it should certainly never cause him to wish harm on his brother.

"When I was a chief and had seen fifty or more winters, the black-robes of the French religion came to the lands of the Huron. We welcomed them as we would any peaceful tribe. We learned from each other and began to build a regard. However you all know the terrible tale. Unknowingly, the black-robes brought disease as we had never seen and a terrible many Huron perished in a few short years. At first there was anger and resentment but we have eventually come to see that it was not their intention; but I have come to believe that it was a sign to distrust their religion.

"It is this religion that tells you what you must do and how you must act, even if your heart is not in accord. I shared my fire for many nights with a holy man from the English people. He told me of terrible persecutions for the purpose of religion. He told me that most if not all wars in the land of the Europeans have been fought over differences in this religion. He told me that his own tribe fled to the new world to escape these terrible acts. But when I asked him how it was now to have freedom of religion, he astounded me by saying that only **his** religion was allowed in his new land. Clearly this man and his people had learned nothing from what they had observed and experienced. Their eyes and hearts were blinded by this word that we do not have, religion, and prevented them from acquiring true wisdom.

"The Indian may war over land or trade or women, but the Indian has never made war over this religion which preys on bigotry and hypocrisy. I use these two French words, for gladly these words do not exist in Algonquin nor do they exist in Iroquois.

"I also fear the white man's use of our land. They do not appear to be good stewards of nature. They cut more trees than they need. They kill more fish and game than they need. They divert the streams for foolish reasons. Mainly they come in more and more numbers than can be counted, and they choose to reproduce as though it were a contest.

"I suppose the Indian would also scar the land if they had such numbers, but we see no need. The tribes of the Indian have always have been the same size. Each woman has two or three children; with the death of some this keeps the numbers equal. They nurse their children for a long time, which forms a great bond and does not produce rapid pregnancy. I cannot conceive of how more people can make the world better. I indicated that the French were welcome if they could stem the tide of the English. It is truly not that I value the French more, but I fear the great numbers of the English. Perhaps one hundred and seventeen winters are too many and I am simply an old man who cannot understand new ways. I wish you *bonne nuit et bon voyage.*" And with that he went to his tent.

In the morning the men rose early and found that the old man had already parted with his entourage walking to the next village.

Chapter 34

Parent checked the Indian weather predictions and finding them satisfactory, he made a bold decision. "We will traverse the Lake of the Huron directly to Michilimackinac. It is more than twice the distance we covered yesterday, but if the weather remains calm and as the moon will be full tonight we can do it and remove a few days from the journey."

The men pushed with all their might and made wonderful headway. Jean-Baptiste* continued to watch his compass and was again amazed at Parent's ability to hold the course with no landmarks and not even any clouds. As night fell the moon appeared, and the way remained calm, but about an hour later they began to hear faint thunder to the northwest. Parent halted the boats and said, "I figure we are three hours from Michilimackinac, but if we head more to the south, we should hit the east coast of Michigauma and safety within two hours." The course was altered and they paddled with renewed vigor and speed.

Unfortunately, within the hour the storm broke and rain began to fall. Even worse was a strong wind from the north. As they were in the northern part of the lake, they would not catch its full fury, but the calm water turned to ripples, then to waves and then to small walls of water. As they battled the waves, their speed dropped dramatically. Eventually the center man had to abandon paddling for bailing with a bucket brought for just such an emergency.

An hour later, Baptiste* checked his compass and told Joseph he thought they were veering off course to the south. Joseph called across to Parent, "I think we should be going more to the north."

"How do you know?"

"I can smell it."

Parent looked down, and back at Joseph, "That's good enough for me." And he corrected the course.

An hour later when the wind was rising but the waves diminishing, the men realized this meant they were approaching land. Another hour passed before they could hear the surf. Fortunately the wind was not directly on shore so the surf was only moderate, but for landing a canoe in the dark, it would be difficult, especially as they were not familiar with the terrain of the coast at this point. Parent shouted to the others that as Pierre Roy was the strongest swimmer, he would jump over when they felt they were close. He would hang to a rope until he could feel the bottom and pull the boat in, thereby trying to minimize damage that may come from rocks.

Soon he began to find bottom, but the news was bad. "Rocks, bad rocks. I will have to swim ashore and direct you to a better point to land. You will have to remain out at this depth until I can light a fire." He was soon ashore where he removed a well-kept secret. Although they were scoffed at by all true voyageurs, Pierre had a French firebox stored in a watertight skin. He found an appropriate dry log under a tree and in two minutes had a fine torch burning. He began to make his way up the beach. The rocks were granite and indeed very bad and would have destroyed the canoes under these conditions. About a mile up the shore he came to a small cove and a short sand beach.

He waved his torch and guided the canoes in one by one. Eventually they were all secure on the beach. The rain had stopped, but the wind continued to build. They made a fire and ate leftover caribou. Parent said to Joseph, "So much for the Indian weather man."

Joseph returned, "At least I found your course."

Parent said, "I never heard of smelling a direction before, even an Indian."

Joseph and Jean-Baptiste* could not deceive their friend any longer and Jean-Baptiste* produced his compass. Parent looked at it with scorn but he laughed and said, "Well, whatever works." And he produced an object from his pocket, an older and more worn version of the same device.

The men had an uproarious laugh when Parent added, "Don't tell anyone but Pierre Roy has a fire box, which is probably why we still have our canoes." The laughter continued. They decided that tonight they would skip the personal story. At any rate it would be hard to compete with the one from yesterday.

The following morning repairs had to be made on the canoes, but soon they were on their way north. The waves remained high still they were able to hug the coast and make way. In early afternoon they reached Michilimackinac.

Jean-Baptiste* was surprised at the lack of progress at the old fort. There were a few small new structures but it looked much like it did several years before. Parent made contact with the commander and arranged to have repairs improved on the canoes. They obtained a few basic supplies and settled in for the evening hoping for calmer weather the next day. In spite of the loss of a day, Jean-Baptiste* was amazed that in two weeks they had made a voyage that took almost six weeks with Cadillac.

That evening Saint-Aubin called on Jean*Laforest.

"My history is not as exciting as the others. My father came from a small village in vineyards of Bordeaux, not far from the home of Monsieur Saint-Aubin. My mother was born in Québec of parents who had fled Larochelle as Huguenot, but they converted in Québec, which was required. Our family lived north of Québec in the Baie Saint-Paul where our long-term neighbor was Pierre* Tremblay. I am sure many of you knew him as before his death he traveled about with his friend Gilbert in early winter and cut trees. There have been many Laforest-Tremblay marriages.

"Myself, I married Marie-Angelique* Rancourt from Québec. Whose mother was Marie* Parent, the sister of Joseph Parent here. Because of the interest in wood, our family has been active in the mills, both wind and water. I have operated windmills in Baie Saint-Paul as well as the great water mill in Montmorency. I have had less travel experience than the others, but as Monsieur Saint-Aubin has told you I am along to help develop mills. I have only met Monsieur Cadillac once and have no fixed opinion."

The following day the group departed in calmer water, but the roll of the waves made going a bit slower.

They made their way past the bay of the Petoskey to the great bay which ran north and south, making camp on the eastern tip, hoping the next day would bring calmer waters for crossing the large bay. That night Saint-Aubin chose Jean-Baptiste* for his story.

"My name is Jean-Baptiste* Allard. My father came from a small village in Normandie and my mother from a small town in Touraine. Her brother is now the Bishop of Tours. My mother was well educated and taught our family to read and write. As a small boy I was attracted to the forest. My father preferred farming but was an accomplished hunter. He learned from a man called Henri who is the grandfather of my friend Joseph.

"Joseph and I have been best friends and have hunted and trapped since we could walk. When we were very young, we stumbled upon an Iroquois raiding party and helped foil their raid on Charlesbourg. We were held in some esteem for the deed, but I must confess we were very lucky. We have had the opportunity to travel with Monsieur Cadillac to both Michilimackinac and Détroit. I agree he is a bit of a rascal but I truly to believe at base he is a great leader who has accomplished great things both for New and for Old France.

"I now have a farm by my brother's farm in Bourg-Royal and a wonderful new family. I plan to return to that life at the end of this adventure."

The next morning the lake was calm and they proceeded easily beyond the small cove where the boys had found the Griffon many years before. As they passed an enormous mountain of sand, Parent told them the Indians referred to as the bear that sleeps, for its peculiar shape. He suggested that they go south of this area to where the forest provided better cover for camp. That night Saint-Aubin assigned the tale to Robert* Reaume.

"My father came from Larochelle. His father was a master carpenter and my father practiced the same trade, spending some years working on the cathedral at Québec. My mother came from the Loire region as *Fille du Roi.* As my father did not farm much, my brothers and I took often to the woods. Indeed five of us are now licensed voyageurs. Some of you know my brother Jean-Pierre who has greatly studied the Indian ways and is considered the best interpreter in New France, although I suspect he is not so good as Joseph here."

"I am now married with eight children. My son Nicolas* here is but thirteen years, but quite strong and capable as you can see. He has been to the frontier many times and I believe we can count on him as on any man. His mother was born in Montreal. Her father is from Larochelle as well as his wife who came with the first boat of *Fille du Roi* in 1663.

"I have visited Monsieur Cadillac at both of his forts. In fact all four of my woodsman brothers have been to Détroit and I suspect that some may settle there. In 1702, I was hired to bring Madame Cadillac and her son to Détroit from Montréal. We were forced to spend the winter at Fort Frontenac. I found her to be a fine lady who endured the winter admirably. I would be a bit more cautious about her husband."

At daybreak as the men prepared to depart, Parent announced that if they worked hard they could be at the bottom of the lake in three days, "From there it is all river voyage and little fear of giant storms and waves. We have been fortunate so far. I hope our luck continues." Joseph Parent was chosen for the night's tale.

"I believe I know most of you well. My father came from Saintes east of Larochelle. He was a butcher and a farmer. My mother was born in Québec as one of the first natives. Her parents came early from Larochelle. As you know, Jean-Baptiste*'s father François*, worked for three years with my widowed grandmother, Anne* Ardouin-Badeau. Our family had some means but it was divided among many children. My parents produced fifteen new Canadians, three of whom are the famous 'Beauport twins'. All boys, exactly alike, Etienne, Jean and another Joseph, I suppose my parents had run short of names.

"We farmed as well as cut meat but I always loved the woods. As soon as I was able, I became a boy for voyageurs and eventually became a voyageur myself. My wife was born in Québec of parents from the north of France. We now have nine children, the youngest born in Détroit where we now live.

"Having spent most of my life in a canoe, I have been to all the outposts as far as Saskatchewan, and have lived with Cadillac both at Michilimackinac as well as Détroit. I was in fact one of the first white men to see Détroit, long before Monsieur Cadillac and certainly the first to live there for a season. I feel that I can call myself the first citizen of the place. Pierre Roy and I have been twice to Louisiana so I suppose we shall be the guides. I can assure you that in the next few days you will see things you would otherwise never have believed.

"As for Monsieur Cadillac. He is indeed clever and capable; however, I would not trust him for a moment."

Morning again rose calm and the canoes made impressive speed. The coast was straight and regular, generally beach with occasional dunes, sand cliffs and always-dense deciduous forest. There were few small coves and the occasional river. They had not seen any sign of life, European or Indian, since the night after Michilimackinac. As they readied for their last camp before the bottom of the lake, Saint-Aubin selected Jacob* Thomas for the story.

"I was born in Ireland, a great island west of England. It is a place of great green rolling hills. The farmland is not so good as in Canada and there are many fewer trees. There is no frontier; I understand this is also true of France. My father was a tradesman and made a tolerable living. Ireland was troubled however by three years of poor crops and a constant threat of being overtaken by England.

"These difficulties were compounded by the fact that Ireland is a small Catholic country and England is a great Protestant one. England had begun to gain some control in Ireland as early as the time of King Henry VIII and the prosecution of Catholics began. This continued for many years, and I was forced to work at farm labor for a local English lord who had gained some control in our county.

"Eventually things became intolerable and seeing no future I chose to leave. I was able to secure passage on a boat bound for Boston where I arrived in 1700. Boston is a city about like Québec in the colony of Massachusetts. To secure my passage I was obligated to sign to two years of indentured service. Indentured service is different in the English colonies compared to the French. It is closer to prison labor or almost slavery. Rather than one or two men working on a farm, the farms are generally enormous estates of the very rich and employ many souls such as myself. The work is hard and there is little if any freedom. At the end of service I was indeed allowed to set out for myself, but it is very hard to start a small farm, as the good land has been taken by the very rich.

"I met a man who had come with a family and some meager means. He too could not find opportunity in the east so he was setting off into the western frontier. He agreed to take me if I would help with the work. We settled in a place called Northampton in the center of Massachusetts where he was able to acquire a small farm and I helped him for two years. We made little progress until eventually he could no longer keep me on. Having no further possibilities, I joined the regular troops attached as militia to the English Army.

"Our first assignment was very ambitious. As most raiding parties went up Lake Champlain to the Richelieu River and on to Montreal, we were to go overland to the Chaudiere River and up to Québec. The trip was grueling and took almost a month. Our leader was an English officer named Johnson who was a fool. Our group had little training and we were lost half of the time. When we reached the southern shore of the Saint-Laurent, we were without a true plan. Johnson decided to hike northeast to the tip of the *Ile d'Orleans,* then cross and come onto Beauport from the north.

"Our inexperienced group was further troubled by the militia of Joseph and Jean-Baptiste* who immediately outflanked us and sent us into full retreat. Fortunately I was wounded and did not retreat. Johnson was gravely wounded and his servant stayed with him. To my further good fortune, the French had no idea what to do with prisoners so we were taken to the camp of Joseph and Jean-Baptiste*. Colonel Johnson died that night, and it was the first time I had met Tom who was the Colonel's servant.

"Ultimately we stayed there and were assumed into the community. Seeing that a poor man could survive in this society, I lost all interest in returning to Massachusetts. As you have heard, I married Toinette Roy, the métis daughter of Pierre Roy and have achieved a happiness and success of which I would have never dreamed in my previous life."

Each night three men were assigned to take turns at watch. This night Joseph had the first watch and sat by the shore contemplating the silence. Jean-Baptiste* who came and sat with him which was not uncommon, said, "I am wondering about Monsieur Saint-Aubin and this odd custom of telling stories each night."

His friend asked, "Exactly what do you mean? I find it very interesting."

"I do as well. I am only concerned about a possible ulterior motive. I am hoping that we are not being duped into a plot against Cadillac."

"Saint-Aubin has said we will not be expected to do anything that would be deceitful."

"It is just that. If we are merely to come to do jobs that could be done by anyone else, why was it so extremely important that it be precisely us and no one else?"

"Jean-Baptiste*, I think you spend too much time thinking. Why don't you go to bed?"

"Alright, but think about this yourself."

Again the morning was fair and calm. The group made excellent progress to what should be their last night before the river of the Illinois.

"My name is Joseph, I am Algonquin. My parents live on the farm of François* Allard in Charlesbourg. My grandfather lived on the farm of Jacques* Badeau and his wife Anne* Ardouin-Badeau. Before that, my family lived with the Algonquin tribes of the region of Québec. The Algonquin are suspicious of families such as mine as they feel we are too French. The French are suspicious because we are Algonquin. My friend Jean-Baptiste* confides in me more than in any Frenchman; and I confide in him more than in any Algonquin, but this is a truly unique relationship.

"My people, the Algonquin, are a simple but wonderful society. They are nomadic and have little concept of property. As Pierre Roy said, the French sometimes consider the Algonquin outside of their society as thieves because they take not so much what they want but they take what they need as this is the way of their society. It is not so much a lack of honesty as a lack of greed. Sometimes I am shamed by this and realize I should not be. However I have long believed that the way of the Indian is to disappear and have continued to move toward the ways of the French. I have married a woman who is métis and I suspect that our children will become even more French.

"Jean-Baptiste* and I have traveled and worked with Monsieur Cadillac both at Michilimackinac as well as Détroit. I know many of you consider him self-serving and not to be trusted; but to be honest, I have always believed these to be traits of most Europeans. Perhaps he is merely more so."

The following morning the weather was very hot and calm. The sky had only wisps of clouds called *la queue des juments* or mares' tails. Parent announced, "Today the weather is to change. If we make appropriate preparations we might use it to our advantage and have some fun as well." Without further explanation he reorganized the canoes with the very best paddlers in the back of each canoe and the next best in the front. The group departed with their usual great effort.

In the early afternoon the northwest sky became black as night and soon thunder and lightning arrived along with heavy sheets of rain. The men, accustom to traveling in rain, merely adjusted their clothing to the circumstance. The rain stopped as abruptly as it had begun and the wind switched violently to the north. As they were a way off shore, they began to experience enormous waves directly from behind, truly great walls of water often cresting at the top.

The experienced men in the front and back of the canoes knew exactly how to handle these giant waves. They would paddle hard to climb the back and then let the wave push them at incredible speed for long distances. The trick was to keep the canoe directly straight in front of the wave as a quick turn to the side would spell disaster. The men, however, knew very well how to 'ride the wave'. As they were already drenched from the rain they did not object to the further drenching from the lake, and the men in the center of the canoes took to full time bailing.

The thrill of the day was such that most lost track of time until they began to see the southern shore of the lake and realized it would soon be dark. Parent corrected the course slightly to the west, which made the maneuvering both more difficult as well as more exciting. As dusk arrived they were at the shore of a long sand beach leading to the mouth of a large river, and managed to 'surf' ashore with no mishaps or damage.

As they made camp Parent announced they were at the mouth of the River of the Illinois and the remainder of their voyage, which was now slightly more than half completed, would be all in the rivers and virtually all downstream. Seeing how exhausted the men were from the day's adventure, Saint-Aubin suggested they would skip the story tonight.

As Jean* Saint-Aubin lay on his deerskin, he made a mental inventory of the men and their stories so far. They had only to hear from Tom and Grosse Pierre and he felt he knew where those two would lay. He figured that of his eleven Frenchmen, counting Joseph and excluding himself and young Nicolas* Reaume, three had no opinion of Monsieur Cadillac, three were indifferent, the other five did not trust him. and of that five three of four disliked him greatly.

Saint-Aubin was an intelligent and educated man. Besides education in books he was educated in how to judge and control men. He had excelled in military school and was held in high regard in the colony. He was possibly the most highly regarded and influential man in the settlement of Détroit and was likely to remain so.

He pondered the days ahead and how he would accomplish his task, realizing that in order for it to succeed, he had not been entirely forthright with the men. This bothered him more than a little. However as a good military man he realized that the objective was foremost.

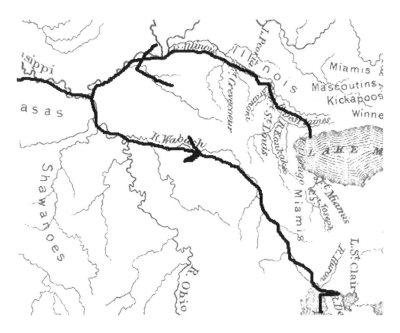

ROUTES TO AND FROM LOUISIANA CENTRAL PART

Chapter 35

The morning broke cool and clear. The waves breaking on the shore were even larger than those of yesterday, and the men were delighted that they would have the wonderful cool day without rough water as the river flowed gently with only a small current and a wonderful breeze, all to their back. Parent told the men they would frequently encounter natives and occasionally voyageurs along this part of the voyage. "Here in the north, the natives are Algonquin and mostly of two tribes, Miami and Illinois. They are generally friendly.

"At this point the river is much like that of the Ottawa and French Rivers. However you will see as we proceed south it will become quite different and quite strange." As the day progressed, Jean-Baptiste* noticed the trees were much more deciduous than in the north. Coniferous trees abounded but not as much as in Québec. He and Joseph examined the river and surrounding areas, and using the wisdom they had received from old Henri, they realized that the potential for fish and game here was incredible.

At midday they stopped at a small Indian camp. Parent took Joseph and they were able to communicate with the group. When he returned Parent reported to Saint-Aubin, "They are Miami, glad to see the French as they have seen some English this year and say there are a few English settlers in the Miami lands east of here but west of the great mountains. They have invited us for dinner."

Saint-Aubin replied, "Thank them but tell them that the urgency of our mission does not allow us to accept their gracious hospitality."

Jean* Saint-Aubin realized this was not entirely wise but felt that as Cadillac had likely already landed in Louisiana, he must proceed with some haste. That night as they made camp Saint-Aubin decided on a geography lesson rather than a personal history, besides he already had learned most of what he needed from the stories. He went to a clearing in the woods where the ground was almost devoid of plant life and outlined a remarkably good map of the eastern part of North America.

"The English and Dutch occupy the lands of the Atlantic coast from very close to the Saint-Laurent going south to, but not entirely including, this southern peninsula. This is called *Floride* and was settled early by France but also by Spain and now belongs in large part to the Spanish. The French control the lands east of this great Mississippi River on which we shall spend many days.

"The English are impeded from westward migration because of France but to be honest, more because of this great mountain range which stretches from the Saint-Laurent southward, but they go only to within 100 miles of the *Mer de Mexique* or Mexican sea. Another peculiar situation is that English colonies are not, as Québec, a unified colony started by the crown. Instead they are many small colonies started by various groups. They all swear some allegiance to the King of England, but are quite varied. For instance, the colony, which borders this 100 miles without a mountainous barrier is called Georgia for their King George. It is occupied to a large part by former prisoners and other low-life individuals and produces a less formidable foe in the eyes of France.

"Part of Cadillac's job and ours is to produce a French impediment to migration through this southern corridor. As we heard from the Miami today, the English have already succeeded in crossing the great mountains and it is up to the French in this part of the continent to stop them."

The next day the scenery remained quite the same. They passed two other small camps, similar to the Algonquin camps along the entire route with mobile tents and similar dress, although these people were more lightly clothed due to the warm weather. The difference in temperature even in early summer was becoming evident. They stopped early as they had run out of provisions. A few of the men went to hunt and Jean-Baptiste*, Joseph and Tom decided to try the fishing.

They merely floated bobbing hooks with maggots, which were always abundant as the previous provisions became older and rotten. As Jean-Baptiste* had suspected, the river was teeming with fish. They pulled in a constant stream of perch and river trout along with a few small fish they had not encountered in the north. As the harvest was becoming routine, Joseph almost had his line pulled overboard. "Is it possible that there are sturgeon in this narrow river?" he queried as he pulled with all his strength on the line.

He eventually brought the monster alongside the canoe and Jean-Baptiste* grabbed it with a large gaff and pulled it into the canoe. "Catfish," Tom announced, "We used to see these in South Carolina, sometimes even bigger."

Jean-Baptiste* and Joseph had seen catfish up north but never this size. When the boat was full, the men returned to camp to the arduous job of cleaning and preserving this large catch.

The next few days were routine. Travel was easy as there was no rough water, high wind, and best of all, no portage. They continued to see Indian camps and occasionally stopped. The people at this point were almost naked and slightly darker in color. Parent explained most of the people in this region were of the Illinois tribes. Vegetation continued to change with fewer oak and maple trees while the coniferous trees began to take on a softer, less dense appearance. The weather was becoming downright hot.

One evening Parent announced they would see the great Mississippi River the next day. Saint-Aubin called the men together for another personal history. He thought he knew what he would hear from the last two men and was certain that it would not alter any plans.

"I am called Grosse Pierre although that is not my given name. I have not told my true story for many years as I had things to fear, but I suspect that is no longer the case and would like to hear it again myself.

"I was born in Paris. My family lived near the Tuileries Palace. My name is no longer of importance. My father was a baron and my mother's father was a count. I was raised in the privileged life of royalty, educated in the finest schools, and played often with the children of the King. My education consisted of years abroad in England, Italy and Spain. I attended the finest University in Paris.

"During my university years I met a young woman whose grandfather was a Marquis but her parents of little social consequence. She would be considered below my social station but we fell in love, and I had planned to marry her when I finished my education. Her name was Monique. I still see her lovely face each night.

"In those days I lived in a stylish house near *l'Ile de la Cité.* Two of my friends had rooms there as well. Both were from families of prominence. Often these two would bring home women of little virtue from the taverns and have their way with them through the night. I was pledged to my Monique and did not take part in these interludes.

"One night as I returned home, I heard a great commotion from the room of one of my friends. I entered to inspect the situation and was shocked to see they had taken my Monique by force, tied her to a bed and were taking the most severe of liberties with her. I was enraged. Even then I was larger and stronger than most and I beat the boys severely. As a result, one of them died.

"The next day Monique's father had her sent to a convent in the Swiss Alps. As it turns out, the boy I had killed was a nephew of the King. My father, fearing for my life and royal reprisals, had me sent secretly to the south where I lived quietly for two years, but the boy's family would not cease seeking revenge. Finally I received word they had discovered my whereabouts. The next day I left for Larochelle where I was able to book passage on a boat to Canada.

"I lived in Montréal for two years, acquired a farm and began the life of a country gentleman under a false name. I was reasonably content but one day a man appeared and accused me of my crime. Before I could be taken, I took to the forest. As I was large and strong, I was able to find employment with people who asked few questions. Since that time I have lived the life of a voyageur and sometimes *coureur de bois*. I have lived this life for now twenty years, and I must say it is here that I have at last met men of truth and virtue. I would not return to Paris to be King.

"As for Monsieur Cadillac, I have no regard or trust for him or his kind."

No one had ever heard Grosse Pierre speak in full sentences let alone perfect French. He was another wonder of the Québec backwoods. That night Saint-Aubin tossed in his sleep. This was one story he had not expected, and it could interfere with his plans.

The Mississippi River - July 12, 1711:

At midday less then five weeks from their departure, the men entered what Parent had called 'the father of all rivers'. There was also an immediate fork to the west he called the River of the Missouri and said it could be followed for many weeks to the greatest mountains ever seen. However even he had only heard of them. They rounded a large broad point where he said Jolliet and Marquette once started a small mission that had disappeared. Beyond this point, the river became wider, deeper with a current of some note. It was much cloudier than the other rivers due to a mud bottom.

When they stopped to camp, Parent announced tomorrow they would pick up the final member of their crew. The following morning as they proceeded, the river became wider and trees became decidedly deciduous. Most of the trees on the bank were weeping willows, which bent gracefully into the water. There were a few very small Indian camps. Eventually they came to a fork which was actually the river going around both sides of a very large island. On the Island was a large Indian camp.

As they came around the eastern edge of the island, it was obvious this was a settlement of some note. In fact it occurred to Jean-Baptiste* it was the largest settlement they had seen since Montréal. They landed in an area that appeared to be a small canoe livery. The area was filled with Indians including many children as well as Frenchmen, priests as well as woodsmen.

Joseph Parent spoke to an Indian he seemed to know. There was a large amount of gesturing after which Parent signaled for the men to follow him. They passed a sizable church and mission with a small school, a small stockade with a trading post and some small houses. Two soldiers were evident but no formal military center. Most of the people, both French and Indian, seemed to live in a large collection of tents outside the stockade.

Parent seemed to recognize the man for whom he was searching and signaled the man who returned the sign, starting toward the group. He was a large rugged sort who looked as much Indian as French. Approaching Parent, he greeted him with an embrace. He also embraced Joseph Gauthier and shook hands with the other voyageurs. Parent then introduced him to the rest of the group as Jean* Gauthier.

"Jean*, as you may recall, is the older brother of Joseph Gauthier. He has lived here with his family for many years and will now be our guide through Louisiana."

The rugged man replied, "Gentlemen, welcome to the great frontier metropolis of Kaskaskia. Please come and meet my family."

The occupied area of the island was relatively devoid of vegetation. Habitations, both wood and tent, were haphazardly located. The mission and church held a central position but the rest of the area showed no sign of forethought or organization. Jean* Gauthier brought the men to a dwelling which was part house and part tent with several thin dogs and a few naked children in attendance.

"My happy home." he announced as a woman in Indian dress but practically naked came out from the tent portion. "This is my wife, Jeanne* but here she is called Capieioufseize*. The lady said in passable French, "*Enchanté.*" The men could not avoid noticing how hard and muscular this woman was. In spite of her dress and

248

dark color she had a vague European look to her and the particular beauty shared by most métis woman.

Gauthier continued, "And here is the brood, Marie age 11, Domothilde age 10, Suzanne* age 6 and Jean one year younger." Jean-Baptiste* noticed that young Suzanne* had a ribbon in her hair while the others wore a small traditionally tied feather. The men had dinner and there was a tribal dance in their honor. They smoked and talked into the night.

The following morning they readied to take off. Joseph Gauthier said that his brother was very familiar with the rest of the journey and would serve as their primary guide. Soon Jean* Gauthier approached followed by his wife. He announced to the group, "My wife thinks it would be best if she accompany us." As Capieioufseize* bent to load their canoe, Pierre Roy came over, "I am not about to voyage with a woman."

At this Capieioufseize* stood and hit Roy on the chin as he had never been hit before. He left the ground and fell flat. He truly feared he could not get up. With this the woman said, "In that case, Monsieur Roy, we shall miss your company."

The laughter was overwhelming. Roy staggered to his feet and said, "I guess one woman would be alright." The laughter continued.

Jean* Gauthier added, "In truth Capieioufseize* knows the country better than any Frenchman and in truth is a more skilled voyageur than any man." And with that they pushed off for the last leg of the voyage.

The voyage proceeded with enthusiasm, but the men could hardly ignore Jean* Gauthier's wife. She wore only a belt with a knife, a small arrow quiver and the dark black hair to her mid back. Her body was muscular to a fault and had the appearance of a sculpture to show the most incredible woman. She had a dark tan but features as much French as Indian. She worked as hard as any man but it was impossible for the men not to dwell on her. By midday, Saint-Aubin realized that he had a problem.

As soon as he had a chance he pulled Gauthier aside, "I believe it would be best if your woman could cover herself some."

The rugged voyageur replied, "If your men are distracted by a naked Indian woman, you are in for a great deal of trouble in the next several days. In addition you may have noticed that my wife has a mind of her own."

That evening as they made camp, Capieioufseize* came to Saint-Aubin. Standing before him with sweat dripping from her perfect body driving even this disciplined soldier to distraction, she said, "Have no fear, Monsieur, by tomorrow night I shall try to solve your problem."

That evening, Saint-Aubin decided to take the bull by the horns and announced, "I have told Monsieur and Madame Gauthier of our custom of personal histories and I have asked Madame Gauthier to tell hers this evening."

He was relieved that she appeared with an Indian blanket on her shoulders.

"I was born in Kaskaskia. This is a settlement of my people, the Kaskaskian tribe of the Illinois. Men named Jolliet and Marquette founded it as a mission several years ago. Marquette died here some years ago. The settlement has moved from time to time but now it is on the island and has become the center of trade in the region.

"My father was a voyageur named Jean* Richard, my mother was a native girl who died at my birth, and I was called Jeanne* Richard by my father although my tribal name was Capieioufseize*. My father was devoted to me and took me on all his voyages. From my third to my twelfth birthday, I had never spent a winter anywhere but in the wilderness. My father taught me all the traits of trapping, trade, and life in the frontier. Unfortunately he died in my twelfth year at the hands of a bear.

"After the death of my father I went to the tent of my mother's brother who taught me the Indian ways in the wilderness. My husband, a voyageur around the mission for two years, one day asked to marry me because he had always wanted to have a woman he could not defeat at arm wrestling." After the laughter died, she continued, "At the time of our marriage I was baptized Marie Suzanne Jeanne* Richard, but I still prefer Capieioufseize*. We have trapped and traded together since that time. We have four children who stay with my uncle's family during the season of the *chasse.*

"One daughter, Suzanne*, is not like the rest of her siblings. She seems French and not like our other children. I believe she was sent by my father to atone for teaching me the ways of the men. Someday I will send her to my husband's family in Montreal."

That night the men could hear Monsieur and Madame Gauthier enjoying each other, and their frustration increased. The next morning they left early and the men could hardly take their eyes from Capieioufseize*. That evening as they set camp she said, "There is a Kaskaskian camp near here that I must visit," and she was gone. She did not reappear during dinner, but as the men sat to smoke after dinner, she reappeared. Looking over the group, she said, "I was correct. There are twenty including the Indians and excluding my husband." Twenty young Indian ladies appeared from the forest and joined the group.

In the morning after they were gone, she said to Saint-Aubin, "Monsieur, I hope your men can now keep their minds on the job at hand."

The men did indeed concentrate more on the task at hand after their night of frolic with the local maidens. The sight of Capieioufseize*, however, continued to be difficult to ignore, but in a few days they began to accept her as part of the scenery.

As the voyage continued south the weather began to get very hot and equally humid. As had been predicted they found the Indians of this region wore as little as Jean* Gauthier's wife. Before long the men had abandoned most of their clothes to better deal with the climate. Capieioufseize* showed them how to apply bear grease to certain areas of their bodies to discourage the evermore aggressive local mosquitoes. She told them these insects carried a number of serious diseases and although most of the natives had developed immunity, it was unlikely that the men from the north would have done the same.

Jean-Baptiste* complained, "I can understand how this works. The smell would discourage any living creature. I thought this group smelled bad before."

That night Saint-Aubin asked for a story from their newest voyageur.

"My name is Jean* Gauthier. I suspect my brother Joseph has told you of our boyhood in Lachine and the fate of our parents in the Indian massacre. I had always been attracted to the backcountry and left as soon as our siblings were settled with relatives and neighbors. In twenty-one years I have only been back to Lachine twice. The rest of my time has been in the frontier.

"I have been far north of Gitcheegumee and to Saskatchewan in the west. I have traveled the Missouri River as far as the great western mountains that few men have seen and none who have not can comprehend. I have been to Louisiana and beyond to Texas in the Spanish colonies as well as several of the Islands.

"I had been many times to Kaskaskia; I married Capieioufseize* there in 1702. It has been our home in the good season since then, although we voyage to trap, hunt and trade regularly. Kaskaskia suits us well. It is equally French as Indian and all the citizens are treated the same. There is really no distinction in anyone's eyes. The camp moved somewhat after the death of Marquette in 1665. The mission has been under Father Marest for some time. It is run to suit the people rather than to suit the church, all in all it is a good arrangement.

"We have worked many times with Monsieur Cadillac, but I think the word scoundrel suits him best. My wife was too ladylike to comment on him. I believe she would characterize my estimation as charitable."

Jean* Saint-Aubin had another restless night.

A few nights later coming to what Joseph Parent expected to be the final week of the voyage, Saint-Aubin called for the last personal history.

"My name is Tom. I was baptized Thomas de Baptiste, but most just call me Tom; however this is way ahead of my story. My father was born in Africa. When he was about twenty he had a wife and a young son. He did not know exactly where he is from but it was near the sea and the sun set into the sea, so it must have been the western coast of that place. His people were nomadic like the Algonquin but quite civilized. His father was an official, what people in the English colonies would have called an elder. One day my father was hunting with other young men, a group of men, other Africans but not the same people, fell upon them with nets and clubs.

"They were tied together by the neck as the Iroquois do, marched a long distance, beaten, and abused severely. When they reached a place along the sea, white men who he believed were Spanish or Portuguese caged them. The captured were branded with a hot iron. Anyone not in good health had his head cut off. Herded to a waiting ship, they began the most terrible voyage. In South Carolina, where I was born, we heard many awful tales about these voyages.

"They were chained lying on a board with others above and below. The board above was only a few inches from each man's nose. They had one hand loosely chained with which they could feed themselves a daily bowl of gruel. They had to relieve themselves where they lay and the waste would fall on to the person below. Each week they would be taken in their chains above deck to have seawater thrown on them. Those dead or near death were removed by cutting off their hands, feet, and heads and throwing the parts into the sea."

"Finally they reached an island where they were unloaded and chained naked in a square where men would come inspect them and level any manner of abuse they wished. Eventually sold to various merchants, they were again loaded on a smaller boat and merely chained by the neck on the deck. From there they came to the colony of South Carolina where they were subjected to yet another market and at this point auctioned off individually. A local planter purchased my father.

"My mother's story is much worse. She lived in a different area of Africa. My father's people were tall and dark; hers were shorter and lighter. My mother was married and had one small son. One day she, her husband and son were bathing in the river when they were taken much in the same fashion as my father. Others from her village were also taken and marched in neck ropes to the sea.

"She had an additional problem, for she was young, healthy, and very beautiful. On the beach her captors began to menace her. When her husband protested, they beat him and then abused her sexually while he was forced to watch helplessly. He became more enraged and was beat unconscious. When they were taken aboard, her son was given to another woman and taken below with the others. She was taken to a small cabin where she was chained and used by the captain and his officers at their will.

"She did not see the others for a few weeks, but was fed and better cared for so that at the mid-voyage she remained in good health. Eventually she was replaced by other women and taken to the hellhole below and chained on a board like the others. Occasionally she was taken above board with other young women and forced to perform terrible acts for the crew. They did not beat the beautiful women so as to prevent marking them and diminishing their monetary value, but they had special means of torturing them in ways that would not show.

"Her son was eventually returned to her but her milk had stopped, and she was unable to feed him. She tried to have him eat gruel but he only became weaker. One day on deck the head slaver looked at the boy and considered him worthless and merely flung him into the sea. She became hysterical and tried to hit the man. He made certain that she would be abused by the men every day hence. Eventually they came to the trading island and were sold, but she never saw her husband again.

"She was sold to a planter in South Carolina, who took a shine to her and had her brought to him regularly for his pleasure. Eventually he became fond of her so she was treated rather well. When she became pregnant and had a son obviously of mixed blood or mulatto as the Spanish say, the planter's wife became angry and had her severely beaten and sold. Fortunately for her, she was quite scarred from the beating, which made her less desirable to white men.

"She was taken alone to a new plantation where she worked the fields and never saw her young son again. It was here she met my father who had come three years earlier. They took each other as husband and wife. My father was very kind, and my mother would often say my father gave her back her soul.

"Occasionally she was called to the plantar for his pleasure as were many of the other women. The slaves accepted that they would have to share their woman if they were to survive. Eventually she had five children, two mulattoes and three black. I was the first child of my mother and my father.

"Life on the plantation was hard although I knew nothing else. Work was as hard as one could work. The older slaves merely died from exhaustion and lack of rest. We were beat on occasion often for no apparent reason. My back like that of most slaves shows the scars. Fieldwork was supervised by a white man who was *patron* or overseer as the English called him. When there was a good overseer, life was better. Occasionally there was a mean one and life was hard.

"The planter's wife was an odd lady who had been educated and decided to try an experiment. My mulatto half-sister and I were brought daily to the house where she would instruct us. It was here I learned good English and also learned some reading and writing. When it became evident I had learned faster, the experiment stopped. As I grew I took a wife and had three children. One day the planter told me that I had been sold to an English officer who wanted a servant who spoke good English. Apparently he paid a premium. I protested about my family but was only beaten and knew it was to no avail. I never saw my family again.

"The officer whose name was Johnson was transferred to New York in the north, where soon after he led the raid on Beauport and was mortally wounded. I was taken 'prisoner'. As you know Jacob* Thomas and I were taken to Jean-Baptiste*'s home where we stayed. I was treated in a fashion I had never conceived of, as a person, as a friend. I learned French and the French ways and married the sister of the wife of Joseph and also took her family name of de Baptiste.

"I had hoped to remain in and a part of the Québec society, but after our meeting with Soaring Eagle I am wondering if I may find a new calling. And, oh yes, I have never met Monsieur Cadillac."

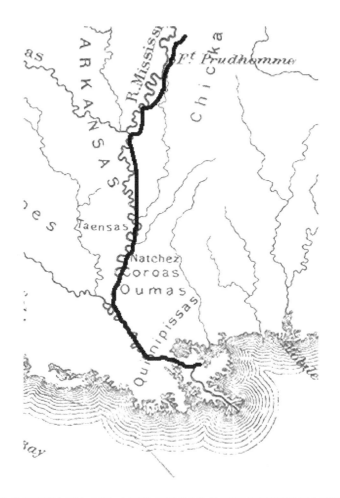

LOUISIANA TO AND FROM SOUTHERN PART

Chapter 36

<u>The Lower Mississippi River - July 19, 1711</u>:

The weather had become extremely hot. With the humidity it was truly steamy. The terrain had changed considerably and trees were now the broad leaf evergreen magnolia and the soft conifer, the cypress. Beautiful and fragrant flowering plants abounded, the azalea, jasmine and orchids to name a few. The forests of the north were dense but these had a density of almost an airtight curtain. As they went south, a strange moss hung from the trees sometimes to the water.

Naked Indians were the norm, and animals common to the north such as white tailed deer, beaver, fox and raccoon were plentiful. One evening as the group sat preparing for dinner, Joseph Parent asked Jean* Laforest to wade out to fetch a strange log. As he waded out the voyageurs knowledgeable about Louisiana began to snicker. As he reached for the log, it became the most incredible monster. Fully ten feet long it snapped at him with its vicious jaws. As the men laughed, Capieioufseize* waded out and grabbed the creature by its jaws when they closed, rendering it relatively helpless. This was their introduction to the alligators that populated the Mississippi from the level of North Carolina south, always in increasing numbers. She explained to the novices that the creature closed his jaws with enormous force but was weak to reopen and thus subdued by her maneuver.

The forest became sparse and the terrain marshy as they proceeded south, resembling in some ways the flat marshlands they had seen some years before north of Détroit in Lake Sainte-Claire. However here the foliage was more tropical. There were channels that naturally cut through the swamp much as in Détroit but here there were strange islands of trees that grew on roots rising from the water and into the air before producing the trunk. There were many strange long necked birds, white, blue, gray, and even pink. One strange fishing bird with an enormous bill had a large wingspan that allowed it to soar indefinitely, much like the eagles of the Saint-Laurent.

When the river turned toward the southeast, they encountered an area of dry land with some trees and an Indian village with a large population of naked Indians who regarded the canoes with suspicion. Gauthier explained quietly, ""This is a band of the Natchez tribe. They are numerous in this area and sometimes not friendly, so we will not stop."

The following day they landed on the northern bank as the river was going directly east. Gauthier explained, "Here is our only portage. The terrain is flat and marshy, and not too long." An hour later they came to a great lake.
"This has been named Lake Pontchartrain by Monsieur Iberville. It is more salty than the river at this point. The river continues south and east for many more miles and becomes very marshy with series of channels, small ponds and marsh referred to as *bayou*, an Indian word with a rather French pronunciation. Our destination is near the eastern end of this lake. We will be there tonight."

Later that day they began to see civilization and soon landed on the south shore of the lake. Although there was considerable activity, the structures were meager, a small stockade with a few interior buildings, a few exterior structures and many tents and lean-tos. They were greeted by a small group of scantily clad, rough looking Frenchmen who seemed to know Jean* Gauthier. They were joined by Joseph Parent and Jean* Saint-Aubin. Saint-Aubin returned and addressed the group, "I am to go and meet with Cadillac. Would Messieurs Allard and Parent please accompany me?"

The men walked to the stockade and entered the largest building. It was well ventilated with many windows all around. Inside they saw Antoine Cadillac looking as dapper as ever, and a few men who Jean-Baptiste* did not know although he recognized Cadillac's old assistant Pierre and a well-dressed gentleman from Québec, Louis Juchereau, a member of the most influential family in Québec. His grandfather had come with Champlaine, and his father had come on the voyage with François* Allard in 1666, but above board in a stateroom.

Cadillac introduced the brothers Pierre and Jean-Baptiste le Moyen better known as Iberville and Bienville respectively, as well as three other well-dressed gentlemen from France. He began, "We all traveled here from France arriving only one week ago today after a horrible storm-racked voyage of more than five weeks. My family accompanied me and is thankfully all here in one piece. We have only started to take stock of the situation. Our first concern is the location, but perhaps Monsieur Iberville can explain."

The older gentleman stepped forward and motioned to a map of the coast of the Gulf of Mexico on the wall, "Our problem is and has always been that the land here moves and sometimes suddenly. The delta land is referred to as bayou; it is filled with rivers and islands that change on a nearly daily basis. We have tried locations far to the east," pointing to a place about 100 miles east, "on the gulf which is called by the Indian word that means 'mobile' because the land is just that, actually more stable than the land here but too far from the Mississippi River. The land to the west is entirely unsuitable due to the changeable marshland. We are now on Lake Pontchartrain which is more stable but not fully accessible to the gulf. Monsieur Cadillac has suggested, and I agree, that we spend the next few weeks exploring and considering other alternatives."

Following the meeting, Jean* Saint-Aubin met privately with Juchereau and one of the men from Paris named Denonville. Saint-Aubin began, "I have heard from all my men. A few have a very negative view of Cadillac. I hope this will not be a problem."

Denonville replied, "Hopefully there will be no problem, but I have pledged to Monsieur Crozat that should Cadillac become a problem we will remove him by whatever means necessary. At this point we will hope for the best."

That evening the group drew up a plan to split into groups and cover various areas. Each group would consist of the men from Québec and someone familiar with the area as well as two natives from the mission. Jean-Baptiste*'s group included Jean* Gauthier,

Capieioufseize*, Tom, Denonville, and two local Indians named Anis and Pedro. There were three groups: one to go east toward Mobile, another west on the bayou, while Jean-Baptiste*'s group was to explore the central region near the current site.

Cadillac instructed Jean-Baptiste*'s group, "Monsieur Gauthier will give technical advice, Monsieur Denonville will observe for the government, and Jean-Baptiste*, you will be in charge."

Anis and Pedro, whose names came from the Spanish missionaries who had baptized them as children, were members of the Choctaw tribe. Although Jean-Baptiste* had heard the tribe was peaceful and friendly to the French, he was worried that he now had two naked Indian women to contend with. Anis was young and attractive but no match for Capieioufseize* who was stunning by any man's judgment. He was particularly concerned about Denonville who, although he tried to keep his aristocratic demeanor, was having obvious difficulty keeping his eyes off the two women. Jean* Gauthier seemed to take it all in stride.

After a tour of Lake Pontchartrain, the group headed north up the eastern shore. Although the weather was almost unbearable to Jean-Baptiste* and Denonville, the others seemed to handle it without difficulty. The lake was salty, but not like the ocean and ranged from meager depths to very shallow, filled with strange fish and birds. The eastern shore had some firm ground yet still looked generally marshy, unable to easily hold a settlement, while the northern shore had more trees and more stable ground. Gauthier pointed out, however, that it was far from the sea.

That night they camped on this dry ground, Jean* Gauthier explained further, "The problem with the lake is that it is filled with thousands of channels and equally drained by thousands of others. Depending on the circumstances, sometimes some channels may flow either way. In autumn, as you will see, although the weather is generally excellent, terrible storms from the sea make it change levels rapidly. In addition, it is too shallow and inaccessible to the sea to be a port."

Before turning in, the Indians spread small dry sticks around the campsite. Jean-Baptiste* asked if this was to warn of other natives, but they only laughed. Some hours later he was awakened by a commotion. He saw Pedro hitting the ground repeatedly with a large stick. When he investigated, the man produced the largest and most incredible snake Jean-Baptiste* had ever seen. The Indian said in passable French, "Here is why we need sticks. Bad poison too, but good to eat tomorrow." And he threw it aside with a laugh that reminded Jean-Baptiste* fondly of old Henri.

The next morning they continued along the northern and then western coasts. The terrain became more and more marshy until it was swamp flats. When they reached the area they had entered with Saint-Aubin, they portaged back to the Mississippi and headed south where the area was filled with marsh and channels, Gauthier said, "This is true bayou, these areas change with every storm. Tonight we should camp at this sand beach that has been trapped by the mangroves," which was the name he had used for the trees that grew from the water on roots that came above the water.

That night they roasted the snake which Jean-Baptiste* thought was not bad. Suddenly during dinner Anis arose and took her bow and shot into a thicket. There was a great thrashing and she went in with her knife. She pulled out an alligator about twelve feet long. It had an arrow directly between its eyes and she had obviously also cut it between the eyes where it had bled profusely. She said, "Must hit right here or he does not stop." Then she fell upon skinning it saying, "Not so good to eat but skin is valuable."

Jean-Baptiste* laughed and said, "The Louisiana Beaver."

The next day they continued down the south end of the Mississippi toward the Gulf of Mexico. The main channel of the river was clear and easy to follow but the surrounding area was filled with small mangrove islands, small channels, and lakes, some rather large. Jean* Gauthier explained, "The main channel can change overnight with a slight change in the river. Sometimes it changes rapidly and moves to where it is hard to find the next day." Jean-Baptiste* could see how that could happen in this incredible marsh.

Two days later they came to the end where the river formed numerous forks, each of which ended in the Mexican Gulf. As they exited, they saw a rather large Indian village. Pedro told them, "These are Choctaw, members of our tribe and friendly." They beached at the village and conversation ensued between Pedro and a few others. Gauthier joined in as well. Upon their return, Gauthier said, "We have been invited for the night. I suggest we stay."

As they sat on the beach Jean-Baptiste* noticed many unusual boats. They had seen some canoes that had been dug out of a great log. As birch bark was not found here, this was the only option. The boats were heavier and less maneuverable than their Canadian counterparts, but they did well in the rough ocean. Many of the canoes here had a second feature which was a smaller hull attached parallel to the main hull with long poles. Some had one on each side. Pedro explained that these 'out-riggers' were added to give the boats greater stability in rough water.

Later Jean-Baptiste* saw some of these boats with sails. They moved at amazing speed. When he questioned one of the natives he was offered a ride. He and Joseph boarded the boat, which had all the aspects of a Canadian canoe except the hull was heavy. After paddling out clear of the shore, the sail was raised. Attached to a mast, a second pole along the bottom edge of the sail allowed easy maneuvering. In the back there was a large oar mounted like a rudder on a large sailing vessel.

One Indian steered while another moved the sail. The rest of the crew moved from side to side to balance the weight. Moving the sail made it possible to sail almost into the wind. The boat was actually faster when the wind was at its side. Jean-Baptiste* realized this enabled them to sail faster than the wind which just didn't seem possible. As they went farther into the sea and the wind increased, the upwind outrigger would actually come out of the water.

When it moved up a good deal, the crew would crawl out onto the outrigger to keep the boat more level. In this condition the speed was absolutely unbelievable. When they returned to shore they saw similar boats a good deal larger and were told these were used in trade to sail distances out to islands in the gulf and could hold more crew and cargo.

That evening there was smoking and dancing after the dinner. Some of the men wore alligator heads as hats as they danced. One of the leaders spoke some French and with the help of Pedro told them some history.

"There are three tribes in this country. Our people are Choctaw we most plentiful. We hunt and trap the marsh and trade with the islands. The other tribes are Natchez from the north and Chickasaw from the east. These people are warlike and fight with Choctaw. We fish the water. We are a boating people. We welcome the French and their trade. We have seen English and do not find them agreeable."

That night as they retired, Jean* Gauthier arranged to have an Indian maiden sent to the tent of Monsieur Denonville. The man seemed to be in a fine mood in the morning and said nothing of the affair. The others joked in private trying to visualize this 'stuffed shirt' with the Choctaw maid.

The next day they began to work their way north up the coast of the bayou country. This was the most dismal swamp of all. They could not even wade without sinking almost disappearing in the bog. At camp on the second night, Denonville lamented, "I don't know how we can find

a place suitable for a village in this God-forsaken place."
He questioned Gauthier and Jean-Baptiste*, but they had no
ideas. Denonville continued but was soon interrupted.

Capieioufseize* had hardly spoken during the voyage
but she interrupted in mid sentence and said, "Why do you
not ask them?" motioning to Pedro and Anise.
Denonville looked up incredulously and said, "Why
them?"
Capieioufseize* continued, "Perhaps because they
live here and their people have lived here for many years."
Undone by being addressed so casually by this naked
savagesse, he turned to Pedro and said, "Well, what do you
think?"

Pedro looked at him and said; "Only suitable place is
a few miles from Cadillac's settlement. It is almost always
dry. The land is stable, from there one can go to lake, gulf
and river."
Denonville looked at him still bewildered and said,
"Why have you not said this before?"
Without hesitation, Pedro returned, "No one ask."

And with that, the decision was made to head for this
location at daybreak. As Jean-Baptiste* readied for bed,
Capieioufseize* came and sat next to him. She looked up
and began to speak, "I am half French but feel almost none
of it. My children are more French than Indian and other
than young Suzanne* they feel little of it. I have always
been amazed by the French. In many ways they are very
intelligent and charming. But sometimes their stupidity
amazes me."

Before midday they arrived at the site. They spent several hours exploring and at dinnertime when they returned to the camp they all agreed that it was by far the best prospect in their exploration. Gauthier said, "Perhaps we should call it New Denonville as he was the only one smart enough to ask the correct question." Denonville gave him a snide look and Jean* continued, "Look at it this way, you can always say it was an inspiration from a beautiful woman."

The next morning the group planned to finish their exploration of the site. Just as they began to organize after breakfast, there was a grand commotion in the brush to the east. When Gauthier went to investigate, he encountered an enormous black man holding a large club. The man said something Gauthier did not understand when Tom came running, "He is speaking English, I can speak with him."

The man was obviously relieved although also surprised to see Tom. After some discussion, the large man limped from the brush with an obviously wounded leg. He then called in to the brush and a young woman holding a child appeared along with two older children. Anise and Capieioufseize* rushed to their aid and soon had them all sitting or lying. They were in terrible condition, obviously suffering from wounds, hunger and exhaustion.

After a short discussion, Anise arose and spoke to Pedro who motioned to Jean-Baptiste* saying, "*Allons,* and bring bow." And the three of them disappeared into the brush. They approached the riverbed and Anise began to gather the leaves of various plants. Pedro took Jean-Baptiste*. They soon encountered two birds that Jean-

Baptiste* recognized as wild turkeys. Pedro said, "You best shot, you do it." And Jean-Baptiste* quickly shot the two birds. They then went to the bank and Pedro motioned to a large fish near the surface. In a moment Jean-Baptiste* had slain it as well, and Pedro took the catch and returned to Anise who seemed to be ready to go with her arms filled with plant material.

Once they had returned to the camp, Anise began with the help of Capieioufseize* to cook and prepare the plants, Pedro started to cook the turkey and fish. They used many of the plants to treat wounds and others to fabricate tisanes or herbal teas, which they began to feed to the wounded. They obtained a milk like substance from the fish and fed this as well to the patients. After the turkey and the rest of the fish were cooked they made a paté, which they fed to the group.

Once they had tended the sick, Tom explained, "I would guess that they are fugitive slaves from the English colonies. They must have been traveling a great while to reach this place. We shall see if they recover enough to give us more information." The next morning all five of the newcomers were improving. The man was quite alert. He was an immense man, extremely black. His lower leg had been badly wounded and Capieioufseize* had wrapped it in a poultice the night before. After he had some herbal tea and a little cold turkey he sat up and began to speak. He spoke English but no French so that his story was translated by Tom.

"I's called Toby. I's born on da plantation in Georgia. Ma woman is Polly and we has tree chiluns.

271

Oldest is Pansy, den mah boy Pork, an his li'l sister Annabelle. We works for a cruel masser, name Misser John. He beats da slaves sumpin awful. He take advantage of all da slave women when he wants 'em. He took ma Polly lots a times. I don't like it but what's a black man ta do? Den one day he come and say he want to have ma Pansy, she ain't but ten years ole. Ah tells im dat jus ain't right, her so young an all. He gives me da biggest beatin of mah life. Nex day ah sez ta Polly, rather be ded than like dis. An we runs off.

"At first dey sets da hounds on us. Dey barkin an chasin us fo days. One big one catch up wit Pork, but I's real strong an I break dat poe dog's neck. We runs an runs as fas as we can. Den one day des no moe dogs. I figures we's free, but we real lost. I knows we gots tah follow were da sun set so we goes on and on. We eats whatever we can finds, bugs, plants and whatnot. The childrens gitten powerful weak. Den we comes on dis swamp like y'all gots here. I gets caught by dis green monster, try to eat mah leg off.

"We figgered we's done fo yeserday, den we sees yo fire. We waits till dawn and comes hopen you ain't slavers."

After Tom had explained the story to the others, Toby asked him, "Who da masser here?"

Tom replied, "Monsieur Cadillac is in charge but there is no 'master'".

"Den whose owns you?"

"Nobody, I am a free man. There are no masters here, we are French."

Toby looked puzzled and replied, "Ain't no free black men in dis land."

Tom reiterated, "You are no longer in the land of the English. This is the land of the French. There are no slaves here."

Toby persisted, "Den who gonna own us?"

Tom again said, "No one, you are now free. You will see. It does take some getting used to."

Toby fell back to sleep and the slaves woke occasionally and had something to eat and drink. By the next morning they had all improved immensely and were deemed ready to travel.

Chapter 37

<u>Cadillac's Settlement - August 1711</u>:

The three exploratory groups reconvened at Cadillac's camp within a few days of each other, and gave their reports in turn. Joseph spoke for the group who had gone to the west, "The terrain is marsh for at least 100 miles. Beyond that there is reasonable land but no harbor and it is too far from the Mississippi. We truly saw no viable options,"

Parent spoke for the second group who had gone to the east, "The land is more secure along this route but there is no harbor until the old fort at Mobile. Even there remains of the old settlement have been destroyed by storms. It is also too far from the river."

Finally Cadillac called on the third group, "Jean-Baptiste*, tell us what you have found, besides more slaves. If you bring more we may have to plant cotton."

Jean-Baptiste* arose, ignoring the comment to say, "We feel we may have found a suitable location not far from here. It has acceptable access to the sea, the river and Lake Pontchartrain. The ground is fairly stable and the Indians say that it has been unaffected by nature for many years."

Cadillac questioned, "What about flooding from the lake?"

Baptiste* replied, "I would like to ask Pedro to explain that."

Rolling his eyes Cadillac said, "Yes, by all means, let us hear Pedro advise the French Empire."

The Indian arose and drew a figure of the lake on the ground. "Many channels into the lake, and many to empty lake. If outward channels remain open, no flooding. If channel is blocked or if man fill the marshes where water drain, big problem. But no one that stupid."

Cadillac asked, "What of the great storms of autumn of which I hear?"

Pedro returned, "Nothing can save what great storms want. In memory of my people, there has been no destruction in this place by great storms."

Cadillac arose and said, "Well I suppose we must go and visit this marvelous place."

The group left the next day and after several days of exploration, it was decided to start the new settlement in this place. Juchereau asked Cadillac what he planned on calling it and Cadillac thought. Then with a sly grin he said, "The Dauphin is now *le Duc d'Orleans*, and he shall soon be the new king." With that he drew his sword and said, "I claim this place for God and the King of France and baptize it *La Nouvelle-Orléans*!"

The next weeks involved moving and construction of the new settlement. The French were amazed by the energy and productivity of their new black inhabitants. Tom remarked, "There is nothing that makes a man work hard as knowing that it is for himself that he works."

Saint-Aubin met again with Juchereau and Denonville. They agreed that the settlement was progressing as hoped and that at this point Cadillac was not a problem.

Nouvelle-Orléans - October 1711:

As autumn descended it became more apparent how different this climate was from that of Québec. The days grew shorter but remained very warm. The stockade had been built and progress was being made on buildings. Cadillac was doing what he did best, other than complaining of the climate, and that was developing trade with the natives. He had also discovered a commodity as useful as Calvados; it came from the islands to the south and was called 'rum'.

Jean-Baptiste* and Jacob* Thomas were busy setting posts for the new home for Cadillac and his family while Iberville watched the project. Pedro came running and pointing to the sky told Iberville, "Big storm soon."
Looking at the clear blue sky and perfect day, Jean-Baptiste* asked, "What do you mean?"
Iberville said, "The Choctaw know at least a day in advance before a storm, we should began preparations at once."

At the direction of Iberville and Bienville, the men were instructed to bring all loose materials into the stockade and lash them securely. The canoes and dugouts were brought far inland and Joseph and Jean-Baptiste* were dispatched with two of the Choctaw to get food for three days. The following day when they returned with several turkeys and other local game the rain began to fall.

The inhabitants gathered inside the stockade and the women and children were sent to the few buildings. Pedro told Jean-Baptiste*, "Storm last one, two, maybe three days." Then sniffing the air, "This one not too bad."

Around midnight the wind began to build and by morning it had surpassed anything Jean-Baptiste* had thought possible. Pedro came to get him and said, "We go check outside before wind get bad."

As they exited the stockade, Jean-Baptiste* thought that Pedro had been joking as the wind could certainly get no stronger. Any loose object, even large cut trees were becoming airborne. The men could scarcely walk into the wind for its force. They inspected the perimeter of the stockade and returned.

Pedro said, "Not bad, one more day."

The next day the wind reached enormous heights, and then died abruptly. Jean-Baptiste* asked Pedro if they could go out.

"We go now to inspect but come in soon. Worst part not here yet."

Outside the stockade Jean-Baptiste* was overwhelmed by the number of uprooted trees and debris. They soon returned to the interior and the wind returned stronger than before. Looking outside a crack to the north Jean-Baptiste* saw trees bent almost to the ground, and then it stopped. Within minutes the day was a clear and fair as they had seen. Everyone returned outside and soon work resumed.

Bienville came over to Jean-Baptiste* and Joseph. "A few times a year we have these strong storms. This was typical. You can now see the beauty of this location"

Indeed they could. The natural harbor of the settlement had its entrance almost due north and away from the wind of the storm. A few miles of bayou protected the entire settlement. Later when they went farther out, they found the bayou entirely changed. Many of the islands and the channels had moved. They could see that the waves had come ashore in places two miles further than normal.

Bienville continued, "This was a problem in Mobile, whereas the land was solid and the harbor excellent, it was exposed to the south. Well, I suppose you should set to work. In a day or two Monsieur Cadillac may emerge from cowering in his new house." With a chuckle he moved on.

Nouvelle-Orléans - January 1712:

Cadillac had called Joseph and Jean-Baptiste* to his office. "I am told that these wretched storms are now over and the weather will remain fair for the rest of the winter. The Indians are sailing to the Islands for trade and have offered to take some of us. I will go, as will Monsieur Iberville, and Joseph Parent. You two will come as my guards and bring your two slave friends as we may need their strength."

Jean-Baptiste* wanted to point out that they were no longer slaves, but he knew that disagreement with this man was always counterproductive. The next day they departed on five large boats They were each basically two large dugouts connected with poles making almost a platform between them. This was covered with a strong net which would allow water to run off but protect losing people or goods. Cadillac had commissioned two of them for his personal use.

With sails launched, the speed of the boats was impressive. The water was a deeper blue than the sky and the rolling waves enormous, but the boats handled them with ease. They were almost four days outside of sight of land, but the sights of the sea were a constant amazement. They were first followed by gulls and then gray birds with wingspans in excess of ten feet that flew all day without moving their wings. Cadillac explained, "The albatross. Sailors believe he brings good fortune."

Jean-Baptiste* was surprised at Cadillac's confidence moving about the boat but remembered he had spent his first years in Canada sailing as a privateer with François Guyon. Later they saw schools of small fish that jumped over the hulls of the boat. "Flying fish," said Cadillac. Large fish with great dorsal fins swam for miles with the boat as if they wished to visit. "*Marsouin,*" Cadillac explained, "said to be the most intelligent of fish, The English refer to them as the porpoise."

On the fourth day they began to see land to the east and to the south. Iberville explained, "The land to the east is *Floride.* It was once a French colony but is now mostly Spanish, although some French remain due to the friendship between France and Spain over the current war with England. The land to the south is our destination, a great and beautiful island called Cuba by the Spanish. We will land near an Indian camp. The black men need to stay close by as there is slave trade elsewhere on the island."

Cuba was indeed beautiful. Fully tropical with rolling hills up to mountains and lush meadows, the island was ringed with hard white sand. As they landed they were greeted by the local Indians who had good relations with the Choctaw as well as with the French. Iberville had made many voyages and was well known to the locals. They were invited to dine. Then there was dancing and smoking of the best tobacco the men had ever tasted.

In the morning Iberville had two of the local Indians take Joseph, Jean-Baptiste*, Tom, Toby and himself on a hike up the mountain. Cadillac stayed behind to make trade arrangements. At the top of the mountain they had a view of the plains of Cuba as well as a mountainous island to the east. Catching his breath from the climb, Iberville began to explain, "The cultivated land here and elsewhere in the islands is sugar cane, much valued in Europe. It is, however, very labor intense and cannot be grown without the use of slave labor. To the east is the island of Hispaniola, the first real island visited by Columbus in his voyage of 1492. Originally it was Spanish, but the Spanish have all moved to the east of the mountain range to a place that is now called *Dominica*. The western side is French and called *Haiti*, an Indian word for high ground. Both sides grow large amounts of sugar cane."

Tom looked perplexed and asked, "I thought the French did not own slaves."
Iberville answered, "In this part of the world all Europeans own slaves."

Tom said something to Toby in English and the group proceeded down.

At camp Cadillac had made great progress. Clearly he had traded for a large quantity of rum, which he planned to trade with local Indians along the Mississippi.

"Old habits die hard," Joseph muttered under his breath.

Later in the day a small European sailing vessel of about sixty feet came close to shore. The chief told Iberville, "These men are slavers, you must take your two Africans to the woods to hide."

Indeed it was a crew of four evil looking Spaniards and their boat carried thirty slaves chained on deck. The Chief explained to Iberville and Jean-Baptiste*, "These men are Spanish slave traders. Their small boat is used to move slaves to the English colonies. The slaves come from Africa on large boats and land in the islands. These men buy smaller groups and transport them to the markets in the colonies. They have stopped to make a repair on their boat. We must ask them to stay the night so as not to make them suspicious of the presence of your two friends."

That night the four Spaniards drank heavily and went back to sleep on their boat. In the morning it was clear something was amiss on the boat. The Indians went investigated and found the four Spaniards hanging from the masts with their throats cut. The slaves were all gone. The chief said, "We must remove this from our camp to avoid trouble with the Spanish." And he had his men set the sails and push the boat out to sea.

The French and Choctaw packed their boats and headed out, however, they made a sudden turn to the west and landed again up the shore. Pedro said, "We need to pick up additional cargo here." They retrieved the 30 Africans from the brush and brought them quickly to the boats. Apparently they were able to communicate enough to convince the slaves this was a path to safety.

Later on the open sea Cadillac complained to Iberville, "I seem to be starting 'little Africa' rather than New France." His countryman replied. "Have you not yet noticed that free Africans are excellent workers to build our settlement?"

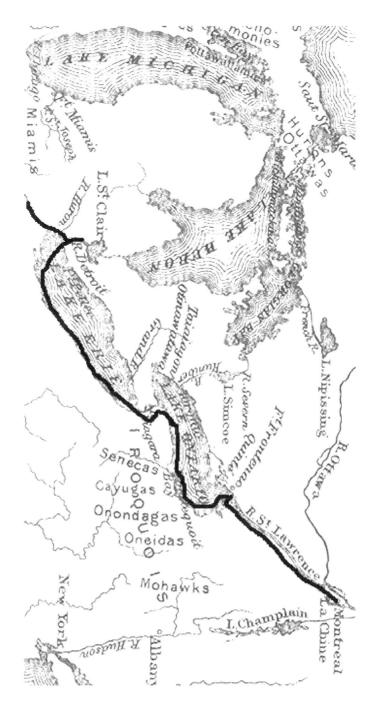

ROUTE BACK FROM LOUISIANA NORTHERN PART

283

Chapter 38

Nouvelle-Orléans - winter 1712:

Iberville was correct and with the new 'free' workers, the settlement progressed rapidly. Cadillac started a prosperous trade making Monsieur Crozat happy in France and maintaining a nice side business in rum, making him richer. It was apparent, however, that the great man was not happy, for he complained constantly about the natives, mosquitoes, lack of society and always about the heat. Even in the winter when the weather was fair, he was always suffering, but not in silence.

As spring arrived Saint-Aubin, Juchereau, and Denonville met again. Saint-Aubin said, "Things have gone smoothly. I am going to announce our departure as I fear some of the men will not tolerate Cadillac much longer. I believe we have fulfilled our obligation to Monsieur Crozat and to the King."

The next day Jean* Saint-Aubin announced it was time for his group to make plans to head home. He had a meeting and told them, "Anyone wishing to stay may, however we have accomplished our goal of securing the settlement, and I promised some of you we would make all efforts to return for planting. I suggest we depart within the week." No one expressed an interest in staying. He continued, "In that case I suggest we go as far as Kaskaskia and head inland through rivers that with some portage will take us to the Maumee River, to the southwestern shore of Lake Erie. Parent, Roy, Laforest, and I can go to Détroit,

284

and the rest can continue to Niagara and on to Montréal and Québec."

He discussed the plans with Cadillac and the others. A ship from France was due at the beginning of the season and the French businessmen would return to France by way of the French Indies. The black family and the rescued slaves were all adapting and learning some French. They and the others were happy to have them stay. Even Cadillac was content with the extra workers.

As they began their voyage north through the lower Mississippi, Jean-Baptiste* reflected on how short the visit had seemed. However he and the others were very anxious to get home to their families. At Kaskaskia they were invited to a dinner and celebration, and in the morning said their goodbyes to Jean* Gauthier and Capieioufseize*. Gauthier told them, "We will likely return to Louisiana this fall for trade. Once our children have grown, we should like to explore the west and see what it offers."

The group soon turned easterly at a large fork and left the great river behind. The inland travel was much different than the large rivers. There was a portage every day or two and frequent forks in the stream. They seemed very confusing to Jean-Baptiste* however the voyageurs seemed to instinctively know the way. Joseph Parent showed him how to read the river and 'usually' select the correct course.

They met several groups of Indians. Most seemed to know the voyageurs and all seemed friendly with the French. All Algonquin speaking, most were members of either the Illinois or Miami tribes. They began to look and dress more like the Canadian Indians the farther north they traveled.

Although the season was advancing, the weather became cooler as they progressed. All were happy to feel cold again at night and nobody missed the particularly vicious mosquitoes. One night at camp, Saint-Aubin said, "I must confess that by the sound of your opinions on the way down, I was quite worried some of you were not going to be so kind and cooperative with Monsieur Cadillac. I would like to thank you all for your cooperation."

Parent, who was trimming callous from his feet with a particularly large knife, stopped and said in his usual informal style, "Well Saint-Aubin, the truth is that we did discuss the old muskrat. In fact, we had a plan to drop his sorry ass a hundred miles into the Bayou wearing nothing but his big sword, but then we decided it was better to leave him suffer in that dismal swamp for the next few years."

The men laughed and Saint-Aubin only shook his head.

The trees and foliage turned more familiar. Most were just beginning to bud for spring when they reached Lake Erie. Proceeding to Détroit they were met by the new commander, a man named Laforest but not related to Jean* Laforest. They toured the settlement which had grown some in the years since Jean-Baptiste* and Joseph were there. There were roads and businesses, many more buildings, and several farms along both sides of the river both north and south of the fort.

Jean* Saint-Aubin, Parent and Pierre Roy remained in Détroit as well as Jean* Laforest. Although he had only been able to start a rudimentary windmill in *Nouvelle-Orléans*, he had plans for a grander device in Détroit. The rest of the group continued up Lake Erie to portage the falls, then across Lake Ontario to the Saint-Laurent and on to Montréal. There they said goodbye to the other voyageurs and Jean-Baptiste*, Joseph, Tom and Jacob* Thomas along with Juchereau, who had hooked a ride, returned to Québec.

They reached the city of Québec on a beautiful day in early April. Juchereau went his way from Port Royal while the four men crossed to the Beauport canoe livery where they stored their craft and made the short walk home. The homecoming celebration at the Allard family farm complex was enthusiastic to say the least. As soon as one of the children saw the group, the word spread and in a few hours, most of Charlesbourg had gathered to hear the tales. Jean-Baptiste* had an additional surprise in the way of a new daughter, Marie-Therese who had been born earlier in the spring. A new son, Georges le Baptiste, also greeted Tom.

The farm had improved considerably over the several months of their absence due to the money as well as the energy of the family. There were now three horses, ten cows and many pigs, sheep and goats. That night Jean-Baptiste* and Anne-Elizabeth* spent the night in amorous revelry so the next morning he awoke more ready to be a farmer than at any time in his life.

Chapter 39

1714 was a fine year for the Allard family. Beginning with the news France and England had settled their differences at the Treaty of Utrecht and the level of local hostilities had dropped to almost nothing. The militias returned to being hunting and drinking clubs while people started to go outdoors without their rifles.

More importantly, the marriages of the last two Allard children occurred within two weeks of one another. Thomas married his longtime neighbor, Marie-Charlotte Bedard on July 11th. They would continue to live on and take over management of François*'s original farm on the Charlesbourg square. Marie-Anne Allard married Pierre Boutillet who had arrived from Rouen and bought a farm in Charlesbourg. They were wed on July 23rd.

Finally Jean-Baptiste* and Anne-Elizabeth* celebrated the birth of their fifth child and fourth son, André Allard. Then on April 28, 1716, Pierre* Allard #337 was born, the fifth son of six children.

1716 brought some unsettling news when Québec learned that the *Roi Soleil,* or Sun King, Louis XIV had died at Versailles in the autumn of 1715 after 72 years as King. He had been the longest reigning monarch in the history of Europe. Having outlived both his son and grandsons, he would be succeeded by his great-grandson, now Louis XV. The boy was but five years old, which meant a regent, probably the boy's mother and/or an influential minister, would control France for some years.

This left a great deal of uncertainty as to the place the colonies would have in the new agenda of France.

Charlesbourg - The Blue Goose Tavern September 1716:

Jean-Baptiste*, Joseph, André, Thomas and François* sat around a table discussing the final days of the harvest and plans for the next year when the door burst open letting in Joseph Parent, Pierre Roy, and of all people, Tom de Baptiste. As soon as he ordered a round of drinks, Pierre Roy started right in, "Well Baptiste*, it seems that our old buddy Cadillac is getting his wish and having his ass sent back to France."

Joseph Parent jumped in, trying to lower the tone of the conversation, "It is true. Monsieur Crozat grew tired of having Cadillac's liquor store interfere with the development of the colony, so he sold the whole thing to a Scotsman named John Law who will now manage it for the King. Well you know those Scotsmen; they don't miss a single sou. He gets the government to haul Cadillac and his whole family back to France. Word is that Cadillac may be in a bunch of trouble, too.

"Fortunately they have put Bienville back in charge and probably he can set things straight. Seems that his older brother, Iberville, has retired and moved to Cuba to live. We were up here visiting when we stopped by to tell you but found out that you were at the tavern. We met up with Tom at your place, and it seems he has some news as well."

Rubbing his palms on his trousers Tom started, "Ever since our trip to Louisiana, especially after the experiences with Soaring Eagle, the slave family and the boat of slaves, I have been considering the destiny of the rest of my life. Joseph and Pierre have indicated that there are occasionally escaped slaves making their way to Détroit. I plan to accompany these men to Détroit along with my wife and young Georges to make our life in there and perhaps help other Africans."

The men indicated they would be sorry to lose the help and companionship of the de Baptiste family but realized this was what Tom was destined to do. They ordered another round and toasted the future. That Sunday a large group gathered at Jean-Baptiste*'s farm to wish well to this amazing man and his family.

Charlesbourg - October 23, 1725:

As had been his habit in the fourteen years since the death of his wife, François* Allard had made a habit of going hunting with his bow when he had free time. Accompanied only by his dog, it gave him time to plan and sometimes to reflect. On this gorgeous autumn day with the forest dressed in its finest, he was particularly reflective. He thought about his life, family and friends in France and what may ever have happened to them, or what might have happened to him had he not gone to Rouen on that fateful day.

He recalled the voyage and Mathurine*, Jean* Renaud, and Jean* Poitevin dit Laviolette. He remembered the early days with Anne* Ardouin and Henri, but he particularly dwelt on his wonderful years with Jeanne* and their children. He sat on an old fallen log. He had not even shot his bow today although he had had many opportunities. Now at 85 years of age, the kill seemed unimportant.

He scratched the ears of his old dog, part Border collie and part wolf, named Rosie. He had named all the dogs of his life after flowers. She was an intent listener and he spoke his memories out loud to her, "It's been a busy life, girl, so full of things wonderful and things not."

He felt a tingle in his chest, thought of his father's medallion, but realized he no longer wore it. The next thing he saw was a face he had not seen in fourteen long years.

Two days later, October 25, 1725, his funeral was held at the chapel of Saint-Charles de Borromée. Much of Québec turned out to say goodbye to this man who had been their friend and neighbor for almost sixty years. Of course none of his old friends were there, Renaud, Henri, Poitevin and the rest. He had outlived them all. After mass he was buried beside his wife in the parish cemetery.

A picnic followed at the old Allard farm on the square. Jean-Baptiste* stood on the porch and surveyed the large crowd of friends and family. His father had been survived by seven children and 65 grandchildren including Jean-Baptiste*'s own brood of seven boys and three girls.

Jean-Baptiste* thought of the past and then of the future as the wind shifted suddenly to the north reminding the Québecois winter would come. At the same moment he felt a tingle in his chest as he did wear the medallion, and a cold wind blew through his heart as he saw Soaring Eagle and heard the old chief, "… and I see great tragedy."

TO BE CONTINUED

EPILOGUE

As in the first book, I have tried to be faithful to the existing facts regarding our ancestors as well as the history of their times. With few exceptions, the characters did exist, although I had to take some license with the Indians due to the lack of good Indian records from this period. I also used license in making Jean-Baptiste* witness to so many events, however, some of our ancestors, generally as included in the book, did take part in these events and voyages; and Jean-Baptiste* may have as well.

LaSalle: His character and events of his life are historically accurate. When I was planning the book, I found an article in the newspaper about a local diver who believed he had found *Le Griffon* in northern lake Michigan. Every few years this seems to happen, but as before, it was not true. It did however encourage me to include this wonderful legend of the Great Lakes with my own twist.

Antoine Cadillac: It would be difficult to tell the story of my ancestors without including this wonderful character who was truly responsible for much of the expansion of New France. His persona of genius and scoundrel are thought to be accurate. It is believed that much of his espoused lineage was fabricated. The details of his voyages to Michilimackinac and Detroit are all from history.

<u>Madame Cadillac:</u> The arrival of the first lady of Detroit is one of the most beloved legends of Detroit history. It is immortalized in the mural on the third floor of the Detroit Public Library as well as in a bronze relief at the Cadillac Square people-mover station. There are several versions of the voyage. I adapted this one from the court records of Joseph Trottier in the Archives of Québec; most current experts believe it to be the most accurate account.

<u>Détroit:</u> The story of the first few years of the city in the wilderness is taken from history. Joseph Parent and Pierre Roy were in residence when Cadillac arrived in 1701. I did take some license with the life of Roy.

<u>Tom de Baptiste and Jacob* Thomas:</u> Both these families will be prominent in future episodes. It is unknown how their descendants made it into early French-Canadian society. This is my explanation.

<u>The plague of 1711:</u> is thought to have been measles but this is not certain. What is certain is that many Quebecois died in this brief period of time including the three Allard wives.

<u>Kaskaskia:</u> Was a hub of the frontier at this time. Today it is a small reservation on the island in Randolph County, Illinois. Jean* Gauthier and Capieioufseize* did live there with their family and I even have a copy of their records from the old hand written mission archives. They are certainly among my favorite ancestors. Gauthier was an active voyageur and traveled widely. His Indian wife did often travel with him. I like to think I have been faithful to their true personalities. Their daughter Suzanne* did

somehow return to Québec to marry and produce children who helped settle Détroit. Jean* and Capieioufseize* did eventually disappear into the wilderness.

Louisiana: This particular trip is of my invention. Most of these people, however, did visit Louisiana around this time, and some men were indeed sent by Antoine Crozat to protect his investment and monitor Cadillac. I did choose these particular voyageurs because most of them, or their descendants, will cross the path of the Allard family in future stories, hence the importance of the personal histories.

The location of the harbor did change many times and was at one time as far east as Mobile, Alabama is today. The current location of New Orleans is the location of Cadillac's settlement in the story. As we now know, they did not take Pedro's advice regarding the canals and the wetlands.

Cuba: Travel to the Caribbean Islands and encounters with the slave trade were common. Iberville did retire to the island after Cadillac was recalled and Bienville was made Governor of Louisiana.

DESCENDANTS OF FRANCOIS* ALLARD
THREE GENERATIONS

1. **Francois* Allard**, b. 1637-1642, Blacqueville, France, (son of Jacques* Allard and Jacqueline* Frerot) occupation farmer. He married Jeanne* Anguille, Nov 1, 1671, in Beauport, QC, b. 1647, Artannes-sur-Indre, Tours, France, (daughter of Michel* Anguille and Etiennette* Toucheraine) d. Mar 12 1711, Charlesbourg, QC, buried: Mar 12 1711, St Charles de Borromée cemetery, Charlesbourg parish. Francois* died Oct 25 1725, Charlesbourg, QC, buried: St Charles Borromée Cemetery, Charlesbourg.

   Children:
   2. i **André Allard** b. Sep 12 1672.
   3. ii **Jean-François Allard** b. 31 July 1674.
   4. iii **Jean Baptiste* Allard** b. Feb 22 1676.
   5. iv **Marie Allard** b. NOV 1 1678.
   6. v **Georges Allard**.
      vi **Marie-Renée Allard**, b. MAY 16 1683, Bourg Royal, QC, d. OCT 10 1684.
   7. vii **Marie-Anne Allard** b. 1685.
   8. viii **Thomas Allard** b. 17 Mar 1687.
   9. ix **Jeanne Allard**.

2. **André Allard**, b. Sep 12 1672, Notre-Dame de Québec. He married Anne LeMarche, Nov 22 1695, in Charlesbourg, QC, b. 1668, Montreal, QC, (daughter of Jean LeMarche and Catherine Hurault). André died Dec 05 1735, Charlesbourg, QC.

> *Children:*
> i **Marie Catherine Allard**, b. Nov 16 1696, Charlesbourg, QC. She married Nicholas Jacques, Nov 05 1719, in Quebec, b. 1691, Charlesbourg, QC, (son of Louis Jacques and Antoinette Leroux).
> ii **Marie Genevieve Allard**, b. Oct 31 1698, Charlesbourg, QC. She married Pierre Chalifou, Nov 07 1718, in Charlesbourg, QC, b. 1692, Charlesbourg, QC, (son of Pierre Chalifou and Anne Magnan).
> iii **Jacques Allard**, b. 1700, Bourg Royal, QC. He married Marguerite Brosseau, 1723, b. Feb 02 1698, Charlesbourg, QC, (daughter of Joseph Brosseau and Marie Anne Gaudreau).
> iv **Pierre André Allard**, b. Dec 21 1702, Bourg Royal, QC. He married Madeline Paquet, Nov 15 1724, b. 1702, Charlesbourg, QC, (daughter of Philippe Paquet and Jeanne Brosseau).

v Thomas Allard, b. Jul 20 1705, Bourg Royal, QC. He married Marie Agnes Belleau, Nov 25 1731, in Ste. Foy, QC, (daughter of Guillaume Belleau and Suzanne Robitaille) d. 1762. Thomas died Jun 26 1762.

vi Jean Charles Allard, b. Feb 06 1708, Bourg Royal, QC. He married Madeline Danet, Nov 12 1731, in Ste. Foy, QC, (daughter of Charles Danest and Madeline Bertheaume).

vii Jean Baptiste Allard, b. May 28 1710, Bourg Royal, QC. He married (1) Marie Elizabeth Pepin, Sep 30 1732, b. 1715, (daughter of Louis Pepin and Elizabeth Boutin). He married (2) Marie Auclair, Aug 01 1746, in Charlesbourg, QC, (daughter of Francois Auclair and Charlotte Martin) d. 1751, Quebec. Jean died May 28 1751.

viii Marie Joseph Allard, b. Jun 22 1712, Bourg Royal, QC. She married Francois Dion, Jan 09 1736, in Quebec, d. 1760, Pointe Aux Trembles, QC. Marie died May 29 1735.

3. **Jean-François Allard**, b. 31 Jul 1674. He married (1) Marie Ursule Tardif, Nov 05 1698, in Beauport, QC, b. 1678, Beauport, QC, (daughter of Jacques Tardiff and Barbe DÓrange) d. Apr 23 1711, Beauport, QC. He married (2) Genevieve Dauphin, Aug 03 1711, in Beauport, QC, b. 1692, Beauport, QC, (daughter of Rene Dauphin and Suzanne Gignard). Jean-François died 1746, Quebec.

> *Children:*
> i **Jean Baptiste Allard**, b. 1699, d. 1699.
> ii **Jean Baptiste Allard**, b. 1701, d. 1701.
> iii **Jean Baptist Allard**, b. Sep 29 1702. He married Agathe Meunier, Feb 28 1729, (daughter of Mathurin Meunier and Madeline Meneux).
> iv **Marie Charlotte Ursula Allard**, b. 1704. She married (1) Louis LaMothe, Oct 29 1727, in Lorette qc, b. 1699, Beauport, QC, (son of Francois Lamothe and Marie Anne Leroux). She married (2) Pierre Protot, 1745.
> v **Jacques Allard**, b. 1706, Charlesbourg, QC. He married Charlotte Godin, 1731, b. 1683, LÁnge Gardien qc, (daughter of Charles Godin and Marie Boucher) christened widow of Vincent Guillot.
> vi **Pierre Noel Allard**, b. 1708. He married Catherine Meunier, Jul 30 1736, in Quebec, (daughter of Mathurin Meunier and Catherine Bonhomme).

vii **Genevieve Allard**, b. Nov 25 1712. She married Jean Baptiste Cantara Deslaurier, Jan 15 1732, ref: ? 196 rjd.

viii **Gabriel Allard**, b. Aug 03 1714, ref: see note, occupation coureur des bois. He married Elizabeth Proulx, Feb 12 1748, in Baie du Fevre, Qc, (daughter of Claude Proulx and Elizabeth Robidas Manseau). Gabriel died Apr 30 1777, Quebec.

ix **Andre Allard**, b. Mar 22 1716. He married Jeanne Giguere Despins, Oct 20 1749, (daughter of Antoiene Giguere Despins and Francoise Jutras).

x **Rene Allard**, b. Feb 02 1718, d. Feb 06 1736.

xi **Marie Louise Allard**, b. Feb 20 1720. She married Joseph Couturier-Labonte, Oct 28 1741.

xii **Marie Catherine Allard**, b. Feb 26 1722. She married Gabriel Dany, Jan 13 1744.

xiii **Marguerite Allard**, b. Feb 23 1724.

xiv **Louis Allard**, b. Feb 22 1726, d. Nov 14 1749.

xv **Marie Ursula Allard**, b. Nov 28 1727, Beauport, QC. She married Francois Proulx, Feb 17 1749.

xvi **Suzanne Allard**, b. Apr. 12 1730. She married Joseph Gagne, Feb 05 1759.

xvii **Joseph Allard**, b. 1732, d. 1732.

xviii **Marie Angelique Allard**. She married François Joseph Prou, Feb 17 1749, b. 1724, (son of Claude Prou and ...).

xix **Joseph Allard**, b. May 19 1734. He married (1) Madeline Harel, Oct 12 1761, in St Michel d Yamaska, (daughter of Pierre Harel and Madeline Tessier) d. 1764. He married (2) Amable Gagne, Oct 01 1764, in St Francois du lac qc, (daughter of Rene Gagne and Gabrielle St Laurent). Joseph died Mar 27 1764.

4. **Jean Baptiste* Allard**, b. Feb 22 1676, Quebec. He married Anne Elizabeth* Pageot, Feb 23, 1705, in Charlesbourg, QC, b. Jan 16, 1686, Charlesbourg, QC, (daughter of Thomas* Pageot and Catherine* Roy) d. Dec 22, 1748, Charlesbourg, QC. Jean died Dec 22, 1748, Charlesbourg, QC, buried: Dec 23 1748, Charlesbourg, QC.

Children:

i **François Allard**, b. 10 Feb 1706, Bourg Royal, QC, d. Aug 28 1728, Charlesbourg, QC.

ii **Thomas Allard**, b. 31 Jan 1708, Bourg Royal, QC, d. Oct 22 1728, Charlesbourg, QC.

iii **Jean-Baptiste Allard**, b. 18 Jan 1710, Bourg Royal, QC. He married (1) Genevieve de Rainville, Jan 22 1731, in Beauport, QC, b. 1712, Beauport, QC, (daughter of Paul Rainville and Marie Anne Roberge) d. Mar 27 1743. He married (2) Marie Plante, b. 1715, (daughter of Francois Plante and ....) christened died at childbirth, d. 1756.

iv **Marie Therese Allard**, b. 26 Mar 1712, Bourg Royal, QC. She married Francois Roi, Jun 04 1731, in Charlesbourg, QC. Marie died Aug 19 1759, St. Michel, QC.

v **Andre Allard**, b. 11 Mar 1714, Bourg Royal, QC, d. Oct 12 1728, Charlesbourg, QC.

vi **Pierre* Allard**, b. Apr. 28, 1716, Charlesbourg, QC. He married Marie Angélique* Bergevin, Nov 5, 1743, in Charlesbourg, QC, b. Oct 10, 1722, Charlesbourg, QC, (daughter of Ignatius* Bergevin and Genevieve* Tessier) d. Mar 18, 1788, Isle Dupas, QC. Pierre* died Dec 27, 1759, Quebec.

vii **Francois Allard**, b. 3 Feb 1719, Bourg Royal, QC. He married Barbe Louise Bergevin, Nov 13 1741, in Charlesbourg, QC, b. 1724, (daughter of Ignatius* Bergevin and Genevieve* Tessier) d. 1794. Francois died 1801, Charlesbourg, QC.

viii **Jacques Allard**, b. 17 Aug 1721, Charlesbourg, QC. He married Ursula Agnes Denis, May 10 1750, in St Michel, (daughter of Joseph Denis and Jeanne Labonte).

ix **Marie Madeleine Allard**, b. 26 Aug 1723, Charlesbourg, QC. She married Germain Bergevin, Nov 05 1743, b. 1719, (son of Ignatius* Bergevin and Genevieve* Tessier).

x   **Marie Charlotte Allard**, b. 28 May 1726,
    Charlesbourg, QC. She married Pierre
    Bergevin, Jan 28 1743, b. 1727, (son of
    Ignatius* Bergevin and Genevieve*
    Tessier).

5. **Marie Allard**, b. Nov, 1 1678, Bourg Royal, QC. She
   married Charles Villeneuve, May 07 1703, in Bourg
   Royal, QC, b. 1681, Charlesbourg, QC, (son of Mathurin
   Villeneuve and Marguerite Lemarche).

   Children:
   i   **Marguerite Villeneuve**, b. 1704,
        Charlesbourg, QC, d. 1720, Charlesbourg,
        QC.
   ii   **Marie Charlotte Villeneuve**, b. 1706,
        Charlesbourg, QC.
   iii **Michelle Françoise Villeneuve**, b. 1707,
        Charlesbourg, QC. She married Michel
        Magan.
   iv   **Marie Madeline Villeneuve**, b. 1709,
        Charlesbourg, QC.
   v   **Marie Renée Villeneuve**, b. 1710,
        Charlesbourg, QC.
   vi   **Marie Teresa Villeneuve**, b. 1712,
        Charlesbourg, QC. She married Francois
        Marie Bergevin, 1732, in Charlesbourg, QC,
        b. 1710, Charlesbourg, QC, (son of
        Ignatius* Bergevin and Genevieve*
        Tessier).
   vii **Marie Angélique Villeneuve**, b. 1714,
        Charlesbourg, QC, d. 1730, Charlesbourg,
        QC.

viii **Charles Pierre Villeneuve**, b. 1716, Charlesbourg, QC.

ix **Joseph François Villeneuve**, b. 1718, Charlesbourg, QC.

x **François Xavier Villeneuve**, b. 1720, Charlesbourg, QC.

xi **Germain François Villeneuve**, b. 1721, Charlesbourg, QC.

xii **Jean Marie Villeneuve**, b. 1723, Charlesbourg, QC.

xiii **Louis Villeneuve**, b. 1725, Charlesbourg, QC.

6. **Georges Allard**, baptized Feb 10 1680. He married (1) Marie Marguerite Pageot, Jan 07 1710, in Charlesbourg, QC, b. 1693, Charlesbourg, QC, (daughter of Thomas* Pageot and Catherine* Roy) d. 17 Mar 1711, Hotel Dieu, QC. He married (2) Catherine Bedard, Jan 30 1713, in Charlesbourg, QC, b. 1680, Charlesbourg, QC, (daughter of Jacques Bedard and Elisabeth Doucinet). Georges died 1755.

Children:

i **Marie Francoise Allard**, b. 1710, Charlesbourg, QC. She married Joseph Collet, 1728, in Charlesbourg, QC, b. 1707, Charlesbourg, QC, (son of Joseph Collet and Marguerite Courtois).

ii **Marie Anne Allard**, b. 1714, Charlesbourg, QC, d. 1714.

iii **Marie Josette Allard**, b. 1715, Charlesbourg, QC.

iv **Marie Louise Allard**, b. 1717, Charlesbourg, QC.

v **Marie Charlotte Allard**, b. 1719, Charlesbourg, QC.

vi **Marie Madeline Allard**, b. 1721, Charlesbourg, QC.

vii **Genevieve Catherine Allard**, b. 1723, Charlesbourg, QC.

7. **Marie-Anne Allard**, b. 1685. She married (1) Pierre Boutillet, Jul 23 1714, in Charlesbourg, Quebec, b. 1677, St. Sauveur Rouen FR, (son of Pierre Boutillet and Jeanne Lemoine) ref: rjd 157, d. 1715, Charlesbourg, QC. She married (2) Jean Renaud, Nov 18 1720, in Charlesbourg, Qc, b. St.Aumario,Perigueux,Perigord(Dordogne, FR, (son of Jean Renaud and Marguerite Anne ...).

Children:

i **Francois Boutillet**, b. Jun 09 1715, Charlesbourg, QC.

ii **Jean Charles Renaud**, b. 1721, Charlesbourg, QC.

iii **Jeanne Elizabeth Renaud**, b. 1723, Charlesbourg, QC, d. 1730, Charlesbourg, QC.

iv **Joseph Renaud**, b. 1725, Charlesbourg, QC.

8. **Thomas Allard**, b. 17 Mar 1687, Bourg Royal, QC. He married Marie Charlotte Bedard, Jul 11 1714, in Charlesbourg, QC, b. 1696, Charlesbourg, QC, (daughter of Etienne Bedard and Marie Jeanne Villeneuve).

Children:

i **Francoise Allard**, b. 1716.

ii **Thomas Allard**, b. 1718.

iii **Nicholas Allard**, b. 1720.

iv **Jacques Allard**, b. 1722. He married Marie Madeline Bergevin, 1751, in Charlesbourg, QC, b. 1734, Charlesbourg, QC, (daughter of Ignatius* Bergevin and Genevieve* Tessier).

v **Charlotte Allard**, b. 1726.

vi **Marie Allard**, b. 1728.

vii **Elizabeth Allard**, b. 1735.

viii **Pierre Allard**, b. 1737.

9. **Jeanne Allard**. She married Guillaume Longpre, b. Quefille New England.

Children:

i **Guillaume Longpre**, b. 1697, new England, christened went west 1721. He married Catherine Bleau, 1720, in Montreal, QC, b. 1699, Montreal, QC, (daughter of Francois Bleau and Catherine Campau).

DESCENDANTS OF HENRI
FOUR GENERATIONS

1. **Henri**, b. c. 1630, Quebec. He married **Angelique**, b. Quebec.
   Children:
   2.   i   **Philippe** b. 1650.

Second Generation

2. **Philippe**, b. 1650, Quebec. He married **Marie**.
   Children:
       i   **Henri**.
   3. ii   **Joseph** b. 1676.

Third Generation

3. **Joseph de Baptiste**, b. 1676, Quebec. He married **Monique de Baptiste**, (daughter of ... and ...).
   Children:
   4.   i   **Toussaint** b. 1716.